HIGHLANDER'S DESTINY
CALLED BY A HIGHLANDER
BOOK X

MARIAH STONE

Stone
Publishing

GET A FREE MARIAH STONE
BOOK!

Join Mariah's mailing list to be the first to know of new releases, free books, special prices, and other author giveaways.

freehistoricalromancebooks.com

ALSO BY MARIAH STONE

MARIAH'S TIME TRAVEL ROMANCE SERIES

- CALLED BY A HIGHLANDER
- CALLED BY A VIKING
- CALLED BY A PIRATE
- FATED

~

MARIAH'S REGENCY ROMANCE SERIES

- DUKES AND SECRETS

~

VIEW ALL OF MARIAH'S BOOKS IN READING ORDER

Scan the QR code for the complete list of Mariah's ebooks, paperbacks, and audiobooks in reading order.

A person is, among all else, a material thing, easily torn and not easily mended.
  —Ian McEwan, *Atonement*

PROLOGUE

Berwick Castle, Scottish territory occupied by England, November 1306

The worst wounds would never heal. They wouldn't leave ugly scars on the body, though he had plenty of those.

Instead, they maimed a man's soul.

The brazier cast an orange light over the rough stone walls of Colum MacDonald's cell. Shadows hid in the creases of the rocks like wee demons. Around him was nothing but stone.

The same wee demons lived in the creases of the scars on his skin.

The demons he'd lived with for the past five months in the six-by-six-foot stone prison deep in the belly of Berwick Castle.

How could the gash from a spear in his shoulder have healed and allowed him to live in this damp, rotting cave? The exit was somewhere beyond the iron grating, somewhere beyond the glow of the brazier.

The iron lock of the door leading to the dungeon gnashed, and Colum glanced up from where he sat on the hard wooden bench. His shoulder ached, as it did after every movement. The sound of shuffling feet told him a guard was coming. Light glowed brighter through the grating, making him squint. The figures of two guards were burned into his vision.

"Hands behind your back," said one of them, sounding bored. "Come to the door with your back to me."

Something was wrong. Normally, they'd bring him a piece of bread and some water. The healer had stopped coming six sennights past. The last time he had had a real visitor was the Prince of Wales himself, future Edward II, the son of King Edward I.

The prince's attempts to persuade Colum to join the English were futile. Colum had been taken prisoner at the Battle of Methven five months ago—the battle that had crushed Robert the Bruce's hope to be a king of an independent kingdom.

Of course Edward wanted Colum to switch sides. The information Colum could give was invaluable. Several Lowland and even Highland clans fought for the English. And if Colum and potentially the whole of clan MacDonald would switch sides, it would help England to find and kill the Bruce.

They would also take advantage of the MacDonalds' naval strength. England, currently weak at sea, would then dominate it.

That was why Edward needed Colum.

"What is it, lads?" Colum said.

The words felt hard in his mouth, the muscles of his tongue and jaws stiff from lack of use. The only interaction he had had for the past several sennights was with his jailer, who had brought his daily portions of food and drink and taken out his night pot.

"Approach the door with your back to me and your hands behind your back," repeated one of them. "You're to come with us."

"Where?" he asked.

"To dine with the prince," said the second one. He was taller and sturdier. Colum could see the two guards better now that his eyes had adjusted. They were new guards Colum hadn't seen before. "An honor you don't deserve."

To dine with the prince... The very idea filled his empty stomach with bile, and he fought an urge to vomit. The prince who'd taken an ax and beheaded his clansmen and sword brothers Rob, Ianatan, and Frangan—friends he'd known all his life. Then he'd commanded another man to execute six more Highlanders and Lowlanders Colum had gotten to know while serving in Bruce's army. Nine honorable warriors and knights were executed with no trial and no demand for ransom, against all chivalric laws.

He scoffed. "Nae. My thanks."

They both chuckled and exchanged an amused glance. "Clearly the barbarian needs someone to spell it out for him," said the shorter one to the other guard, then turned to Colum. "Let me put it this way. Either you come here with your hands behind your back, or we come in and drag you out with what little brains you have scrambled."

Colum glared at them. They had no bloody idea. He wasn't afraid of them or of a wee roughing. He'd welcome unconsciousness and his brains smashed over the floor.

His nine friends and sword brothers had been quartered, beheaded, and had their entrails scattered all over the fields and villages while he had been spared. Despite his prayers for his shoulder wound to rot and kill him, it had stubbornly healed.

Ever since that day, something dark and deadly had grown in the depths of his psyche. Something angry and poisonous. Something that waited under a great cast-iron lid.

That thing made of shadows and memories had him stand up from the bench and walk to the door with his back to the guards and his hands behind his back.

"This barbarian is trembling in fear, lads," he said. "Go on, then. Let's go and dine with Prince Edward."

When they put the shackles on him and opened the door, Colum stole a glance over his shoulder. The guard's position was too advantageous. He was all in armor. His sword's hilt was too far for Colum to reach. The second guard was too alert, and covered with armor from head to toe.

The dark, angry snake inside him would have to wait.

If he was led to dinner with Prince Edward, the snake might have a chance to strike then. For all his friends who had been dealt an unfair death. For Scotland. For his king, who had been ambushed before he could recuperate.

They walked through dark corridors, fires jumping from torches along the stone walls. From behind one of the corners, he heard female cries, and his gut twisted.

They took another turn, and the struggling shadows cast against the rough rock prison walls raised bile in his throat.

The screams came from a figure just underneath a large man with shoulders as broad as a log. Next to them stood Prince Edward.

With the sharp bone structure of an angel, he was handsome, tall, and muscular. His face was the perfect example of a male beauty—with well-proportioned eyes, a straight nose, and a perfect mouth within his short beard. His hair had been cropped to his ears, curly and blond.

Edward watched the wriggling figures with a distinct, fascinated distaste. By his side, a girl of eleven years old whimpered and cried. She was almost the age of Colum's cousin Anna, the bastard daughter of Robert the Bruce and a bright spark in Dunyvaig Castle. God, he missed his clan and his home.

Colum didn't realize at first who the struggling figures on the table were, but his gut wrenched in an instinct to protect the woman, and he jerked his arms against his guards.

His shackles rattled and Edward looked up at him. "Ah. There he is, the MacDonald who lived."

"Stop," screamed the woman underneath the large shadow. "Please!"

Holding her down, the man pulled his arm up. With it, the skirt of her dress lifted. To Colum's shame, he could see a round buttock and a naked leg. When the man turned to him, he recognized Sir Henry de Bohun, one of Edward's most prominent knights. The man had been known to crush everyone he'd jousted.

"Stop it!" Colum yelled.

He thrashed against his captors, but they held him too strongly.

"Let her go, ye bastart!" he screamed.

Whoever the lady was, he couldn't tolerate the abuse about to happen in front of his eyes.

Prince Edward met his gaze and grinned. "Oh, you don't want her to get raped, do you?"

Something was odd about it all. The lass by Edward's side, crying into her palms, her wee back shaking. The woman stretched over the table, and the large man looming over her. With a sickening feeling, Colum saw the braies of the man fall and his buttock appear under his tunic. One hand against his groin, his buttock moved as he searched against the woman's behind, his second arm flat over her back.

Then the woman turned her head to him, and his whole being froze in horror.

She had a clear face with a low forehead and thin eyebrows. Her dark blond hair was in disarray.

Colum had seen that head wearing a crown only nine moons ago.

Queen Elizabeth, the wife of Robert the Bruce.

Panic and humiliation darkened her eyes. She squeezed them shut, locking him out. The wee lass by Edward's side must be Marjorie, Bruce's daughter from his first marriage.

Christina, Bruce's sister, had been taken prisoner, as well, he knew. Was she here in Berwick somewhere, too?

All that mattered in this moment was that his queen was here, and the man towering over her was about to rape her.

Colum roared, pulling and twisting with every bit of strength left in his body. But the shackles would not budge.

An easy, satisfied smile spread on Edward's face. "Ah. I see you understand what's going on."

The smell of sweat and fear was thick in Colum's nostrils. In March of this year, he had sworn his loyalty to the King and the Queen of Scots.

But even before then, since his birth, his allegiance had been to his clan.

"Swear your allegiance to England, and this will stop," said Edward. "The queen and Marjorie will be taken to a safe location and kept in good conditions as noble ladies should. Their safety will be ensured."

Nae. He should be saying nae. He should be protecting his clan. If he swore his allegiance to England, something in him would break.

But what of his queen? What of Marjorie, who was still just a child?

Scotland's king and queen were nae but eight months on the throne. What would happen to the spirit of the country whose queen had been raped and dishonored by its enemy?

He shook as his very soul split in two. He, whose whole life had been dedicated to honor. To loyalty. To his clan.

To his country.

What was more important? Could there be a choice at all?

The battle fought between two parts of his soul. Choose the vow to his clan...to his family...

Or the honor of the queen.

And his country as a whole?

Bile churned in his empty stomach. He shook so fiercely, the shackles gave a metallic rattle.

He'd never wished as fervently that they had killed him as he wished it now.

"Stop it," he growled.

He sounded vicious. Pure anger, pure fury.

"Ah, do not be this way," Edward purred. "We don't need you broken. There's nothing wrong with swearing your allegiance to

England. The MacDougalls did it. The Cadwells did it. The Comyns. Almost all the Lowland clans..."

"They can burn in hell," he roared.

There was very little that held his humanity against that dark, poisonous thing that had been brewing within him all this time. Wildness had been seeping, flowing through the gaps in his self-control like water through a sieve. One good thing about his mad raging was that the man about to rape Elizabeth stopped moving and stared at him. Elizabeth stopped whimpering. And Princess Marjorie stared at him with a mix of awe and fear, as if he were a wildcat.

The smugness on Edward's face disappeared. "Well." Edward took a step back. "We need you to make a decision about this. Or he will continue."

Sir Henry stared at him.

"So?" Edward said. "What's it going to be, MacDonald? Will he take your queen, or will you swear your allegiance to me?"

Colum shook. His shoulders slumped. The light was blown out in part of his soul.

"Aye," he said.

The voice didn't belong to him. This body that had just agreed to be loyal to his enemy didn't belong to him.

"Nae..." the queen cried. "Nae!"

Edward pulled his chin up and looked down his nose at Colum. "Drop to your knees, kiss the ring, and swear."

As though this wasn't enough humiliation... The prince had to push him to his very limit.

Colum stood and stared at the prince. "I already said aye..." he growled.

"It's not enough. Drop to your knees." He held his hand out, and the ruby ring glistened in the firelight like a drop of blood. "Kiss the ring and swear to serve England."

As though to make the point, Sir Henry shook the queen, then grabbed the back of her dress and cut it with a knife. The ripping of the fabric was like thunder. Queen Elizabeth whimpered again, and Marjorie started crying.

"Ye bastart," growled Colum. "Ye son of a whore..."

Edward took three large strides and hit Colum in the face with the ring. A sharp cut sliced across Colum's cheekbone. His face turned to the side, pain exploding through his head.

"That's for calling my mother, Queen Eleanor of Castile, a whore, you damned Scottish mongrel."

Colum turned to him slowly. Hate boiled in his gut. Warm blood trickled down his face. "Ye can beat me all ye want. Ye can maim me. Ye can kill me. That wilna make me betray my honor."

"But I know what will..." Edward said. "You already agreed. All you need to do is drop to your knees, kiss my ring, and swear your loyalty to England."

"Please, sir," whispered Marjorie, eyes wide and glistening with tears. His heart broke.

She reminded him of Anna. There was a similarity between their features, as half sisters. If Anna had stood before him like this—broken, terrified, traumatized—he wouldn't hesitate.

He shouldn't hesitate for this wee lass, either. Nor for the woman who was being humiliated, treated like meat, stripped of her humanity.

He should have died with his sword brothers. This was worse than death. He was betraying the very core of what made him who he was, giving Edward power over him.

Because once he swore his allegiance to England, he'd mean it. He couldn't do otherwise.

He forced his legs to bend and dropped to his knees in front of Edward. Complete silence fell on the room, except for the wood crackling softly in the braziers. Edward moved his hand closer to Colum's face. He stared at the damned ruby. He could see his own blood smudging the golden rim.

Pushing his humiliation and revulsion down, he leaned forward and kissed the ring.

"Swear," Edward said.

There was a cool triumph in his voice that boiled Colum's very blood.

Nevertheless, he straightened his shoulders. He would never be the same again. Old Colum, the golden lad of the clan, the lad everyone respected and loved, would be dead.

"I swear to serve England," he said.

The words were like a noose around his neck. He hung his head. As footsteps shuffled and Edward left the room, Colum knelt, empty and hollow.

Who was he now that he had betrayed the most sacred thing —his clan? How could he live with himself now that he was a traitor?

CHAPTER 1

LANDS NEAR STIRLING, June 2022

THE VAST LANDS OF BANNOCKBURN SPREAD OUT BELOW WHERE
Danielle Field stood on top of a hill. It was nice to breathe in the
fresh air that smelled of trees and grass and flowers. She recognized thistle, Scottish bluebells, and the small white flowers of
cow parsley blanketing the grassy hill.

The town of Bannockburn, with its gray and orange roofs,
extended over a large area. These days, it was part of the city of
Stirling. Back in the Middle Ages, this was the site of the famous
Battle of Bannockburn. The reenactment of the battle would
take place in a bright green field where triangular and round
canvas tents and a few pavilions had been raised. Dozens of
people in medieval clothes trained on swords, shot arrows, and
made formations commanded by horsemen. People lined around
the perimeter, watching them rehearse for the reenactment, on
June 23.

As much as Danielle loved plants, her sister, Jamie, loved
history.

"You see the statue of Robert the Bruce?" Jamie asked,

leaning towards Danielle and pointing at the statue close to the Bannockburn visitor center. Jamie worked in the museum at Stirling Castle, and was excited to be one of the coordinators of the reenactment for the first time.

By her side stood a medieval warrior. He wore chain mail and a chain mail coif and watched the practice with a dreamy expression. A local actor named Liam, he certainly suited the role, with his ear-length red hair and short beard.

When Danielle had arrived to visit Jamie at the visitor center, he'd volunteered to come for a walk with them. Based on the glances Jamie kept exchanging with him, there must be something going on between him and her little sister. Alarm bells rang in Danielle's head. Could she trust this bloke to treat her sister well? She scanned him for any signs of there being something off. But he seemed a regular chap who was too much into history.

"Yes, I see it," Danielle said. It was a large bronze statue of Robert the Bruce on a horse, atop a tall pedestal.

"Fun fact," said Jamie, her crystal-blue eyes sparkling. "It was built in 1964 by Pikington Jackson for the Earl of Elgin."

Liam nodded seriously. Danielle giggled and hugged her sister by the shoulders. She was as tall as Danielle and built in a similar way: narrow hips, barely any waist, flat chest. The mean girls in high school had called her a stick.

"Only you would call that a fun fact," said Danielle.

Liam looked at her, puzzled. He must have found it fun, too.

Danielle grinned. "I missed you. It's good to take my mind off work."

Jamie looked at her. "Yes. Work. You came to visit so suddenly. Don't you have some important operation or something?"

Danielle crossed arms over her chest and shifted her weight. The best way to spoil the mood was to think about work right now. "Not anymore."

"Where do you work?" asked Liam.

"She's in MI5," Jamie told him conspiratorially.

Liam blinked at her and looked her over. "You? A spy?"

Danielle gave him a forced smile. This was why she was glad she didn't meet many new people outside of work. Because she either had to lie about what she really did, or she would get reactions like that. She had told Jamie and their parents not to tell people, but of course they did.

"I'm not a spy. I'm an investigator."

He whistled. "A real-life female James Bond."

"She really is!" Jamie said.

No, Jamie. She really must like this man if she kept trying to make sure he was impressed.

"Not James Bond, Liam," Danielle said. "I help prevent cyberattacks and sit at the computer all day. It's quite boring, actually."

That was what did the trick to tone down the curiosity in people like Liam who asked too many questions.

"But didn't you have a special operation in Venezuela...or Colombia or something?" insisted Jamie.

Danielle tensed. Jamie shouldn't know more than she was supposed to. Not only was Danielle now under investigation at work, but she might also get fired in less than a week. Yes, she had had an operation in Venezuela. Her informant, Juan, had gone missing. He'd since been found and was now in the UK receiving psychological care. She was on suspension while her bosses led the investigation. The hearing was in five days, and she was going back to London tomorrow for the first interview. Truly, it had been her own mistake in judgment.

The mission was meant to prevent a large-scale cyberattack where hackers planned to break into UK bank security systems to steal private information and money. Juan had gone to meet with a known and highly sought-after hacker.

And hadn't come back.

And the cyberattack had happened, but they'd managed to stop any money being transferred. The hacker was still out there.

After disappearing for a month, Juan had been found, suffering from PTSD. And who knew what he had told the cybercriminals?

They worked with a local gang that took care of roughing up anyone who crossed them.

"Darling," Danielle said, "you know I can't talk about details with anyone."

Liam put his hands on his waist. "Jamie Field, what other secrets do you have?" He shook his head, an admiring grin on his face.

Yes. The bloke liked Jamie. Protective instincts had Danielle clench her hands into fists.

His face fell when he looked at her. "Wait...Field..." He frowned, and Danielle's gut twisted. "Danielle Field, right?"

Danielle swallowed hard. He'd made the connection surprisingly quickly.

"You're that girl, right?" he insisted. "That girl that got kidnapped and kept in a basement by that psycho?"

Jamie's face got a worried look. "Um..." she said.

Danielle spread her hands wide. "Yes, Liam. I'm that girl."

"Oh. Bugger." He looked her over with different eyes now. Surprise. Pity. Suspicion that something may be wrong with her. Those were the typical things she'd seen on people's faces once they found out. "How are you?"

She gave a fake smile. "I'm fine, as you can see. I'm alive."

Well, that was debatable. She was alive. But she had no life. No friends. No relationships. No boyfriends.

It was better that way. Trust was what had led her into that bastard's basement. Sixteen years ago, he'd taught her a valuable lesson. To never trust anyone.

So her work was perfect, really. It was about keeping her distance and being observant and studying patterns. And since she didn't want relationships anyway, that was just as well.

"She's fine," said Jamie with a nervous smile.

"God, I remember that story," said Liam. "It was all over the news. Your whole town went searching for you, didn't they? Not just the police. And you were right next door at your neighbor's the whole time. I remember telling my mum I wanted to go and help. She didn't let me, of course. You were down in London. I was here in Stirling. But when they found you, every newspaper wrote about you."

Danielle nodded and pursed her lips. Not everyone in Britain remembered that story, but apparently Liam did.

"Yes," she said, trying to focus on the groups of people that marched in round formations across the field. "They did. Listen, Liam—"

She was about to tell him she didn't want to talk about it, when Jamie's phone rang loudly.

"Hello?" she answered, clearly relieved not to talk about Danielle's kidnapping any longer. "Oh, yes, we'll be right back."

She hung up and looked at Liam. "We need to go back." She squeezed Danielle's hand. "Sorry, hun. But you have the key for my flat, and I'll meet you there later after work. We'll go to the pub and have dinner."

Liam looked sheepish. "I'd like to join, if that's all right?"

No, it wasn't. Her sister was her best friend, and she longed to spend time with her.

"Great," Danielle said.

Jamie beamed. Liam was important to her, Danielle could tell. Ah, well. More chances to check this man out.

"Okay," Jamie said, kissed Danielle, and the two of them were off down the slope. Danielle watched them walk into the distance, then looked around. While they had talked, the sky had become very dark. Wind picked up, and droplets of rain hit her face.

There was a grove of trees five hundred or so feet away. She picked up her purse and hurried there to hide from the weather. As she ran, the rain started pouring down, and as she gained the protection of the trees, the scent of rain reached her nostrils. Raindrops battered against the leaves above her. She didn't have an umbrella, but standing in a clearing under the thick branches wasn't that bad.

She walked to a boulder and sat down. Looking around, she saw there were several large boulders and the barely noticeable remnants of old mortar between rough rocks. Why hadn't Jamie mentioned anything about this? Usually, she'd be chatting about how this was a remnant from the ninth century or however old it was.

Danielle looked into the grayish curtain beyond the line of the tree crowns. She'd wait out the rain and then go back to Jamie's flat. She'd also try to be more understanding and trusting about Liam.

Gazing around, she noticed some sort of a carving on one of the stones. Curious, she approached it. The rock was very old and crumbled, but she could just make out a carving of a hand-print. The other carvings were worn away, too, looking more like wrinkles in the stone.

She put her hand on the rock. It was cool and smooth. A vibration went through her, like a small earthquake. The carvings began to glow.

She snatched her hand back and stood up.

Glow? Stone?

Then there was a sharp scent of grass and lavender, and as though out of nowhere, a woman appeared next to the rock. Danielle stared at her, carefully watching for signs of danger.

The woman beamed at her. She had the pleasant appearance of a girl next door, with a round, strawberry-shaped face, a pointy nose, and big green eyes. She had long red hair that streamed from under a hood. And a medieval dress was visible under her green cloak.

"Did you come from the reenactment practice?" Danielle asked.

The woman giggled. "Ye can say that." She had a strong Scottish accent and a melodic voice.

Was that a yes or a no? Maybe she was Liam's friend, or

maybe she knew Jamie. "Right," she said. "Well. Looks like we're stuck here for a while."

"We dinna need to be. My name is Sìneag. I just opened the tunnel through time for ye. Ye should go through it."

Danielle laughed. "What?"

"Did ye see the stone glow?"

"Yes."

"It means the tunnel is open for ye. If ye put yer hand on that rock, ye will go into the tunnel through the river of time. At the other end, there's a person that's destined for ye."

Danielle couldn't believe her ears. She'd heard a lot of interesting stories and explanations through the years, but never anything as ludicrous as time travel and tunnels through time and fated mates.

She crossed her arms over her chest. "Right. Humor me. Who's that person?"

"Colum MacDonald. A Highland warrior. A man of honor. A man ye can trust."

Danielle raised an eyebrow.

"Because ye dinna trust anyone, do ye?" Sìneag said, narrowing her eyes at her. "Even yerself. 'Tis why ye let that man take ye and hold ye captive."

Danielle felt her face fall. "How do you know? Did Liam tell you? Jamie couldn't have done this to me…"

Sìneag smiled. "I can see into yer heart, love. Ye're lonely. Colum is lonely, too. Together, ye are two parts of a whole. Ye can help each other heal."

Danielle shook her head and scoffed. "Look…it's an interesting story and all, but come on. We're both adults."

"Ye dinna believe me?" Sìneag's eyes glistened with mischief. "Ye dinna trust me."

"No, of course not."

"So what's the harm in trying, then? Prove me wrong. Prove 'tis all children's stories. Touch the stone."

Danielle froze. Her gut told her not to do it. It twisted and turned and churned. Like back when she was sixteen and Sebastian, the new, young neighbor she'd had a crush on, had invited her to play chess with him and prove she could beat him.

The next time she'd leave that house would be about a month later, under the protection of the police, rolled out on a gurney towards a waiting ambulance.

But her logical mind kept telling her this was impossible. Some woman she'd never met before came and told her about a soulmate who was back through time?

"Nonsense," Danielle said. "Sure. But once I touch the stone, would you please not talk about soulmates and time travel and so on?"

Sìneag smiled, and Danielle didn't like the glint in her eyes at all. "Aye, lass."

Danielle sank to her knees by the rock, and there it was, that strange pull again. *Don't do it!* her gut yelled. But what did her gut know when there were no signs of anything being the matter? She didn't trust herself. The strange woman was right about that.

She placed her hand into the handprint. But she found no stone under her palm. Instead, there was cool air, and something sucking her in, and she was falling, tumbling down headfirst into the darkness. Panic squeezed her stomach, and shock hit her like an icy wave. Her gut was right. Whatever this was, she shouldn't have done it.

And then there was only darkness.

CHAPTER 2

L ANDS NEAR S TIRLING, June 1314

W HEN D ANIELLE OPENED HER EYES, IT WASN'T RAINING anymore. She sat up, her head heavy and sluggish, aching.

She was near the ruins. It was quiet under the trees—leaves rustled in the wind, birds sang. Sheep baaed in the near distance, and she could now smell animal dung. She winced and shook her head.

What the bloody hell had happened? She distinctly remembered talking to Jamie and Liam, and then it had rained and then... Oh right. That woman, Sìneag, had told her she'd opened a tunnel through the river of time. And that if Danielle went through it, she'd travel through time and meet the love of her life... What was the name? Colum MacDonald.

Damn her brain. It couldn't forget anything.

Danielle sighed and rose to her feet. Why had she needed to prove a point by touching that stone? Of course she couldn't have traveled through time, but something odd had happened, with her touching empty air instead of a rock. And the feeling like she was falling... And she'd passed out.

All that was very odd, but it could have been an illusion... Or something...

She looked around searching for her purse but couldn't find it. She should return to Jamie's flat. Maybe she'd pick up some groceries on the way, something for the train to Edinburgh tomorrow. Then she had to catch the train to London.

She walked back out onto the grassy hilltop where she, Jamie, and Liam had talked probably half an hour ago.

The sound of bleating was louder now, and she saw the first sheep just beyond the curve of the slope leading down. Right. This was where she had stood, watching the preparations for the Battle of Bannockburn reenactment. Stirling and the town of Bannockburn had stretched down below, tiny houses and roads clearly visible.

Except...

There were no tiny houses. There were no roads. There were no squares and rectangles of farmland surrounding Stirling.

There was nothing but woods and grassy fields. Stirling Castle was still visible in the distance on a rocky hilltop, but there was no city around it. Just a tiny village.

The only other sign of life was the reenactment site—except it wasn't on an open field anymore but seemed to be hidden in between the trees. New Park forest, as she remembered Jamie telling her, looked much bigger than when she'd stood on the hill looking over it with her sister and Liam. Tents were white patches in the clearings across a large area. So many tents. And many more men... In one large clearing, they made formations, grouping together in tight squares or circles, their pikes sticking out as if they were a huge hedgehog.

She remembered Jamie telling her those were called schiltrons. Robert the Bruce had spent months training his men to make these anticavalry formations and move quickly as needed, knowing England would come with a huge force of cavalry.

"What the hell is going on?" she muttered.

Panic ripped her gut apart. Was she even in the right place? What had that stone done? Had she been drugged?

She needed to find out. On shaky legs, she ran down the hill, maneuvering between grazing sheep that darted away startled. One of them ran right under her legs, and she tripped over its back and tumbled down the hill, hitting the ground hard with her shoulders, her back. She rolled onto something squishy. She tried to stop herself, but couldn't.

When the grass and the sky finally stopped turning and she lay flat on the ground, pain radiated through her whole body. And she smelled terrible... Oh no, please, please let her not have rolled into sheep dung...

She sat up, and...sure enough. Her denim jacket was completely smeared with shit. Some of it was even in her long, blond ponytail.

"Eeeeeww..." She wriggled out of her jacket, trying not to touch it, then threw it onto the ground and stood, a little chilly in her black tank top. Gratefully, there didn't seem to be any shit on her jeans or sneakers.

She stared at her jacket and just couldn't bring herself to take it with her. She pulled a paper napkin from her jeans pocket and cleaned her hair as best she could.

"You mates can have my jacket," she said to the sheep that now watched her carefully from up the hill. "I need to find out what's going on. And where the hell I am."

She walked through the woods in the direction of the camp. It must have taken her ten minutes before she started hearing the grunting of men and clashing of iron. Men talking, yelling battle cries. Horses neighing.

This must be a reenactment still. Maybe she had passed out for longer than she'd anticipated. Maybe someone had knocked her out or drugged her and, somehow, she'd been moved to another location altogether, albeit one that looked similar. The thought of someone doing that against her will, just like Sebastian, sent a shiver through her.

She locked the feeling away. She needed to think logically and not give in to her fears. Besides the ruins and the hill she had stood on and Stirling Castle, there was no indication it was the same place. Perhaps it wasn't even Stirling at all. It could be another castle.

She walked out of the woods and into the camp, passing by the men who trained with swords and pikes and axes. Some of them stopped to watch her with odd looks. They were dressed like Liam, wearing tunics and long, heavily quilted coats. Some of them wore chain mail, but most didn't. They all looked much shaggier than Liam, with long beards and unbrushed hair.

She had an odd sensation of danger in her gut.

"Ye lost yer clothes, lad?" said a man with long, blond hair and a build as muscular as a bull.

Lad...he thought she was a man? Excuse her! She didn't have the greatest boobs or the best curves in the world. And she did have defined muscles because she worked out a lot and went to krav maga. But plainly assuming she was a man?

Who cared? She was cold and her jacket had tragically fallen in the battle with the sheep dung.

She nodded. He rummaged in a chest next to a tent and gave her a tunic.

While she put it on, he asked, "Ye came to join Bruce's army? He welcomes everyone—farm lads, shepherds, butchers. Ye would need to train of course, but 'tisna too late."

The tunic slid over her head and covered her to the knees.

"Ye lost yer coif, too? And yer girdle, I see?" He held them out to her.

She wasn't sure she wanted to put anything else on that didn't belong to her, but it was no doubt best to blend in considering there was something strange going on. With a nod, she took the things from him.

She tied the belt around her hips and put on the simple linen coif. None of them were new, but they were clean at least.

"Ye ken where ye go to find the commanders? Sir Keith, James 'Black' Douglas, Aulay MacDonald, and the rest?"

She shook her head.

He pointed at the large tent closest to the center of the field. "There's Bruce's tent. Someone will give ye a sword and a shield over there."

She nodded her thanks and headed over there. Something was very wrong and very fishy. The man was way too serious about this whole reenactment thing... *The Bruce welcomes everyone...* And he'd given her, a complete stranger, some clothes. No doubt he was one of the actors for the reenactment and wanted to ensure she had a proper costume.

As she walked among the tents and the formations of training men, she realized this was quite primitive. A lot of the tents were shelters made of pine branches and simple wooden sticks. Some were made of canvas. People cooked at fires with cauldrons over them. There was not a single thing she'd expect to see from a modern camp: no camp stoves, no canned beans, no signs of modern life.

The only reasonable explanation was that people were super dedicated.

The big pavilion was just like one she'd seen Jamie organize at the reenactment site. As she was about thirty feet away from it, a group of eight men marched towards it. They were all dressed similarly to the rest of the men she'd seen. The only difference, perhaps, was that they had better swords, based on the condition of the sheathes and the hilts. Their quilted tunics were in better shape than most. They had an air of leadership and power around them. But they all had beards and long hair that ranged from ear length to shoulder-blade length, like hers.

"Yer Grace," said one of them. "There are six thousand of us now, but we need more men and women to hunt, forage, and trade with the locals to supply the army with food."

"Robert, he's right," said a huge man in his fifties, quite attractive, with shoulders like boulders. "Let me ride into the villages and ask people to contribute since they may be freed from the English in two sennights."

Robert... Yer Grace... Was the man he was addressing supposed to be Robert the Bruce? She narrowed her eyes, studying the man. He was dressed like the rest of them, no crown, no jewels, no other signs that he might be a royal. He was tall, muscular, clearly proud, and had an air of authority about him. His dark, shoulder-length hair had a few silver strands, and his beard needed grooming. He had a pleasant face with high cheekbones.

"Aye, Aulay, 'tis good," the man they called Robert said. "Do that. We canna let our men starve."

Then they disappeared inside the pavilion. All her spy instincts told her everything she needed to know was inside. Her heart beat faster. So far, she hadn't encountered anything that explained what was going on or where she was. On the contrary, all evidence suggested she was in Robert the Bruce's camp before the Battle of Bannockburn. And it didn't look like a reenactment at all.

A poisonous voice reminded her that Sìneag had said if she touched the rock, she'd land here...and she had touched it. Only, what rational person would believe she'd traveled in time?

She looked around. No one paid any attention to her. She moved closer to the pavilion and sat on the ground by its side and listened. Thankfully, the walls were canvas, and the voices were only a little muffled.

The men gave him reports on the progress of the training. Someone told him Edward's army was almost complete at Berwick and that they would soon make their way to Bannockburn for the battle. They discussed the terrain and the choke points. Some men named Craig Cambel and Angus Mackenzie had a lot to say. It all sounded authentic. If they were actors in the reenactment, she'd expect them to discuss other things, like how to follow scripts and how long it was till the lunch break.

They'd probably wonder if what they were doing was historically accurate.

But there was none of that. Her blood grew colder.

"What are ye doing?" came a male voice behind her.

She jerked and turned around.

Above her, the most gorgeous man she'd ever seen blocked the small patch of blue sky between the crowns of the trees. He had a face so handsome, angels must have cried when they created him: high cheekbones, sharp, slightly slanted eyes, a short beard covering his square, chiseled jaw. He had dark hair tied in a tail at the nape of his neck.

Her death was written in his dark eyes.

And the tip of his sword was one inch away from her nose.

CHAPTER 3

THE MAN GRABBED her by the collar and dragged her away from the pavilion as though she were a sack of potatoes. She kicked and wriggled, trying to get away from him. Honestly, how could a man be so strong as to just drag her...?

But then, she remembered, a man could. Even a man who didn't look strong at all could have power over an unsuspecting person.

Panic she hadn't felt for a long time crept over her. The panic of a dark room and a closed door and the scents of mold and stone and old, damp bed linens. *Hold on. Don't give in to it...*

"Let me go!" she yelled, kicking, trying to stand up.

He lost his grip on her and she ran. She didn't make it far, just ten feet between the tents and shelters, before a huge weight fell on her. Her breath was knocked out of her. He sat on her back, pressing her face against the ground. She tasted the mud on her tongue.

"Who are ye, man?" came a cool voice from above her.

She growled, trying to wriggle out from between his thighs, which straddled her. He thought she was a man, too. What was wrong with these people? Was it her jeans? She'd never had this happen to her in London.

He pressed his arm against her back. "And why were ye eaves-dropping on my king?"

"This is getting out of hand!" she groaned with the little air that remained in her lungs. "I'm done playing these games. Let me go!"

Suddenly, the weight and the pressure were lifted and she was flipped around, facing her assailant. He straddled her, thighs pressing into her ribs.

"What did ye say?"

God. It was hard not to stare. She'd seen he was gorgeous before, but now she was mesmerized. His thick eyebrows gathered together in a perfect line of fury, eyes throwing daggers at her above a straight nose. A strange, curled scar led over his cheekbone down to his beard like a silvery hook. She couldn't breathe, forgot how to move. She hadn't expected to be affected like this by the man who had just mishandled her.

He had broad shoulders under his long, quilted coat and was twice as big as her, it seemed, towering over her like a mountain.

"I said, let me go!" She kicked again uselessly. And his thighs held her so tight, she couldn't get an arm out from under him. She could use a self-defense technique and get him good in his family jewels; they were right there at her chest. But she couldn't, goddamn it. "I'll call for help, for the police. Jamie is in charge of all this. Go ahead, call for Jamie!"

The man froze, and the animosity in his face was washed away by bewilderment. "Who's Jamie?"

"You have got to be joking!" she yelled.

"Jamie... 'Black' Jamie Douglas?" he said. "Ye ken him?"

She wriggled some more. "Unbelievable. Honestly, I'm so tired of people assuming women only have a certain look, certain names. What's *your* name?"

He was still staring at her blankly. "Colum MacDonald," he said, seeming a little dumbstruck.

Colum MacDonald...the name rang a bell, but she didn't have time to dwell on it. He was clearly distracted now. This was the time to make a move. She exhaled sharply to hollow her lungs. Then she lifted her hips and the two-hundred-pound man with her torso—thanks to her daily workout routines—then freed her arms and punched him in the bollocks with all the strength she had. He groaned, and his thighs relaxed, letting her go. She wriggled out from under him, but the moment she was on her feet, he caught her by the arm. She whirled to kick him with her foot, but he was faster and ducked down.

She got her arm free and took several steps away, panting, working hard to catch her breath. "I'm leaving. And, rest assured, I'll tell her about your behavior. You just attacked a visitor."

He narrowed his eyes at her. "Ye're English."

"Yes, and you're Scottish. What does it matter?"

He picked up his sword from the ground and pointed it at her. Good God, why was this guy taking his role so seriously? "Ye were spying, were ye nae?" he demanded.

He wasn't playing the role of a knight like Liam was, she realized. He was actually ready to kill her. Was this how Juan had felt when he'd gone to the meeting and been taken hostage?

"Just trying to understand what is going on," she said.

"Of course ye were. So that ye can take yer information back to yer blasted king." He pressed the tip of the sword against her rib cage. Horror spread from that cold, sharp tip through her veins. "Walk."

She was shaking. She remembered staring down the barrel of a shotgun, the one that was licensed for clay pigeon shooting and deer stalking, that Sebastian had held on her when he'd told her to go into the basement. The cool, sleek drip of sweat that had run down her spine.

Oh God, oh God, oh God. This was a bit too far for a reenactment. There was no one crying out commands. There were no people checking safety. No electrical generators, wires, cookers, heaters. The weapons and armor all looked alarmingly real.

She swallowed hard. She needed to get out of here. The last

time someone had pointed a weapon at her, she was held captive. "Look, you needn't act like this with me. Like it's all real. You're being a bit too much."

His eyes were cold. She'd seen those kinds of eyes on people who'd known real darkness. On war survivors. Torture victims. She'd seen that look in her own mirror.

"Walk," he said.

She walked. The tip of his sword was pressed against her back. She could almost feel it breaking her skin, ripping through her muscle, the blood flowing down from her wound. She walked along the pavilion wall, and when she passed by the entrance, he said, "Enter."

She opened the entrance of the tent, and men stared at her as she walked in. Robert the Bruce, the man called Aulay, and six others. They stood around a table with a large map on top of it. They were all in that armor she'd seen before, somber, battle-forged faces astounded as they watched her.

As a good spy, Danielle knew she should let them talk first, see if what they said could help her gain ground.

"'Tis an English spy," said Colum.

Well, not that. This was exactly the type of bad situation a spy could be in. She knew enough of history to know being English in a Scottish camp during the Wars of Independence was not a good thing. She was the enemy spy before a decisive battle, so she knew they'd act like they were furious with her.

Please, let this be some sort of a hard-core cosplay. She told herself not to listen to that gut feeling that something was terribly wrong.

"Who are ye?" asked the man playing Bruce.

"No one," she said. "I was just visiting Jamie."

"Here's Jamie." Colum pointed at a man in his thirties. "James 'Black' Douglas." Right, this was supposed to be another famous historical figure. He was medium height and had the broad shoulders of a warrior. A light-brown beard framed his face, and shaggy hair of the same color reached his shoulder blades. "Ye ken this man, James?"

The man playing James Douglas came closer and looked her over. For a moment, his eyes landed on her chest, and she froze. Would one of them finally recognize she was a woman? But the baggy tunic hid any hint of femininity.

"Nae," said the actor playing Douglas.

"What is yer name?" asked the man playing Bruce.

They all assumed she was a man. At least that would maintain some sort of a cover. She wasn't sure if the fact that she was a woman would make her situation worse. "Daniel," she said.

"Aye. Sassenach," said a man with a sharpshooter's eyes.

"Ye're right, Craig," said the Bruce. "The accent. Though he kens Gaelic well enough..."

Danielle froze. *Gaelic?* Bloody hell, they'd all been speaking Gaelic this whole time—and so had she! How could she explain that?

"Look," she said. "I know I'm supposed to be the enemy in your script, but can we just stop this for now? I really don't want to play any games. All I want to do is find Jamie and get the hell out of here."

"Who is that Jamie ye talk about?" asked another tall, handsome blond warrior.

"I am Jamie," said James Douglas, "but I dinna think the lad means me. There must be two of them, Owen. There must be another spy in the camp."

"Aye. Look for the spy, lads," said the man playing Bruce. "And ye, Colum, take this one to the cage."

"Aye, Yer Grace."

"And, Colum?"

"Aye?"

"Ye've done well, lad." The king squeezed his shoulder.

Colum grabbed her by the elbow and dragged her out of the tent.

CHAPTER 4

THE PRISONER GLARED at Colum through the wooden bars of the cage. Served him right, the English pig, snooping around, spying.

The lad must be sixteen or so, judging by the lack of a beard and the voice, which was a wee bit high for a man. His shoulders weren't broad, but he was tall, and he wouldn't be comfortable in the low cage with thick wooden bars. It wasn't big, barely tall enough to sit and wide enough to sleep curled into a ball. There were several of these in the middle of the camp, standing under the canopy of the New Park forest. They had been prepared in advance for English hostages—there would always be important nobles and knights to be captured...

Of course, if they were victorious in the battle to come.

Despite the lad's slender figure, he was strong judging by the resistance he'd given Colum. His big blue eyes were dark with fury, his chest rising and falling quickly as he sat with his back against the cage, long legs bent at the knees and feet propped against the bare ground.

If anything, the lad looked a wee bit feminine. Even his movements were graceful. His face was very bonnie for a lad, with long lashes, high cheekbones, and full, sensual lips. It wasn't unusual; Colum had seen lads like him. He'd been thin and scrawny for a while before his own body could grow some muscle. Despite his femininity, there was something fierce about the lad—a strength he couldn't help but respect.

And yet, the lad was an English spy and a liar. The enemy.

He served the cruel king who had pillaged Colum's land, hammered his fist over innocent people. The king whose men raped, killed, and stole.

The king who had forced Colum to betray his people back in 1306.

King Edward II.

And Daniel served the bastard.

A young sentinel guarded Daniel. Colum eyed the prisoner, who kept glaring back at him, not budging, his steely blue eyes like blades.

They needed to increase their sentinels. This English spy had just walked in. Had he come on foot all the way from Berwick? And where was his partner, this Jamie?

A shadow appeared next to him, and when Colum looked to his side, he saw Robert the Bruce eyeing Daniel.

"Yer Grace," said Colum.

"Colum." Bruce nodded and folded his arms over his chest. "Did he say anything?"

"I didna ask."

"Well, ask. But be careful. The way he's watching ye, I wouldna be surprised if he'd bite yer hand off."

Colum nodded and stepped forward. The lad raised his chin up.

"How many are in Edward's army now?" asked Colum.

Daniel said nothing for a few moments, just glared at him. "I don't know," came his eventual reply.

"Edward must move soon," said Bruce to Daniel, stepping closer. His dark eyes glistened. "'Tis only sixteen days till John the Baptist, which is the date by which Stirling must be freed by the English, or it comes into my hands. Is Edward waiting for someone else?"

Daniel shook his head. His blond eyebrows gathered at the bridge of his straight nose. "Are you even aware what kind of trouble you're going to get? Jamie is going to kill you."

Kill Bruce...

All the hair on Colum's body stood. Bruce went completely still by Colum's side. And when they looked at each other, there was the same exact thought on Bruce's face. "Jamie is an assassin," said Colum quietly. "He's here to kill ye, Yer Grace."

Colum's hand lay on the handle of his claymore and he cast a quick glance around. Daniel shook his head in disbelief and rolled his eyes. "If this is the game you still want to play..."

Colum moved closer to the cage. The lad followed him with his eyes, his face stoic. When Colum lowered himself by the cage, his face was a few inches away from Daniel's. He could smell the lad's strange, flowery scent that was too pleasant for a farmer, but it was mixed with the scent of sheep dung, and that was true. His skin was far too smooth, no scars or blemishes, though he had a few smudges of dirt on his face. From this close, he could see long, curly, blond eyelashes that gave the lad that feminine look.

"Where is this Jamie ye talk about?" he asked.

"I don't know. If you give me a phone, I'll find out."

"A phone... What is that?" he asked.

Daniel bit his lower lip as though to stop himself from smiling, and Colum's upper lip curled in a snarl.

"Ye arrogant wee prick." He grasped the bars of the cage and rattled them. The sound of wood cracking made him let go. "Like all English, ye think we Scots dinna ken yer fancy words, do ye? Ye think we are all uneducated, wild barbarians?"

The smile fell off Daniel's face, and fear flashed through his eyes for a moment, but he stubbornly stuck his chin forward. "I do not want to play in your reenactment," he said, slowly pronouncing every word.

Reenactment? What in God's bones was that? It was as though they spoke different languages even though they were both speaking Gaelic.

Bruce laid his heavy hand on Colum's shoulder. "Lad," he said. "Dinna let him get to ye. He's trying to confuse us. He's succeeding."

Colum rose to his feet, still fuming. Daniel watched him with a wild ferocity. Colum had managed to scare the shite out of him. Well, good.

He and Bruce walked out of Daniel's earshot. "Coming here, spying, bringing an assassin—" Colum mumbled, then went completely still as an idea struck him.

If Edward could send spies and assassins to the Scottish camp and they could enter so easily, what stopped Bruce from doing the same? Edward was coming with a huge army. It might be even bigger than any army his father, Edward I, the Hammer of the Scots, had ever brought.

"Yer Grace," Colum said. "If Edward sent an assassin to kill ye, ye must be on yer guard."

"Aye. I ken that."

"And it means ye can send an assassin to kill him first."

Bruce was silent in shock. "Colum, ye dinna mean that."

"I do. Send me."

Bruce sighed heavily. "'Tis a suicide mission. I wilna send ye to yer sure death."

He was right. It would be dangerous. But Colum had nothing to lose. His clan still didn't trust him because he had betrayed the most valuable thing for a Highlander—his clan. His honor. His very soul.

Aye, they didn't know why he'd had to do it. They didn't know he had lived every day for the eight years since with a cracked soul. And he couldn't tell anyone the real reason why he'd had to break his word. He couldn't inflict such a terrible embarrassment on the queen, to have people know how compromised she'd been. Had Edward not done what he had to Queen

Elizabeth...had he not been ready to force a wee, innocent lass to watch the rape and beating of her stepmother while her father, the king, was missing and possibly dead...

Colum would have gladly died before he'd swear his allegiance to England.

But there were worse things than death.

"Yer Grace," Colum said. "Ye ken what I had to do in Berwick."

He had told Bruce what he'd seen in Berwick because he needed him to know his wife and daughter were safe. He also wanted him to have this information to make the best decision about what to do. The Bruce had then asked him to keep this secret to protect the queen's honor.

"I do. And I will never stop thanking ye for what ye did for my wife and daughter."

"And I'd do it again. I'm nae saying it to ask for yer gratitude. What I mean is, I ken them. I lived with them for almost a year. I can sneak in—"

Bruce's nostrils flared. "Colum, nae."

Colum threw a glance at the cage. Daniel sat and stared at the two of them, his arms straight over his knees, fiddling with a strand of grass. From this distance, the baggy tunic was like a sack over his slender body. Colum could almost feel poison seeping from the lad's eyes.

Around them, the camp was alive with sound: wooden swords knocking as men trained, commanders yelling as they taught men military formations, horses neighing, someone cutting wood for the campfires, arrows swooshing and thonking against straw targets.

It was a hot June afternoon, and the air was heavy with moisture from the ground and grass.

At some distance, he heard "Clann Domhnaill! Clann Domhnaill!" the war cry of his clan. That meant they were training, too. Not under his command. They might never accept him as their next laird.

But it wasn't that that worried him about this whole situation. It was the deep ache of his soul. The need to be forgiven. The need to be part of his clan again. To serve his people, his community. His family.

"Yer Grace. Ye're the only one that kens what happened. When my clan came bursting through Berwick Castle, ready to kill and die for me, they found me dressed in English armor. Wearing a surcoat with three golden lions. They risked their lives, and some of them died—and for what? For a traitor."

Bruce gave a long sigh and looked at his feet. He brushed his fingers through his dark, wavy hair and looked at Colum. "I ken, lad. I appreciate yer silence to them. I asked ye to nae tell the truth. The only person that I told is yer uncle Aulay, and I ken he'd die before he betrays this secret to anyone."

"Aye. I wouldna have told anyone on my own accord. Yer queen's honor is more important to me. But if I can redeem myself, I will. Let me go to Berwick and kill Edward. Then this whole battle wilna happen. We all ken how many lives it would save. Yer life is on the line. Eight years of war and hardship, thousands of lives lost to keep ye on the throne. All that is at stake now. Let me do this for ye."

Bruce's face was unreadable. His small, dark eyes were on Colum like two shiny currants. Then he shook his head and clasped Colum's shoulder. "'Tis in God's hands now, Colum. There's no one more loyal and courageous than ye. But I canna send ye to yer sure death when we can all win together. We've been preparing for months. We can do this."

Colum opened his mouth to say it wouldn't be a sure death and he wouldn't mind dying for his country and his clan and his king, but Bruce interrupted him. "Nae, Colum. I command ye to stay in the camp."

Defeat had Colum hanging his shoulders. He stared at Daniel a few long moments. His king was way too honorable, way too loyal. That was why Colum respected him and was ready to die for him. But Colum knew he was right about this. If Edward was pig enough to send an assassin and a spy, Bruce should do the same.

Colum would take the hard decision away from his king. He must disobey him for the greater good. If Edward II was dead, the battle might never happen. There would be chaos and quarrels, and if Colum did his job right, mayhap he would put the English nobles at one another's throats if they didn't know who killed the king.

He met Bruce's eyes and had to lie to his king for the first time in his life. "Aye."

Bruce nodded and clapped him on the shoulder. "Good. 'Tis better this way."

As his king left, Colum looked around. No one was nearby, save for Daniel's guard. Colum nodded at him and walked to the other side of the cage where he wouldn't hear. He sank into a crouch and wriggled his finger to Daniel. Daniel frowned at him and moved closer. "Daniel, do ye want me to free ye?" Colum asked quietly.

The lad's eyes widened in surprise. "Yes, of course."

"Then ye will have to come with me to Berwick and tell me about the English camp."

CHAPTER 5

IT WAS night and the camp was quiet as Colum moved without a sound among the shelters and the tents whitening in the darkness. An owl hooted somewhere in the black shape of the woods around the camp. Men snored. The scent of woodsmoke lingered, and the campfires of the night sentinels glowed orange.

When Colum came to Daniel's cage, a different young guard stood, leaning against his spear, barely keeping his head up. Daniel scrambled to the front of the cage, holding the grating.

"Ye're relieved, lad," Colum said to the sentinel.

The guard's eyes flew open. "Aye?" he said hopefully.

"Aye. I'm supposed to switch with ye for the night watch."

The guard looked around. "Really? But my watch just barely began..."

"Ye worked hard today," Colum said. "Yer commander told me ye need to take a rest. I'll take over."

The lad sighed in relief. "My thanks. Och, I dinna mind a bed." He shoved the keys to the cage into Colum's hand and left.

When the lad was out of sight, Colum retrieved the travel sack he'd hidden behind a nearby tent on his way here. Then he walked to the cage, the key in his hand. He met Daniel's eyes.

"Ye remember our agreement, aye? I let ye out of the cage. Ye come with me to Berwick and tell me everything there is to ken about entering the camp."

"Yes," Daniel said. "I remember. Go on, let me out."

Colum retrieved the shackles he'd found earlier. "Put yer hands through the grating."

Daniel's eyes were wide on the shackles. "What? No! I won't let you put those on me."

"'Tis the only way ye're coming out of the cage. I could go by myself and leave ye here to rot."

"You're mad!" the lad whisper-cried. "I'll scream and tell everyone you were about to let me go."

That was such an odd thing for a soldier to say, he was caught off guard momentarily. He shook off the feeling. This lad had to be an English spy. There was no other reason for him to be in the camp. And he certainly looked like he was willing to kill.

"Ye wilna because ye will stay in this cage forever."

Daniel's mouth became a straight, angry line, and his delicate nostrils flared as he breathed in and out. "Okay."

Colum frowned. "What?"

"Yes." Daniel put his wrists through the gap in the grating. "You mad arsehole."

Colum scoffed at the insult. It was a funny one. He hadn't heard it before. As he put the shackles around the lad's wrists, he marveled at how thin and dainty they were. He was just young.

He remembered the moment his own shackles had been removed. It was right after he'd dropped to his knees in front of Edward. His oath had been ironclad, binding him stronger than any restraints. He'd thought he would serve England for the rest of his life, and he'd hoped it would be a short one. How could he raise a sword against his countrymen? And perhaps one day against his own clan?

He'd found out quite soon. Eight months later, Berwick Castle had been stormed at night. Like other warriors, Colum had been woken up that night by screams and clashes of metal. He jumped to his feet and put on the chain mail and surcoat. He grabbed his sword and shield, and he left the barrack and went to battle with a heavy heart, knowing it must be the Scots that attacked Berwick. It must be the king he had loved but no longer served.

When he ran out into the bailey, the shadows of the battling warriors cast by the fires of burning arrows were black demons dancing their wild dance. Blades flashed with orange and red. In the darkness, it was impossible to see what clan these men were from. A large man who had just finished an Englishman with his two-handed sword turned around and sprinted towards Colum, raising his sword.

Colum roared, calling the rest of his shattered honor to come and serve him. And if he was lucky, he would die under that claymore that headed for his neck.

He raised his own sword, ready to strike.

The man was only three steps away when Colum froze in silence. The man's face came to view in the light of a nearby torch.

It was a face Colum had known his whole life, the face of the man who'd taught him how to hold his very first sword, how to navigate a birlinn, and how to sprint through the Highlands and stalk the enemy like a wolf.

His uncle Aulay.

Turned out, there was an oath Colum couldn't break. An oath that ran deeper than anything he'd promised to Edward. Queen Elizabeth and Marjorie had long ago been taken to another castle, and Colum didn't know what had happened to them or Bruce's sister—didn't know if they were alive.

His uncle stopped, too. He looked him over, as though not believing his eyes. Trying to make sure he'd really seen the English lions on Colum's surcoat, the English sword in his hands.

And then Colum dropped to his knees for a second time,

handed his uncle the sword, and put down the coif and bowed his head, exposing his neck.

"Do it, Uncle," he'd said. "Do it."

But Aulay hadn't. And now Colum was here.

So aye, he knew the desperation of being captured and trapped by the enemy, just as Daniel did. As he slid the key into the lock, he realized it was also the enemy that had made him who he was. He had no limits now, he knew as he turned the key and the lock gave a metallic click.

He was ruthless. As merciless with the enemy as they had been with him. As he opened the cage door and Daniel walked out, he grabbed the lad's elbow and led him quietly through the sleeping camp to kill the king who was destroying his country and who had destroyed his honor.

And he would probably die there.

He was going to his destiny.

CHAPTER 6

"W OULD ye like to kill me, lad, is that it?" asked Colum as he stopped chewing.

They sat on a log by the side of the old Roman road leading to Edinburgh. Around them, the woods were sparse, but a few tall trees shot into the sky, their crowns shielding the sunlight.

They had paused for a cold lunch after riding Colum's horse, Gaisgeach—which, for some reason, she knew meant "warrior" —for the whole night and well into the next day. They'd passed by woods and fields and bogs. The landscape was beautiful and wild, with hills and occasional cliffs. She'd seen some plants she could have foraged for food had she been camping...and not in shackles.

What she hadn't seen were any signs of civilization. No asphalt roads. No electric power lines. No planes in the sky. No sounds of vehicles in the distance. Only the wild scents of nature —greenery, flowers, occasional animal scat, the manure of the horse. Bees and flies buzzed by. Birds sang in the treetops.

The pain in her bottom from sitting on the horse for so long, and of the shackles on her wrists, was hard to ignore.

Despicable man, taking her hostage. The blade of his sword had been like the barrel of Sebastian's shotgun pointing at her.

Even after sixteen years, panic had gripped her by the throat in a clawing, icy grasp. Just like it had back then. And suddenly, she wasn't a thirty-two-year-old woman who had carefully built an impenetrable wall guarding her trust and her heart.

She was once again a helpless teenage girl who'd trusted the wrong man and now suffered the consequences.

The sword was just a prop. It couldn't really hurt her, she'd told herself. She was at a reenactment that had gone too far. She hadn't time traveled.

But her gut had wrenched in panic. And deep down she'd known the sword was real. She'd seen the death sentence in Colum's eyes. No one could be that good of an actor.

And so she'd walked.

And when he'd locked her into that cage... She'd been a cornered animal, ferocious and desperate. Like back in Sebastian's basement when she'd banged on the door of the room he'd locked her in and cried for help. Her parents had been only thirty feet away in the house next door. How was it possible that she'd been kidnapped by a neighbor?

The same shaking panic, the same trembling desperation had thundered in her gut back in that cage. There'd been no concrete walls and no metal door, she could see everything that was going on around her, but the feeling had been the same. She shouldn't have touched the rock. She should have never gone into the camp.

Colum raised his eyebrows as he waited for her to reply. She bit the piece of bannock he'd given her and chewed. It was hard and stale, but she was hungry and this was food.

He still thought she was a man, which was good. At least he wouldn't be tempted to rape her.

"Kill you...?" she replied. "Well, I wouldn't mind if you dropped dead just now. Let me go!"

Colum chewed more. "Dinna ye try to escape again. Next time ye try, I will have to give ye a good beating. I dinna want to do it, but ye're asking me to show ye the boundaries."

Danielle blinked. The bastard had tied her shackles to his waist after she'd tried to escape the first time. She'd gotten so close to the goddamn rune-covered rock, she could see the top of the hill when his strong arm had dragged her down... The second time, she'd gotten only about five steps away from him when his large, heavy body had pinned her to the ground. For the first time she'd felt more than hatred towards him. Heat had rushed through her body where he'd covered her. There was something animalistic about him combined with military training. It was fascinating to watch him move, walk in his confident, collected warrior's swagger. He was handsome, lean, and muscular like a tiger. But she knew better than to drool over a man who was keeping her captive.

This could be Stockholm syndrome, and she knew about that all too well.

The stream gurgled, and the woods around them rustled. The scents of wildflowers and wet mud were strong here. It was peaceful, almost idyllic if not for the giant, despicable Scotsman glaring at her.

At least she wasn't in the cage. But she still wore the heavy, iron medieval shackles that made painful indents in her wrists. Once again, she was a captive. There was a part of her that was horribly close to breaking down.

And not just because of the shackles.

Because now almost twenty-four hours had passed since she had touched the blasted rock and come to a different version of the camp. She hadn't seen any signs of modern life. And she spoke Gaelic, goddamn it! How could she speak Gaelic?

She was seriously considering accepting the impossible.

That she had traveled in time, just like Sìneag had promised.

Only, Colum MacDonald could not be the love of her life. He was the hate of it.

So she had to escape. She still could. She just needed to be smarter about it. It would be easier to escape with one man guarding her rather than the whole camp waiting to catch her.

She took another bite of the tough bannock.

"When will you let me go?" she asked.

"After I complete my mission."

His mission... He didn't know it, but she had heard every word he'd exchanged with the Bruce. She knew what his mission was.

And she knew it was a suicide mission. Jamie had told her a bit about the battle. Twenty thousand men were in Edward's army against about six thousand Scots. The best knights—not just of England but of Europe—were gathered there, chasing glory and riches. There were five thousand archers and spearmen from Wales alone.

"Your mission..." She chuckled. If she had to go on this mission, she might not return.

She wondered for a moment if she'd had Juan go into the exact same situation in Venezuela...if it *was* all her fault. Yes, Colum's plan was suicidal.

The only way he could survive was on a team. He needed a partner. He needed someone who spoke English without a Scottish accent, who knew the camp. Who could be trusted.

Her.

But she'd never do this. She'd never help him. And he'd never trust her, anyway.

She decided to be straight with him. "You will never succeed. They'd never let you kill the King of England."

That she knew because that was not how the Battle of Bannockburn had gone according to historical texts. However, she remembered the story of a kamikaze Highlander who had been caught, killed, and quartered.

He put the last piece of his bannock into his mouth and wiped his fingers against each other to brush off the crumbs. "We'll see. They definitely didna succeed in sending ye to our camp, did they?"

She shook her head. "I was not sent by anyone. I'm not serving Edward II. And there's no assassin trying to kill the

Bruce! What is happening is that you kidnapped me, took me captive, and now are dragging me across Scotland so that *you* can get killed."

"Dinna fash, Daniel," Colum said, his voice low, his eyes like bullets. "Ye ken how ye can get free. I may be going to my death, and if I take a wee shitty spy like ye to the grave with me, so be it."

CHAPTER 7

As they continued the next day, Danielle's mind kept racing. The hard torso of the Scot against her back and her bum were distracting. And sitting on the horse, rocking with its movement and feeling Colum's rock-hard body against her, his muscular arms holding the reins on both sides of her body made her brain melt into goo.

It became harder to think about new ways she could escape. Especially disturbing was that her body had all these hot feelings and desires towards him while he was her captor who hated her with the ferocity of a hundred suns, and who thought she was a teenage boy.

But she had to keep her cool. She'd been trained to keep her cool, not to be affected by emotions. And for most of her career, she'd been very successful in that. A perfectly cool slab of rock she was.

She had gone on dates with attractive, tall, muscular men. She had had sex with attractive, tall, muscular men. It had never been great, not for her. And never in her life had she felt as if she were about to melt and burn in any man's presence.

Until Colum.

She needed to take control. This was the ultimate test, and she was failing. *Get it together, you cream puff.*

As they rode past the swaying trees of the forest, she tried to reason with him, to convince him to open her shackles and let her go. He remained as stony and silent as a blasted mountain. Then finally he'd said her tricks wouldn't work on him.

She breathed her frustration out in a long sigh. Bribery. She hadn't tried that yet.

"What would it take for you to free me?" she said.

"Ye helping me when we get there."

"What about money?" she asked. Her wallet was not with her, but she was positive she could find a way to get him some coin if she had to.

Good God, was this how Juan had felt, desperate and ready to go to any lengths to get back home? To safety?

She had begged Sebastian to let her go, too. Just like now, she had offered him money. Sure, her accountant dad and her school-teacher mum didn't have a lot, but surely they'd come up with something. But Sebastian hadn't wanted money.

What he'd wanted was a girl completely in his power. What he'd wanted was to watch her, observe her, and keep her like a pet, all under his control.

He had explained to her it was a similar sort of desire as collectors of insects or cars had. To find something unique and beautiful and have it. Only, instead of cars and insects, he collected girls. She was the third one he had caught. The first two hadn't survived their captivity.

A shiver of revulsion went through her. That feeling of being diminished to a thing with no voice, no will. An object to be owned.

She'd need to ask Juan about his experience if she ever saw him again. She'd already missed her first interview, and it was only three days until her hearing, where she may be sacked.

Then she would never have a chance to talk to Juan again because her contact with him would be forever cut. She wanted to tell him how sorry she was this happened to him on her watch. That she understood how it felt to be kept captive. That the whole reason she went into MI5 was to protect others.

"Money?" Colum scoffed. "There is not enough gold in England to buy ye out, lad. Besides, where would a farm boy get any money? Unless there's something ye arenae telling me?"

She needed to divert him. "What then?"

If he knew she was a woman, she could try to seduce him. Well, he might be into men, too, but there would be a problem with that—namely the lack of a penis and the presence of, however small, boobs.

She needed to find out what was important to him. Clearly, money wasn't. That was sort of new. Most people in the twenty-first century would be tempted by a large enough sum.

She tried to recall what she knew about him. He was loyal, a patriot dedicated to the cause and to his king. Damn, it was hard to work with such values. But there must be something.

"Why are you doing this?" she asked.

"'Tis clear why, nae?" he said.

"I like my country, too, but I don't go around trying to kill other kings," she said. "There must be more there."

Behind her back, he was stiff and silent. *He'd* be a great spy. "Is it your clan?" she asked.

She felt his thighs tense around hers, and his chest, which had risen and fallen evenly against her back as he breathed, stopped moving. She must be right.

"What about your clan?" she asked. "Is it in danger?"

"'Tis nae of yer concern."

So it was the clan. Her mind raced to remember anything about clan MacDonald that Jamie might have told her or she might have read. She would remember something. "What if there's certain information I could offer you?"

"What information?"

If only she had Jamie's knowledge. All she remembered was that Robert the Bruce would win using guerilla tactics and the strategic position of Bannockburn to his full advantage. They had dug pits around the road the English would appear from and created a choking point, which allowed them to win against a force four times stronger than them.

She was sure they were already working on all that.

Still. She could come up with something generic. "You'll have to make a deal with me. Free me and I'll tell you."

He scoffed. "Wee liar, are ye nae, lad?"

"What makes you say that?"

"And a bad liar at that. Ye dinna ken a thing about my clan, about my king, or about me. Grow a beard first before ye try."

He was stubborn, but he was right. She didn't know a lot. But he didn't know much about her, either. In fact, everything that he thought he knew about her was wrong. She wasn't a lad, and she wasn't even from this time.

He also didn't know being captive wasn't new to her. And unlike before, she wasn't in a windowless basement with a metal door locked and bolted. This time it wasn't four walls that held her captive. It was one man and his body around her. Even shackles wouldn't really stop her. She could run with them on.

It was he who imprisoned her.

God, how she hated him. And he hated her, too, it was crystal clear. It was a different kind of situation from sixteen years ago. Sebastian didn't hate her. He was fascinated by her. In his sick way, he had even loved her like collectors love their precious, rare possessions.

But she wouldn't be owned and controlled anymore. She wasn't a scared, vulnerable teenager. She was a trained MI5 investigator. She'd stopped four large cyberattacks on the UK in her career.

What was a medieval Highlander compared to that? She'd find his weakness. Every mountain had a pass to climb it. Maybe not now, but she'd probe and try until he lost his cool and his control. Then she'd slip out.

Only, knowing that he was going to be killed out there in the

English camp made her wish she could change his mind. His death would, of course, free her. But he wasn't a sick psycho or an evil man like Sebastian. He was a warrior who did what he did out of loyalty to his country.

So no, she didn't wish him dead. She just wished he'd let her go.

They went farther and farther south, farther and farther from her way back home. When orange sunrays peeked low through the leaves and branches in the west, they made a stop. She could hear the sound of running water nearby, and the ground was rockier than it had been, the vegetation less abundant.

He helped her get down from the horse and tied her to a tree. Pleading with him hadn't helped. Now it was time to do something physical. Like knock him unconscious. She'd watch for an opportunity to do just that.

The horse grazed peacefully ten feet away. As Colum bustled about setting up a campfire, she watched him. There it was, the blasted key, on a ring around his girdle. He had his back to her, his broad shoulders rounded as he worked.

His mistake. He had become soft and relaxed around her. Thought she was a wee farm lad. Holding her breath, Danielle looked around. There were plenty of old, dry sticks and pieces of wood.

She needed a branch big and heavy enough to hit him. She felt sorry to strike his handsome head, with that black hair in soft curls to his shoulders.

But he should have let her go.

Slowly, soundlessly, never looking away from Colum, she reached out with both her bound hands and grabbed the branch. It felt harsh and prickly against her skin.

The length of the rope tying her to the tree would be just enough to do it. The world froze. The trees stopped moving. Her middle tightened with the apprehension of a trapped animal before a volcanic eruption.

Silently, she rose to her feet above him, careful not to make the dry leaves rustle as she moved. She brought the branch back and swung at him.

The sound was like a rolling pin against an overturned bowl. The impact was hard and knocked her back a little. He swayed, but didn't fall.

Blast! She needed him to be unconscious!

She couldn't lose a moment. He was disoriented.

She lunged at him and wrapped the chain of the shackles around his neck and started choking him. She wouldn't kill him. She'd just choke him until he fell unconscious. He roared and pulled at the chain.

God, he was strong. She tightened her grip and pulled the chain towards herself harder. He was choking, and the terrible sounds he made almost made her stop...

Almost.

No. He was her captor, and she wouldn't give in to Stockholm syndrome.

But he was still stronger. Double, maybe triple her muscle mass.

He tore the chain off his throat. She tried to pull it back in place, but he threw his hands over his head, blocking the chain, and turned, quick as a lion. Teeth bared, eyes red and bulging with fury, he threw himself at her and pinned her to the ground.

He pulled her hands up and over her head and held them with one hand, towering over her like a raging mountain. His face was red, the traces of the chain darkening on his neck.

"Ye fucking bastart, ye almost choked me!" Colum roared into her face.

She struggled, wriggling, bucking from under him. She kicked with her legs and tried to turn. Her tunic kept creeping higher and higher, but she didn't care.

Nothing mattered but getting away. Going home. Back to her life, to defend her position and keep her job.

She was hot and something was brushing so pleasantly

against her chest. The struggle, the fight, the rubbing against him, her fury with him, the desperation to get out, all mixed up in a hot cocktail. Suddenly, she found herself not that furious but bothered and warm and aching.

Something was wrong. In the semidarkness of the dusk, Colum wasn't yelling at her anymore, nor was he pressing against her. He was looming over her and looking down at her chest.

That's when she realized—her tunic had crept up to her neck. From all the wriggling and struggling, the spaghetti straps of her tank top had been pulled down.

And he was staring at her naked breasts.

CHAPTER 8

THE LAD HAD BREASTS...

Small, bonnie, round breasts with pale pink nipples that puckered in two perfect buds.

But lads didn't have wee bonnie breasts, not typically.

Not that he ever heard of.

Nor did they have a thin waist under a strange clinging black garment that curved into feminine hips. Not the broad hips best for childbearing, but bonnie feminine hips nonetheless.

He looked up at Daniel's face. He—she—lay perfectly still, lips round and red, blue eyes dark and glistening on him. His—her—cheeks were flushed, long strands of blond hair had come out of the coif and were plastered to his—her—face. This was a look he'd expect to see on someone who wanted him...who was aroused and aching for him.

He became aware of her long, pleasant, warm body under him. And he didn't want to fight her anymore. Because his own body liked having her there.

Still holding her wrists, he grasped the coif and pulled it down. Long, blond hair, the feel of it silky and thick. Long hair wasn't unheard of for men. But he—she—didn't have a single hair on his—her chin. And now that he saw the face...in combination with the body...and the voice, which was high for a man and perhaps a lower cadence for a woman...

This was not a lad called Daniel.

This was a woman. A goddamn woman and an English spy. She tricked him. What a wee vixen!

He yanked her tunic down to cover her nakedness and stood back up, his eyes never leaving hers. "Ye're a lass!"

Slowly, she sat upright and glared at him from under her eyebrows. All the glistening desire in her eyes was gone, and the same menace he'd seen since he put her in the cage had returned.

"Your observational skills are unheard of," she concluded. She undid a tie that held her hair in a tail behind her head, and it fell around her face in golden locks, framing her high cheekbones and softening the hard edges of her features.

"Ye lied to me," he said.

Now that he saw her in this way, he could hardly imagine how he ever assumed this creature with a long, lean body and the gracefulness of a wildcat could be a man. It was her attire, the tunic and the coif and the breeches she'd been in, that had confused him. And the fact that he'd caught her eavesdropping on his king in the middle of a war camp. He'd just assumed...

"I didn't lie to you," she said, standing up. "You assumed I were a man. I went along with it."

He ran his fingers through his hair. His head hurt where she'd hit him. God's bones, she was strong. His neck ached, and it was painful to talk. She'd almost strangled him.

"Why?" he said. "Ye're a lass...a bonnie lass..." he blurted out and shut up.

The antagonistic glare on her face disappeared, washed away by a bright blush on her cheeks. Her mouth fell open in surprise. For just a mere moment, she looked open...and almost shy. The feral wildcat able to choke an experienced warrior disappeared, and from underneath it, emerged someone vulnerable.

She opened her mouth to say something, then changed her

mind. She pulled her chin up, closed her mouth, and straightened her shoulders. The blush was gone, and she was once again his enemy.

Bonnie lass or not, she was a spy serving England. And if she was able to trick him into thinking she were a lad, what else was she hiding?

And she'd goddamn almost killed him.

"A lass spy is a clever move," he said. "I never heard of such a thing. Women are usually cooks and cleaners in the camp. Healers. Nae spies."

They also typically didn't fight like she fought. Didn't have the physical strength she did. And didn't dress like men.

Owen Cambel's wife, Amber, was who this woman reminded him of most. Amber was a warrior and a military strategist from the caliphate who had helped Bruce win the Battle of Brander six years ago.

"So ye're nae Daniel," he said. "Which *was* a lie ye told. Who are ye then?"

"My name is Danielle. Danielle Field."

Danielle... Need she have a bonnie name, too?

"And I do not spy for the King of England," she added.

He scoffed. "I find that hard to believe. Tell me the truth, *Danielle*. Admit it."

A battle fought on her face, some conflicted emotions he craved to know. She bit her lip, was silent for a short while. Her chest rose and fell quickly. Then he saw the decision made as her face relaxed.

"Right," she said. "You want the truth? I shall tell you the truth. You're right. I am a spy. But not for the King of England." She took a deep breath in and said, "I'm from the future."

From the...what? He shook his head. Did he hear her right? "What?"

"I know it sounds mad! But I was born in 1990. In 2022 I met this woman...at Bannockburn. She told me about time travel through a certain stone...about a man that is meant for me..."

"Who?"

A bright blush covered her cheeks. "You."

He blinked. "Me?"

She blew air out of her mouth in frustration. "I know. She must have been mad or something, that Sìneag."

He scoffed. "Aye. Never would I be the right man for an Englishwoman that lies and cheats and spies."

She rolled her eyes. "Excuse you. You took me hostage and still are keeping me captive and dragging me across the country against my will. Do you think I'd ever go for someone like you? Besides, you're a medieval man."

"Is that another word for 'barbarian'? Ye Sassenachs never miss an opportunity to call us Highlanders that."

She shook her head in confusion. "No, that's not what I meant... Anyway. What happened was, I put my palm against that handprint in the stone and went through time."

He stared at her, waiting for her to say more or for a sign she was jesting. But she kept looking at him with those big blue eyes.

Who did she think he was? A bairn?

Of all the things she could have said...of all the things she could have lied about...she chose *time travel?*

He laughed. He laughed for a long time, letting the joy and the ridiculousness of the situation roll over him. It was almost a physical release. The relief of a careless laugh. He didn't know the last time he'd allowed himself to laugh like that. It had definitely been before Methven. Before he'd betrayed his clan.

He wiped the tears from his eyes and sighed, letting the last laughs bubble up and calm down.

She shook her head, looking very displeased. "I knew you wouldn't believe me."

"I kent a spy would come up with an explanation, but never in my life did I imagine to hear a story like this."

"If I were a spy sent by Edward II, wouldn't I have thought of a better cover story?" She pointed at her shoes. They had hard, rounded noses and thick soles of a strange material. They were laced like a lady's dress. The material of her breeches was odd, too. He'd wondered about it for a while. It was blue and hugged her legs closely.

He studied the breeches and shoes, no longer laughing. Aye, he admitted, those looked very different. Then he remembered another person who everyone thought was so different—Jenny, Aulay's wife. She'd had that unnaturally bright dress and an accent he'd never heard before. And all those different notions about medicine. She'd even questioned their healer, Bhatair.

Nae. There must be another explanation. Something else must be going on.

"I'm nae glaikit," he said. "Yer shoes look crafty but mayhap 'twas a master in England that made them."

He observed her long, sculpted legs in her blue breeches. What to even call this fabric? It looked like nothing he'd ever seen before. But it didn't prove she was from the future.

"Tell me who ye really are."

She shrugged. "Whatever I tell you from here on would be a lie because you don't believe the truth."

CHAPTER 9

LATER THAT EVENING, Danielle blew on the steaming trout lying on a piece of bark that she held in her hands. The shackles hurt her skin, and she threw an angry glare at Colum. He'd kept her tied to the tree while he went fishing in the small river nearby. The fish was a welcome break from dry bannock, but she'd do anything for a fresh salad. Between the stones and rocks, she could see dandelion and yarrow and some wild garlic growing. Would Colum let her pick some of the dandelion and garlic?

Seeing the plants she recognized made her heart squeeze for her old life, a life that was starting to feel like a dream. Every day she thought about her dad. Her mom. Jamie. They all must be going mad searching for her—again.

The thought made a cold shiver run through her. Sebastian hadn't happened just to her. He had happened to her family, too. For a month, they had been looking for her, not sleeping, not eating, organizing searches, and going around the neighborhood asking if anyone had seen their daughter.

And now they'd lost her again. She worried for her dad's weak heart. And for her mom's PTSD. And for Jamie, who may think she was the one who had lost her sister.

She needed to run, get back to them, right now. And her job... The hearing was fast approaching, and if she lost her job... Money was one thing, but if she didn't even turn up for her own hearing, she would hardly be employable. Being stuck here any longer could ruin the remainder of her career.

She picked up a piece of fish with her fingers and put it in her mouth and chewed. "Needs seasoning," she said.

Colum sat across from the campfire and ate his fish, his shoulders rounded. She supposed she should be grateful that, despite his absolute hatred of her, he was still honorable enough to feed her. She also noticed he gave her the juiciest part of the fish and left the bony tail for himself.

He didn't look up at her as he kept chewing the fish, his movements businesslike.

"Excuse the barbarian for the bland dinner," he said with his mouth full. "Salt and saffron dinna grow on trees here in Scotland."

"I meant, there's wild garlic right there." She pointed at the green stalks with white flowers. "The whole plant is edible. If you dig it up, clean it in the river, and chop it, it will go nicely with the fish. And we can eat the dandelion leaves as a salad."

He looked where she was pointing. Then back at her. "Nice try, lass. I would rather ye eat bland fish than try and trick me once again. If ye didna notice, I dinna believe a word ye're saying."

"Sure. Stubborn Scot. Why would you listen to reason?"

"Lying and cheating Sassenach. Ye wilna trick me nae more. What if ye want to poison me?"

"They're not poisonous. I spent a lot of time camping and foraging—I know which plants are edible and which are not."

He scoffed. "Exactly."

She'd learned foraging and basic survival skills after she was released from that basement. Camping and spending time outdoors had helped her cope with the fear of being trapped and caged. Her dad had taken her out to the Lake District after she'd kept waking up from nightmares where she was trapped in that small concrete room with the iron door. She and Dad had stood on top of a large hill and looked over the vast landscape of hills and woods, and there was nothing but sky and air. It had been the first time in months that she'd felt free.

Ever since, she and Dad had camped often. Even when she'd moved out and gotten her own flat, she'd continued going on camping trips with him and sometimes by herself. Together, she and her dad had taken survival courses that had included foraging for plants and mushrooms. She knew how important it was to identify things correctly and would never eat anything she wasn't sure of.

"Well then, just untie the rope and let me go and get it and see me eat it first. It's just wild garlic. It's really good for you, and it will be excellent with the trout."

He shook his head, looking at her heavily. "Nae. Just eat yer fish, lass."

She sighed and did exactly that. The trout was excellent, actually, even though some salt, lemon, and garlic would make it amazing.

When they were done with the dinner, she felt better. It was good to have something warm in her stomach, and as she watched Colum throw fish bones into the fire and brush his hands together to remove the last bits of fish, she said, "Thank you, Colum."

He froze and frowned at her. "For what?"

"For the food."

He didn't say anything for a while, then threw the flat piece of bark he'd used as a plate into the fire. "Ye dinna need to thank me. Prisoners are fed and taken care of. I dinna strip anyone of their humanity and honor. I ken what 'tis like."

Something squeezed in her as he said that. What had happened to him? Was that thin scar on his cheekbone the result of a battle, or was there something more to what he told her?

He wasn't a sadist, and he never did anything to humiliate her or harm her in any way. Even though he considered her his enemy, he still treated her with respect.

No, stop this, she told herself. This must be Stockholm syndrome talking. She shouldn't sympathize with her captor; she should be very careful.

Remember what happened last time?

By the end of the month with Sebastian, when the police had come and freed her, she had pleaded with them not to hurt him. He'd managed to convince her he had done what he had done because he appreciated her. She was the most beautiful girl he'd ever seen. He was so alone and his mother had raised him in strict obedience, and he never could have anything he wanted because he was a bad boy who couldn't behave.

She couldn't allow herself to let that happen to her again.

"So if you don't want to strip me of my humanity and rights... can I have a bath?" She looked towards the river.

"A bath?" He followed her gaze, and his eyes narrowed in suspicion.

"Yes. I've now been a captive for three days. My hair still stinks of sheep dung. I reek of sweat."

And she could try to swim away, let the river carry her downstream, or cross the river and run. She remembered how he'd stared at her breasts when he had first seen them. So that she'd felt desired. Maybe he fancied small boobs. And if he stared at her naked again, maybe he'd get distracted and she'd have a chance to run.

Maybe reminding him that she was a woman would help. Maybe he'd even be embarrassed enough to look away...

Internally rolling her eyes at her own words, she said, "My lady parts need some basic hygiene."

He said nothing, only his jaws worked under his short beard. "Yer lady parts," he said through his teeth. Then he gave her a nod. "Well, if yer lady parts need a bath, who am I to refuse them?"

He marched to her purposefully and undid the rope that had been tied around the tree. "But if ye think ye will trick me, ye're sorely mistaken. I wilna let ye out of my sight."

As she walked with him towards the river, she wondered if that was a good thing or a bad thing. And why did the recently mentioned parts warm and burn and tighten at the thought?

The shore was rocky, and a lot of reeds and grasses grew along it. She stretched her arms towards him. "I need you to remove the shackles."

He scoffed and gave her a crooked smile. "Of course ye do." He didn't move a muscle, only stood there holding the rope.

"So, will you? Or I can't remove my clothes."

He shrugged. "Then bathe with yer clothes on."

She swallowed and stared into his dark eyes. "Please, Colum. You said you wouldn't strip your prisoner of their humanity and honor."

"Aye. I am allowing ye to go to the river, am I nae?"

"Remove them just for a moment, until I can pull the blasted tunic off. Then put them back on before I go in."

Then she could hit him in the bollocks and just run for it.

He studied her for a while, then nodded, and his hand went to the key chain on his belt. "Aye."

With time stretching to eternity, she watched him undo the key ring and insert the key into the hole on one shackle. It clicked, and the shackle around her wrist opened and fell. Her heart beat hard in her ears as she watched him insert the key in the second shackle. Her whole body tensed, ready to move the moment she was free. In the single moment between the key turning with a click and the shackle falling, she stopped breathing.

Then she was off. She pushed her feet hard against the ground and broke into a run.

Only, she didn't get far. Strong arms wrapped around her waist in a steellike embrace and lifted her off the ground. She kicked her legs and clawed at him. He pressed her to him tightly, as if clamping her to a bloody stone wall.

"I told ye I wilna let ye run, lass," he growled into her ear as he wrapped the rope around her waist and tied it. She clawed and pushed his arms off, but he tied the knot around her and let her go.

He secured the end of the rope to his belt and stood with his arms crossed, watching her. "Dinna betray my trust again, lass, or this will be the last kind thing I do for ye. Go on and wash yer lady parts."

She was furious with herself. If only she had waited a bit, she could have found a way, perhaps from the river.

"Fine," she said through gritted teeth.

Without looking away from him, she lifted her tunic. It was a bit of a struggle to pull it out of the tightly tied rope. She pulled it up and over her head. Fresh air cooled her naked shoulders. His eyes never left her and went over her body as he frowned, studying her spaghetti strap tank top.

Right. Let him watch, the bastard. He wouldn't look away, and neither would she. And she'd be damned if she would be embarrassed stripping in front of him.

Still looking straight into his face, she undid her jeans and slid them down her legs. She hadn't shaved them before her trip to Stirling. Well, even better. If he was offended by a bit of hair, served him right. She undid her walking shoes and pulled them off. Then her socks. Then she kicked her jeans off her legs. Her feet pressed into the firm ground, the feel of small pebbles and grass prickling. Now she was in only her knickers and her top in front of him.

And she didn't feel that angry or smug anymore. His expression changed, too. From cold anger, his gaze was now dark and dangerous. He kept his eyes pointedly on her face. It didn't help that his sleeves were pulled up to his elbows, and his giant, muscular forearms bulged where they were crossed over his chest. He was all male gorgeousness with his broad shoulders, huge biceps, narrow waist, and the most perfect, long, fit legs spread in a wide stance.

There was no way to back out now. She'd need to strip naked in front of him. Her breath caught.

She tugged the edges of her top out from under the rope and pulled it over her head. He visibly swallowed but still didn't let his gaze drop below her chin. Her skin covered with goose bumps when the next soft gust of wind blew, and her nipples hardened.

Despite herself, heat crept to her cheeks. She would go into the water like this, but she didn't have any other knickers, and the idea of sleeping in wet knickers was horrible. She pulled down her knickers and stepped out of them. She wished she were one of those confident women who loved their bodies and knew the effect they had on men. But no.

Ever since Sebastian, it was as though she'd lost the ability to connect to her own body, to trust it and to enjoy it. It seemed, along with the dark and fearful emotions that she'd locked up deep within her psyche, she'd locked up the ability to experience many enjoyable things.

Like pleasure from sex. Orgasms.

Except, standing now naked in front of this gorgeous man, she felt all kinds of things. Heat in her face. Her heart beating fast and strong. And odd burning and squeezing deep between her legs.

"Go on now, lass," he said, still keeping his eyes on her face, his voice low and rasping.

She turned around and, carefully balancing on the uneven ground and rocks, walked into the slow-moving river. Cold water took her breath away. She stepped on muddy pebbles. Despite the cold, she kept going. The Highlander's unmoving gaze was on her back, and she felt hot where he watched her. Finally, when she was shoulder-deep in the water, feeling weightless and enjoying the feel of water supporting her, she turned around to face Colum. He stood on the riverbank, connected by the rope still around her waist, his dark eyes never leaving her.

As she began washing herself with the river water, he watched her every move. But whether it was because he fancied her physically or because he didn't want to take a chance that she would escape, she didn't know.

CHAPTER 10

THE NEXT DAY...

"BE QUIET," COLUM SAID AND FELT DANIELLE TENSE AGAINST his chest.

He pulled on Gaisgeach's reins and the stallion stopped, nodding his head. The edge of the woods opened to farmland with oats waving in the wind. They were under the cover of the trees and bushes and shouldn't be visible at first glance with the thick woods behind them.

At the end of the field was a croft, including a home with a thatched roof high over low stone walls with no windows. There was also a byre and a shed. An older man and an adolescent lad worked with rakes, cleaning the byre. A cow chewed hay from a pile. Smoke rose from the hole in the roof of the main house.

Six hundred feet away from Colum and Danielle, three riders wearing red surcoats bearing three golden lions over leather armor galloped towards the farm from the west.

"What's going on?" Danielle asked.

The riders stopped at a gate in the simple wooden fence that surrounded the croft and the farm buildings.

"Yer friends are paying a visit," he said.

The riders descended from their horses and tied the animals to the fence. The farmer and his son stopped working and straightened their backs, watching them. A woman appeared in the door of the house, a wee lass of five or so by her side, holding her skirt. The Englishmen unsheathed their swords and marched confidently towards the farmer and his son, who backed away.

"God's bones," Colum spat out through gritted teeth and dismounted. "Ye need to stay here. Get down."

Danielle, still in shackles, stared with worry at the farm. "Are they—"

"'Tis a raid. Yer bloody countrymen are raiding this farm. Go on, climb down. I'm going to tie ye to a tree."

"What? Why?"

"I'm going to help the farmer, and ye are going to stay here until I return."

She swallowed. "Let me help."

He scoffed. "Help? Do ye take me for a fool? Ye will join yer friends, will ye nae? Make haste, or I will drag ye down from this horse. Ye are wasting the farmer's precious time."

She looked pale, and her eye were wide on the farm as she climbed down. He dragged her towards a tree and tied her shackles to the trunk and then the rope around her and around the tree. That should keep her in place for a while.

She opened her mouth to say something, but he didn't have time. One of the Englishmen raised his sword to the farmer's throat. Mounting his horse, Colum saw with a sinking horror that one of the Englishmen had taken his sword and cut the cow's throat. As it fell in a large heap, the woman's scream pierced the air. They'd killed the only cow this farmer had. A single cow was a treasure, and killing it was taking away a large source of food and also profit.

"Hya!" Colum cried, spurring Gaisgeach. "Go on, lad!"

Gaisgeach flew through the field as Colum watched the third

man disappear into the house and return with a stick lit on fire. Nae! He was about to burn the farm.

As he worked his thighs, Gaisgeach's powerful body moving under him, he watched the farmer and the Englishmen argue. The man with the stick waved it broadly like a threat. The woman pushed him, and he hit her in the face so hard that she fell.

Fury roared through Colum's veins. He was close enough for the Englishmen and the farmers to hear the drum of Gaisgeach's hooves.

Their heads turned. He unsheathed his sword as he let Gaisgeach jump over the fence, and with a single swing cleaved the head off the nearest Englishman. A fountain of gore sprayed from his body and the head rolled around the garden like an overripe cabbage.

He had the advantage of being on the horse and of having surprised the bastards. The Englishman who'd slaughtered the cow still stood by its corpse, pointing his sword at the lad, who held his rake and watched Colum with his mouth open. But the third Englishman, the one holding the torch, was the most dangerous. If he set fire to the thatched roof, he would destroy this family's home.

The man stood at the doorstep, and Colum spurred Gaisgeach towards him. The man's eyes widened, then his eyebrows drew together, and his teeth bared in a snarl. He marched towards Colum, the torch in one hand, and his sword in the other. He wielded the torch like a weapon as he moved forward.

Too late, Colum realized what the bastard was doing.

He was going to scare Gaisgeach with fire or even hurt him. It was working. Five steps away from the man, Gaisgeach came to an abrupt stop and neighed, bucking and rearing. Colum balanced on his back as the force of the scared horse threw him back. The man shoved the torch towards the horse, and Gaisgeach bucked and kicked harder. Colum lost his grip and flew through the air, the impact of the ground against his body forcing all the air out of his lungs. There was a sharp pinch of pain and a crack of bone in his arm. The hooves of his horse thundered away into the distance.

A shadow moved over him, and he barely had time to raise his sword to block the attack. Heat flashed against his skin as he kicked back the torch. The blade of the sword came for his head.

"You killed Rodric, you fucking Scot!" the English warrior yelled as Colum rolled out from under the blade.

He scrambled to his feet, only to jump back as the Englishman swung his sword diagonally, aiming to open Colum's gut. Colum blocked his blade and pushed him back. The Englishman staggered, and Colum attacked, sweeping his sword up towards the man's neck, but the man blocked it.

Cries and grunts sounded from where the farmer and his son last were, and Colum saw that the two of them were using their rakes to fight the raider who had killed their cow.

As he fought the Englishman, he knew something was wrong with his arm. It hurt with every movement. He didn't think he'd broken it, but it was hard to wield a sword. As he raised the sword again, he knew he was too late. Pain made him slow, made him weak.

The blade was coming for his heart.

Only, it didn't come. A figure flashed behind the Englishman, who grunted and stopped, his face distorted in pain. The farm woman pulled a knife out of his neck and stabbed him again. He fell on his chest and didn't move.

She must be around thirty-five years old, with strands of gray in her hair, and she was lean from many years of hard farmwork.

"Thanks," Colum panted out.

"Nae," she said, wide-eyed. "Thank ye."

He looked towards the final Englishman. He was running for the gate as both the farmer and his son chased him. He climbed onto one of the horses and was off.

The other two horses neighed and stepped from side to side as the man galloped past them.

Bastards. Gaisgeach was long gone, and Colum would not likely find the stallion without a lengthy search, if then.

The farmer and his son walked towards him, both breathing hard, rakes in their hands. "Thank ye for yer help," said the farmer.

"They killed Thistle," said the lad regretfully, staring at the dead cow.

"Aye, I am sorry for ye," said Colum. "But they didna kill ye. And ye get two horses for that."

"But yer horse got away," said the woman. "Take one of their horses, then."

Colum eyed the beasts. They were good, tall English horses. Not warhorses, but perfectly fine for traveling long distances. "Are ye sure?" he asked. "I do need to travel quickly to Berwick. And I have a..." What could he call Danielle? He couldn't say he had a prisoner. "A companion."

The farmer shook his head. "Why do ye go to Berwick?"

"To stop the army these three bastarts came from."

"Ah," said the farmer. "'Tis good. 'Tis time they left our country. The English army is getting impatient and cruel. We were raided before, just a sennight ago. We gave them all the food we had and all the coin. We wilna be able to pay the next rent."

There was a loud pounding in Colum's ears. His hands twitched and curled into fists. "Bloody bastarts," he growled out.

"Ye should avoid the main roads," said the woman. "The English are everywhere down south from here. And ye shouldna go anywhere near Edinburgh."

"Aye," he said, shaking off the anger. At least he was able to help them now. "Thanks. I wanted to follow the old Roman road, but mayhap 'tis best to keep to the deep woods."

"Aye," said the farmer. "Can we pay back yer kindness somehow?"

"Aye," said the woman. "Yer horse must have taken everything ye had with ye. What do ye need?"

Colum smiled at her, then looked regretfully at the woods. Somewhere in there was Gaisgeach with all his things—his provisions, sleeping roll, field medicine.

"A blanket would be good if ye can spare one. My companion gets cold."

CHAPTER 11

As Colum galloped away to the farm, Danielle struggled to free herself. She'd hardly get a better chance to run away.

But she couldn't untie the rope, and she had no knife to cut it. She searched for any sharp stones that might be lying between the grasses and the roots of the tree he'd tied her to. The woods were not as dense here. The ground was covered with a thick layer of old, dry leaves. Bushes and grass grew here and there. But there were no rocks.

She growled in frustration. With every day passing here, she was putting her family through more trauma, and her parents were older this time, their health weaker. And her job... There was no way she could make it back in time for the hearing even if she did manage to get free now, and by not even showing up, she was losing her last chance to keep her job.

Still struggling to break loose, she watched Colum rush to fight the raiders, saw the raiders kill the cow, and whimpered in sadness. They didn't have to do that!

And then Colum killed one of them. And fought the other one—the one with the torch—while the farmer and his son fought the third raider with only rakes. She found herself cheering for the farmer's family and for Colum.

There was another side to him. This kind, protective, selfless side that she didn't realize he had before. And she hated the raiders; of course, what they did was wrong. Now, she could really understand why Colum hated the English so much.

And she was English...

When he was thrown off the horse, she screamed, worry for him piercing her chest like a spear. She shouldn't be afraid for him. She should be glad if he was wounded because then the farmer could free her, and she could finally run back to Bannock-burn and return home.

Colum was her captor. She shouldn't feel anything for him. She shouldn't give in to Stockholm syndrome.

But then it was over, and despite herself, Danielle sighed with relief. She had seen Gaisgeach gallop away. How would Colum take it? He loved his horse and cared for him well. Every night before going to sleep, he brushed the horse's neck and talked to him.

She supposed it was good they were now without a horse, though, because it would slow them down and give her more chances to escape.

When he rode back on another, taller horse she lost that hope. Colum descended, and she saw something was wrong with his shoulder. He held his arm close and didn't move it. Her stomach tightened, her mouth dry. She clasped her hands together.

"Are you wounded?" she asked.

He didn't reply but untied the rope from around the tree and tied it to his waist. "Get on the horse," he said. "I need to hurry and see if I can find Gaisgeach."

She walked to the horse and looked over her shoulder at him. "But you're unwell..."

"Why, lass, are ye nae happy they didna kill me? Are ye looking for an opportunity to finish me?"

She breathed out sharply and shook her head.

"Get on the horse, lass, or I will put ye over its back."

She sighed out and obeyed, putting her foot in the stirrup and swinging her leg over the horse's back as she lifted herself into the saddle. He took his place behind her, then clicked his tongue and the horse trotted through the woods.

But something thundered in Danielle's chest. She was done with him being so defensive and mistrustful. She'd seen how horrible the English could be to the Scots. She'd seen how protective and strong and kind he could be.

"Why can you not imagine that some English are not on the side of violence?" she asked. "That even though I'm English, I may not be your enemy?"

"Life taught me better than that," came his reply, his breath warming her ear.

That echoed in her soul. Life had taught her to mistrust everyone, too. To shove people away before they could hurt her like Sebastian had.

"Are you wounded?" she insisted.

"Nae, I'm just holding my arm as a jest."

She brushed off his sarcasm. "What happened?"

"I fought. I hit my shoulder. I'll be fine on the morrow."

"It was a nice thing you did for them. If it weren't for you—"

"I dinna need any appreciation from ye, lass. I canna trust anything that comes out of yer mouth. Mayhap ye're trying to get on my good side and trick me with yer sudden sweet talk."

She didn't say anything. They searched for Gaisgeach for a while but couldn't find him. She could feel frustration and anger radiating from him like heat. She felt sorry for him. Gaisgeach must have meant a lot to him. Finally, by the time dusk fell, he stopped the horse by a stream and tied it there, close enough to drink.

He secured her to a tree once again. She sat on the ground and watched him untie two sleeping rolls from the saddle and put a full sack of something on the ground. He was still wincing when he used his left arm. "Come on," she said. "Let me look at it. I know the basics of first aid. Maybe you need a splint or something."

He glanced at her as he lowered himself in front of the sack. "Ye think I will trust ye to come near me, lass?"

He rummaged in the sack and pulled out a bannock, then stood and walked to her and crouched before her. He handed her the bannock, and she took it with both hands.

His eyes met hers, dark and glistening. "Thank you," she said, and licked her dry lips. His proximity warmed her like a red-hot furnace.

His gaze softened in surprise, and his lips parted. He watched her for a while, then his expression hardened. "Thank the kind farmer that gave me provisions and two sleeping rolls, one of which is for ye."

Yet another kindness he had done for her. No doubt he'd asked for two sleeping rolls, thinking about her comfort. Maybe she wouldn't need to sleep sitting tied to a tree anymore?

"Again," she said, "thank you."

He went back to the sack and found a bannock for himself, then sat on a fallen tree and ate, watching her. It got quiet in the woods. The birds chirped more softly, their calls dwindling. A stream gurgled nearby. The horse snorted quietly.

"Ye can thank me by telling me about the English camp and helping me orient there. Taking me to the king."

She inhaled deeply and pursed her lips. "Unfortunately, I can't, even if I wanted to."

He scoffed and shook his head in disappointment. "I guess we'll have to wait and see."

Later that night, she was allowed to sleep on her own bedroll, but she was still tied to the tree, far away from him, from the campfire, and from the weapons. At least she was warm, covered in a woolen blanket and feeling the warmth of the fire even from here. She watched him lying on the deer hide a few steps away from the campfire. His face was illuminated by the fire, and he stared into it, his expression a mixture of ache and thoughtfulness.

What haunted him behind his eyes? Huddling into his blanket, he took out one fist and looked at it like it was a demon that had emerged from the darkness. Then he started saying something, touching every knuckle on the fist.

She'd seen him do this every night before he went to sleep, but only now was she close enough to hear the words: "Rob MacDonald. Ianatan MacDonald. Frangan MacDonald. Alexander Fraser. David de Inchmartin."

Every time he said a name, he touched a knuckle. Then he winced and pulled out the hand of his injured arm and kept going: "Hugh de Haye. John Somerville. Alexander Scrymgeour. James Barclay."

He paused over the fifth knuckle, just looking at it.

Then he pulled his other hand out and started over: "Rob MacDonald. Ianatan MacDonald. Frangan MacDonald. Alexander Fraser. David de Inchmartin." Then the other hand again: "Hugh de Haye. John Somerville. Alexander Scrymgeour. James Barclay." Then pause.

And again: "Rob MacDonald. Ianatan MacDonald. Frangan MacDonald. Alexander Fraser. David de Inchmartin." Then the other hand: "Hugh de Haye. John Somerville. Alexander Scrymgeour. James Barclay." Then pause.

Danielle's chest tightened as she kept listening to him chanting out those names methodically, thoughtfully. It was like every name was a bead on a rosary only he could see. Nine names. Over and over again. Like a prayer. Like a memory. And then there was that empty pause at the tenth knuckle, like a gap in the rosary.

She wanted to ask him who they were, these nine men represented by his knuckles. But she couldn't interrupt him. She had a feeling he may not want her to witness this. That she was peering into a part of him he didn't want anyone to see.

Did he know she heard him and saw him now? Did he think she was already asleep?

Or was she so unimportant to him that he simply did not care because once they reached Berwick, he'd never see her again. Either because she'd finally be free and leave.

Or because she'd be dead.

Or...because he would be?

He kept chanting, and his voice was so beautiful and so deep...and she was warm and comfortable and her aching body melted into the deer hide underneath her. And just before she drifted to sleep, she thought that he had finally stopped chanting and simply looked at her.

And there wasn't any hatred in his eyes.

Maybe that was why she abandoned caution and looked him straight in the eye, and asked, "Who are they?"

She thought he wouldn't reply, thought he'd dismiss her and tell her he'd never reveal that to an enemy.

Instead, he said, "My sword brothers. Those with whom I should have died."

Her throat tightened in sadness for him. "Why do you say their names?"

"So that their memory can live. So that I can keep living with myself."

She nodded slightly and cuddled deeper into the blanket he'd brought for her from the farmer. Then they both said nothing, but they also didn't look away. His dark, haunted eyes were the last thing she remembered before her heavy lids closed and she slept. And she didn't dream of the nine Scotsmen who had died.

She dreamed of the one who had lived.

CHAPTER 12

SHE WAS GETTING out of here. Today. Now.

With every day, they got farther and farther away from Stirling. From her job and her family. And yet, there was nothing she could do to escape while they rode on the horse and Colum was right behind her, his arms around her.

But she was determined to find a way now that they had stopped for the night near another river.

Trees shot high into the darkening sky around them. Occasional mosquitoes buzzed by her ears. The scent of grass and woods was thick. The horse grazed nearby.

Colum crouched, setting out his sleeping roll. His arm was getting better, thankfully. After last night, there wasn't as much animosity in him when he spoke to her.

Part of her liked that and wished she could get to know him better.

Not Colum her captor.

But Colum the protector and man of honor. The man who had brought her a blanket and let her bathe. The man who whispered the names of his dead friends every night before going to sleep. The man whose eyes had darkened in desire when he'd seen her naked.

The man who took her breath away and made her feel warm things. Burning things. Dangerous things.

Things that may just work to break her free.

She needed to try something she'd never normally have tried. She didn't have confidence in herself when it came to sex. She was not even sure she could do this. How far was she willing to go?

Flirting had never come naturally to her. She'd never enjoyed sex, never had a serious boyfriend or experienced true intimacy. No one had ever said that she was sexy or especially feminine. How could she even try to seduce Colum?

But try she would. She'd seduce him and steal the keys.

He took out his fire steel and began striking it to start a fire. She nervously tapped her foot against the ground and threw a quick glance at the river. It didn't look inviting at all. The air was chilly, too, so she'd be totally freezing.

"I need a bath," she said nevertheless, her voice high and awkward and not seductive at all.

Colum turned to stare at her over his shoulder. Good.

"Again?" he asked.

She nodded. With her wrists still in shackles, she grasped the edge of the tunic and of her top and pulled them both up.

His mouth fell open. Well, at least she got that. Then his face disappeared behind the edge of the fabric as she tugged the tunic and her top higher and higher, awkwardly attempting to pull them both over her head.

"Stop, lass!" Colum said and his steps sounded closer to her. "I didna say ye could bathe tonight."

Awkwardly, she managed to pull them over her head, but the fabric bunched around her wrists. The cool air prickled the skin on her breasts, her waist, her shoulders. She could see his face now, and he looked her straight in the eyes, like he couldn't look down, not an inch. He was completely still. His upper chest right under his collarbones rose and fell in quick, shallow breaths.

She locked her eyes with his. She was affecting him. She could do something with this.

Her nipples tightened from the cold wind...definitely not from the thought of him being affected by her.

Feeling a bit more confident, she put her hands down, the tunic tangling at her wrists, and slowly walked to him.

"Would you like to join me?" she asked when she stopped directly in front of him.

Surprising her, he closed his eyes tight. She wondered why he was doing so now when he'd kept them open two days ago when she had been completely naked before him.

"Ye wilna distract me," he said. "I ken what ye're trying to do. Please, put yer tunic on."

There were his lips, right there, framed by his short, dark beard. She stood so close to him, she could smell his manly musk mixed with the scent of the woods and of the horse. Her nipples tightened till they ached, and this time she knew it wasn't from the cold.

It was from the closeness to this man. From knowing that if she wanted, she needn't stop. She could lean forward just an inch and kiss him. She could feel his tunic against her naked breasts, the hardness of his chest against her bare skin. She could find out whether his arms felt as strong around her body when he was kissing her as they did when he held her captive.

But she didn't.

Because he was a fool. He had his eyes closed.

She grabbed the key, and it came off his belt surprisingly quickly. She hurried to insert it into the hole on her shackles, but she needed to fight through the layers of her tunic and her top tangled around her wrists.

He grunted and tried to grab the key back, but she was faster and avoided his hands. She needed time to unlock the shackles and to untie herself from the tree. Then she could run for the horse, and he'd never catch her.

She pushed him back. He staggered but didn't fall. He waved

his arms, trying to reach for her, but she stepped back and to the side and kicked him in his solar plexus.

He fell to the ground, struggling to breathe. She needed to restrain him. If she could put the shackles on his wrists, she'd be able to escape.

She jumped on him and straddled him, pinning his own hands high above his head like he had done to her before.

Still gasping for breath, he struggled weakly to free his wrists. He was strong, but she was also strong. She knew krav maga. Despite his incapacitation, keeping his wrists in place while trying to insert the key into the keyhole was hard.

Awkward.

She could see the hole and the edge of the key right there; she just needed to connect them...

But Colum had finally gotten his air back. He moved and wriggled his wrists and pushed back.

Then something felt quite strange at her chest area. There was some pleasant warmth and a sweet ache in her breasts. Freezing her efforts, she looked down at him. Her breasts hung right over his face, and he stared at them, bewildered. His mouth open, he looked at her chest as if mesmerized.

Something clenched within her as an odd thought came. How would it feel if he took her nipple in his mouth and sucked...hard?

She stopped struggling. Stopped breathing.

His eyes came up and met hers.

His eyes were as dark as her desire. The heat from his body was so intense she couldn't take another breath.

There was just one thought.

There he was. His eyes like liquid amethysts. His mouth was so close. His body heat scorching her through the tunic, making her breasts ache and her insides clench and for the first time in her life...ache for him to be near, to thrust into her.

As though reading her thoughts, something between his legs, hard and hot, pressed against the apex of her thighs.

Danielle felt herself clench and wet in response. His scent, so primal and masculine, tickled her nostrils, and as she inhaled it, never wanted to let it go.

For the first time in her life, she wanted a man. Very, very much.

She should keep trying to open the shackles. She should forget him. Rejoice at the fact that she had managed to seduce him.

Instead, there was this feeling in her gut. A burning ache she couldn't explain, that only he could satisfy. She had ignored gut feelings her whole life.

But she didn't now.

She leaned down and kissed him.

There was a moment of stillness when her lips met his. A moment of shock, like there was a wall that now separated her life before the kiss and her life after. A moment of surprise at the pleasure a simple touch of the lips could bring. It was silken and soft, and it injected honey into her veins.

The next moment, he was devouring her like she was his last meal on earth. There was no more hesitation, only pure, unapologetic desire. His mouth opened for her, his tongue stroking hers, caressing, sucking gently.

She was melting. Evaporating like water on a hot pan.

But before she knew it, the kiss was broken. A force hurled her over and down, and he pinned her against the hard, cold ground.

Over her loomed an angry, humorless Scot, his eyebrows drawn together, thunder raging behind his eyes. He reached for the tunic and pulled it up her arms, over her head, and down her body.

"Nice try, lass," he said.

Her body still ached for him. Now, being pinned to the ground, his wrists on hers, his weight heavy and sweet and all around her, her body wanted to keep going...her body wanted more.

But there was no more.

Her mind cleared. No! She'd missed her chance of an escape because of what...a kiss?

She growled in frustration. "What would it take for you to bloody let me go?"

And why did it feel so good to have him tower over her like that?

"Nothing, lass. I dinna make compromises when it comes to honor."

He picked up the keys and stood, putting them back on his belt.

"Honor?" she demanded.

"Aye. Yer king made me suffer."

She sat up, huddling in the tunic that now covered her chest. "What did he do?"

"He took me and my fellow warriors captive. Then without following the chivalric law, he quartered and killed everyone without trial or a chance for ransom. But he spared me."

She frowned. "Were these the nine men you talked about last night?"

He nodded. "God kens he shouldna have spared me. And then he did something...he found a way to force me to switch to the English side. To pledge my loyalty to him."

A sharp pain in her chest made her wince. Her throat tightened and she swallowed an aching lump.

Had she been captured by another government and they'd found something to hold over her, some way to make her switch sides, would she have done it?

"I didna do it because I wanted to," he said. "I did it because I had to save someone. But he humiliated me with that. He made me break my vow to my clan. And when I did, he chipped at my soul. Ye're a Sassenach. What do ye ken what honor means to a Highlander?"

Pain hit her core. "Why do you assume I don't know what honor means? You don't know anything about me. You assume because I have an English accent, I have no honor and I'm your enemy. You laughed at me when I told you the truth. And you are keeping me captive, stubbornly dragging me to Berwick when I have no way of helping you with your insane mission. Nor will I take part in a disastrous assassination attempt, which will fail and result in your sure death."

"I ken ye're resilient. I ken ye're strong and cunning and very imaginative. Ye wouldna have stopped at anything to get the information ye're after and help yer friend Jamie to kill my king. I also ken that ye're nae an ordinary English lass, and yer plan would have succeeded had I nae caught ye. I ken ye're beautiful and mayhap 'tis yet another weapon ye'd have used had I nae dragged ye away."

Had he actually complimented her? She wanted to be angry with him but couldn't bring herself to. "Oh yeah? You only caught me because I thought I was on vacation and had my guard down. Had I been on a mission, I'd have never allowed this to happen."

Confusion flashed on his face for a moment, then he shook his head. "If ye try to run away again, I will tie yer feet and throw ye over the horse, and ye will continue the journey in a much less pleasant state."

CHAPTER 13

THE NEXT DAY...

COLUM DIRECTED THE HORSE CAREFULLY OVER THE MUDDY soil between the pools of black standing water. Its hooves made wet sucking noises.

Grasses and reeds rippled in the wind over the plains of the vast marsh. Endless saw grass grew in clumps. Snags and logs stuck out of the water. A heron stood in the grass and lowered its long neck to snatch a fish from the water.

Frogs croaked. Wind rustled the grasses. The scent of rotten eggs coming from decaying plant matter was thick in the air. Mosquitoes and midges buzzed around them, and Danielle waved her hands to scare them off.

"'Tis worse over there," he said and looked towards the area at the center of the marsh. She followed his gaze. "The water there is deeper, with lots of traps and sinkholes. Dinna fash. We'll stay well clear of the middle. We just need to cross over to that side." He pointed to the woods that must be a mile away from them. "Wilna be so many wee buggers."

She slapped her thigh with her bound hands. "Thank God. Must we really go through a marsh?"

"Aye. We must stay away from the road. 'Tis what the farmer said."

He wasn't sure why he wanted to reassure her, to ease her discomfort.

Just like he didn't know why he let her watch him do his nightly ritual. Why he didn't stop or turn away from her. All he knew was that sharing it with her made him feel better. Lighter. Like it lifted some of the burden he'd carried for the past eight years.

The wee seductress. He didn't want to feel any desire for her. He didn't want to feel anything but the hatred he'd have for any English spy.

And yet, she must be the bonniest lass he'd ever seen in his life. She had the face of an angel with her high cheekbones and pale pink lips to kiss and to cherish.

And those eyes...good God gracious, those aquamarine eyes, so translucent as though they were two pools of the clearest seawater. So cool now, he couldn't believe that just a few hours ago she'd been kissing him as though she were dying and he were her last cure. She had a long, elegant neck and the proud posture of a warrior—that was one of the things that had confused him. And her body...good God, that body. Tall and willowy but with defined muscles everywhere. And her arse was so delicious he'd craved to bite it when he'd seen her proudly walking down towards the river in front of him. The sight of her breasts round and wee and bonnie, with those pale nipples the color of sunrise blush, would forever be burned into his mind.

Why did he need to show kindness to her, his enemy? Was it because he was attracted to her? He had no trouble having a lad sleep in the cold or on the hard ground. But he couldn't bring himself to treat a woman the same way. He knew it was his weakness, his Achilles' heel. The whole reason he'd betrayed his clan in the first place was because he wanted to protect the queen.

A flock of geese shot into the sky, spooked by something. Colum stopped the horse and looked around. It was quiet, not a sign of man.

"Mayhap an otter," he said.

Danielle stared into the black water two feet away from the horse's hooves.

"Gave me a fright," she said.

The lass who had tried to break free from him repeatedly, the fierce warrior, sounded unnerved. That was one of the things he admired about her—her relentless courage. Her inventiveness. Mayhap all those midges and mosquitoes had worn her down.

For a moment, he wondered if she could have told the truth when she'd said she traveled in time. She'd told him she wasn't his enemy. He'd seen her worry about his shoulder, which surprised him. He'd seen her wish to help the farmer, too.

If she was telling the truth, he was keeping an innocent woman captive.

But that was exactly what a spy would do—poison his mind with her strange ideas. Make him trust her, feel for her.

Which he already did, more than he'd wanted to. He felt lust. He felt protective. He felt empathy. He also felt curiosity.

But he shouldn't give in to those feelings. He was stronger than that. He also knew better, after what her king had put him through.

For eight years, Colum had remembered the nine names of his sword brothers. For eight years, the last, the tenth knuckle had been left untouched, waiting for his own name to be placed there.

But for the past few days, he'd caught himself feeling alive. More alive than he'd been since he'd been captured at Methven. He even wondered if it was such a good idea, after all, to go on this suicide mission.

The memory of the Battle of Methven, with fires orange and

bright against the black night, burned Colum's inner vision. The screams, the flesh being ripped by blades, the panicked neighing of the horses being gutted to get to their riders.

Robert the Bruce had been king not even three months, and he may have already died.

Dead bodies on the ground. Reflections of flames lunging in pools of blood that shone black in the night. As Colum fought on in the darkness, he saw his uncle Aulay and the MacDonald warriors as well as the Cambels and Mackenzies make a formation around Bruce about a hundred feet away. It was a thick wall of loyal men, ready to die before they let the English and the MacDougalls, MacDowells and other Lowland enemy clans touch the Bruce.

As the circle of men backed away from the carnage, trying to move the Bruce to safety, Colum cut his way through the enemy towards them. His eyes locked with Aulay's while the formation backed up.

"Come on, lad," Aulay screamed. "Get over here! Come on!"

But a small warrior was in his path. A lad of fourteen or so, sword raised. The lad backed up, stumbled, and fell on the ground. Flames reflected from his shiny armor and his young, fearful eyes in which Colum was, no doubt, a wild animal that was about to attack and kill.

Alexander Fraser, who had been fighting next to Colum, raised his sword over the lad to finish him when Colum stepped in front of him. His fellow warrior's eyes were wide and glistening with battle rage.

"Stop!" cried Colum. "He's just a lad."

"He's an *English* lad," growled Alexander.

"Please..." came a voice, and a man in armor knelt by the lad's side. It was Philip Mowbray, one of the Lowland Scottish nobles who had fought for England. Colum recognized him because he had visited Islay a few years ago to negotiate a trade deal with the clan. "He's my nephew. He's only fourteen. Let him go."

Colum nodded curtly, his chest rising and falling quickly with exhaustion. Alexander nodded. "Aye. Ye're right, he's a lad. I didna think he was so young in that armor."

Philip helped his nephew up and pulled him away from the fighting. The formation around Bruce was farther away now.

"Come on, Alexander," he said. "We must aid the Bruce."

Alexander nodded and sprinted forward through the darkness. Colum hurried after him when something hot and sharp pierced him from behind and he saw the point of a blade sticking out of his shoulder. Colum gasped and froze, then fell.

He struggled to remember much afterwards. Just the darkness and the fires and the screams. And the hot, agonizing pain in his shoulder.

Then the prison together with Alexander Fraser, Rob MacDonald, Ianatan MacDonald, Frangan MacDonald, David de Inchmartin, Hugh de Haye, John Somerville, Alexander Scrymgeour, and James Barclay.

And then the day Prince Edward had sentenced them to death, and the ten of them had stood in the inner bailey of Berwick Castle, Philip Mowbray was there.

One after another, Colum watched them die. He said his final prayers, preparing himself. He didn't want to die, but he knew he would.

And when his turn came, Philip Mowbray went to Edward and whispered something into his ear. Both threw glances at Colum. And when Philip was through, Edward gave a shake of his head to the executioner.

Someone came and grasped Colum by the arms and led him away. And shamefully, regretfully, there was a small, cowardly part of him that was glad he was alive.

Perhaps it was the same part that had been glad to be alive for the past few days, as well. Only, it didn't feel shameful or cowardly this time. It felt bright and hopeful. But why did it have to come from an enemy?

CHAPTER 14

DANIELLE'S INSIDES melted as Colum's face spread in a beautiful smile she hadn't seen before.

It was like a light bulb had come alive within the darkness in her chest. Gosh, he shouldn't have done that.

Didn't matter. She wasn't on his side. There wouldn't be any future for them, even with a smile like that.

Later that day, finally clear of the horrid swamp, the woods became thinner. Through the gaps in the bushes and trees, she saw thatched timber buildings and rough stone walls. They must be about five hundred feet away.

Which meant there were people. People who could help her!

Danielle tensed. He must have noticed them, too...

Though he hadn't shown any sign that he had.

God. She hated to betray the thread of closeness that had developed between them. But she needed to get going. The hearing was today, and even though there was no way she'd make it home for several days, she might still be able to explain herself, say she'd been in a car accident or something. Plus, she wasn't ready to die alongside Colum in his suicide mission, no matter how much she was starting to like him.

Ignoring a hard, heavy stone of guilt sinking in her stomach, she opened her mouth and yelled, "Heeeelp!!! Heeeelp!!!"

He hadn't expected it. Nor, it seemed, had he noticed the rough stone walls through the trees.

She had tricked him.

A rough hand closed over her mouth.

"Lass, what are ye doing?" came his hot whisper over her ear.

Betraying you, came a guilty thought.

The horse stopped and shook its head.

Too late.

Someone yelled back, "Hey-ho! Who's there?"

"Dinna make a sound," Colum demanded quietly, his breath scalding the tip of her ear.

She could feel the heat of his anger, of his confusion, the bitterness of her betrayal.

Colum was as still as a rock pressed at her back. For a few moments, nothing happened. Birds called to one another. Branches swayed in the wind, rustling and whispering. Flies and mosquitoes buzzed around.

Then something swooshed past Danielle, and an arrow thunked a few trees down.

"God's bones," Colum murmured, wrapping his arms around her as though to shield her.

He spurred the horse away and into the woods. It galloped between the trees, the two of them hunching low over its back.

But she wasn't his enemy, she wanted to say. She didn't mean for him to get harmed, for the hooves of his real enemies to drum behind them as they rode.

The horse went faster and faster, and she bounced harder against its back as they rode.

The sound of galloping hooves behind them grew louder. Then multiplied.

There were many of them.

So many.

And then they were surrounded. The circle of riders forced them to stop.

Colum unsheathed his sword.

There must be ten of them—men in chain mail and plated armor, on their mighty warhorses that snorted and tossed their heads. They wore helmets over chain mail coifs. The blades of their drawn swords flashed. One of them had especially good armor and a tall horse. They all wore red surcoats bearing three lions over their armor.

Just like the three raiders back at the farm...

The English.

So many of them...so much better armored.

Worry for Colum completely crushed her. What had she done? What the *bloody hell* had she just done?

They'd kill Colum! She didn't want him harmed. She just wanted him to let her go.

Despite being so overwhelmed, Colum still fought. Real steel blades came for them. Slashed. Moved. Clashed. Metal rang against metal as Colum tried to protect himself and her.

But it wasn't enough. They were everywhere, and they were about to wound him.

"Stop!!!" she cried in English.

The warriors looked at her. "Are you in danger?" one of them asked. "Is the Scot holding you captive? Do you need to be freed?"

God, she did. And maybe it would stop them from hurting him.

"Yes," she said.

This was working! They'd stopped fighting him, so if only they'd just let her go and not harm him, she'd be on her way.

"I'm English, and he holds me captive." She raised her shackles into the air.

The faces of the warriors darkened.

"Free him, you damned Scot," said the one who had the best armor and the best horse, pointing his sword at Colum's throat.

"You're at Blackhaugh Castle. And from now you're a captive of England."

Another man took Colum's sword. She looked over her shoulder. Colum's face was cold, and pure fury raged behind his eyes. The muscles in his square jaw flexed and clenched. He was still being held at swordpoint while another man helped her descend from the horse.

She was almost free. She could almost go back to her time. She could make sure her parents knew she was fine. She might be able to keep her job.

Walking on the ground without a rope tying her to anything made her heart drum and warmth radiate through her whole body.

But when she met Colum's dark eyes, her heart squeezed with regret. He was now a prisoner of the English—again. She knew what it was like to be a captive, partially because of him.

Yet she didn't want him to suffer or be harmed. She cared for him—more than she should. More than she'd ever allowed herself to care for anyone.

She'd kept people away so carefully. Afraid they'd betray her. Fool her. Try to break her like Sebastian had.

This man had treated her like an enemy, but she still saw the good in him. And he was her enemy because he'd kept her captive.

And now she'd finally gotten what she wanted. She was free of him.

So why could she not bear seeing him like this?

CHAPTER 15

DANIELLE'S HANDS shook as an Englishman hit Colum's face. The sound of flesh hitting flesh made her sick. The warriors had descended from their horses and two of them held him by the shoulders as he grunted and jerked in their arms. Blood flowed from his nose and a cut over his cheekbone, where a large bruise was forming.

The woods around them stayed indifferent. Trees and branches swayed gently in the wind, and the scent of plants and flowers and horses was thick. Birds sang cheerfully, unaware of the human misery below.

"Ye English pigs, ye canna fight me man to man," Colum growled.

Danielle's stomach churned. This wasn't the Colum she'd known for the past few days, an intelligent man and proud warrior, his shoulders straight and head held high.

No. There was a wildness in his eyes, the agony of a cornered predator that would slash with its claws and sink its teeth into its attacker.

"No one here needs to fight you," said the Englishman who held Danielle's shackled wrists in one hand and Colum's key in the other. "You already lost, you Scottish filth."

He held the key to her freedom, literally, and yet those words made her fists clench in an urge to hit him. She didn't, of course. She just needed to wait a minute more and she'd be free. Then she could leave and go home.

The Englishman was a knight, Danielle thought, based on the shiny plates of a full suit of armor. His muscular neck bulged from a lowered chain mail coif that pooled on his shoulders. Straight blond hair was plastered to his forehead. His gray eyes were narrowed on Colum. High cheekbones and a straight nose, a clean-shaven square jaw, and a firm mouth made him look handsome, the perfect image of a noble knight. Danielle bet he was very popular among the ladies.

And yet, he made her feel sick. He reminded her of Sebastian, with the same immaculate appearance. And she knew better than to trust pretty boys and slickly handsome men because of Sebastian.

Colum thrashed and roared in the arms of the men as if he'd come unhinged, chilling Danielle's blood. Tears welled in her eyes. It was so easy to imagine herself in his place. She'd be thrashing and growling and clawing her way out of the arms of her captors.

As she had been doing for the past few days...

"Did he hurt you, boy?" asked the knight as he turned to her and finally inserted the key into the keyhole.

"No," Danielle said, watching the key turn. It clicked and the first shackle fell open. She felt her pulse accelerate, seeing her wrist free, feeling the weight and the harsh metal of the shackle finally gone from her body. She threw a quick glance at Colum. He, no doubt, had heard the knight call her boy.

Would he say something, betray her to the English? Raise their suspicions about her, make them change their minds about helping her?

But Colum had stopped thrashing and silently panted, watching the knight and her.

"No, he didn't hurt me," she said again.

The knight shook his head disapprovingly as he inserted the key into the keyhole of the second shackle and turned it. It didn't move, and he squinted his handsome eyes as he applied force. "What did he want with you?"

She swallowed hard. She could just tell the truth, that Colum had taken her hostage to bring her to the English camp. Tell him Colum wanted to kill their king.

And watch them kill Colum...

Her throat contracted, the words stuck. "He thought I was sneaking around and stealing."

The English knight stilled, and he cocked his single eyebrow and threw a suspicious glance at her. "And were you?"

"No. No. I got lost and he caught me. But he didn't believe me and wanted to bring me to justice..."

She felt Colum's eyes burning holes in her skin. She cleared her throat as the knight's hand twisted the key and the shackle finally opened with a *click*. It fell on the ground with a soft *thump*, and Danielle sucked in a deep breath of relief. She stepped away from the man and rubbed her wrists. She could leave. She could say thank you and leave. She looked back at the woods. Then at Colum.

He knelt, held by the two warriors, his face bloody and angry and desperate under sweaty strands of hair. Her feet chilled. What would happen to him once she left?

Just say thank you and go. Leave!

But her feet didn't move. "What's your name, sir?" she asked instead.

"Sir Geoffrey de Beaumont," he said with a ceremonial nod, "at your service, boy."

"Thank you, Sir Geoffrey," Danielle said.

The knight chuckled and went to mount his horse. "No thanks necessary," he said. "It's my duty as a knight of the realm to protect the weak."

The rest of the warriors were getting back on their horses. The warrior who had hit Colum before went to him with a rope.

"Put your hands out," said the man to Colum.

She should feel satisfaction. That was how she had felt days ago when he'd put those damn shackles on her wrists. She should rejoice in seeing her captor being captured. Instead, she was horrified, her stomach tight and hard.

It's Stockholm syndrome. You should know better.

Colum gave the man a hateful glare from under his eyebrows, then raised his chin and spat into his face. The Englishman grunted in surprise, then kicked Colum in the stomach. He doubled up with a low groan. The other two gathered his arms together while he helplessly gasped for breath, and the third Englishman secured his wrists with the rope. He tied its other end to his horse. The other two Englishmen mounted their horses. Danielle stood there, clenching and unclenching her fists, fighting the urge to run to Colum and help him.

The English horse he'd picked up at the farm neighed as the last man tethered it to his horse. They were leaving. The horses walked slowly away and towards a forest path. The rope tying Colum to the horse strained, and although he was still doubled up, he was forced to stand up and walk after the horse.

"Where are you taking him?" she called after Geoffrey.

He turned his head to her over his shoulder. "To Blackhaugh Castle. He stole an English horse. He's a dirty Scottish enemy, he must be dealt with."

Dealt with...

Killed.

She swallowed hard as she watched Colum follow the horses, stumbling, wobbling. She looked the other way, at the other end of the road where there were no angry Highlanders putting her in shackles and dragging her with them on suicide missions. Where somewhere a few days away from here was her way back home.

Forget him. Go.

But he had saved the farmer and his family. He was an honorable man, unlike the English soldiers raiding the farm. Unlike the

English king, killing Colum's companions rather than ransoming them. Clasping her hands, she watched the line of horses slowly walking away.

Bloody hell. She couldn't live with herself if she let him be imprisoned and die like that. She hurried after them.

"I can ride that horse for you!" she called. "Is there work at the castle? Just for food and shelter. I'd like to pay you back for saving me."

Geoffrey looked at her again, frowning. "I suppose. There's always work in the kitchens. Stables and the latrines need to be cleaned."

As she walked past Colum, he shot her an angry, confused glare. She sent him a meaningful glare back, trying to tell with her eyes that he should just shut up and go with it.

When she drew level with Colum's English horse, she put her hands on the saddle and swallowed her fear. She'd been on the horseback for the past few days, even though Colum's reassuring back had always been behind her. "Great," she said as she put her foot in the stirrup and swung her leg over the saddle. "I'm coming with you."

The man untethered the horse from his saddle.

Remembering how Colum had behaved with horses, she clicked her tongue and pushed her heels into the horse's sides to draw level with Geoffrey. "How far is Berwick, do you know?"

Geoffrey glanced at her. "Why? Is your master there?"

"Yes," she said, her heart racing. "In the army. He sent me with a message, but this wild Scot kidnapped me, and I don't know the way there anymore."

"It's three days on foot," he said. "Don't you go thinking you'll keep this horse."

"No. Of course not. Are they still there, though? The army?"

Geoffrey scoffed. "They are. Do you think it's easy to get twenty thousand men organized? We're expecting them to pass by in about a sennight. My men and I will join them."

"Oh, are you going to fight the Scots?"

"Yes, of course. This battle will be written in history books for generations to come. I will not be excluded from eternal glory."

Eternal glory...if only this bloke knew...

"Are they ready, do you think?"

"No. Not all of the Welsh archers are there yet. The king knows there's no more powerful long-range weapon than the English longbow. He won't move until they arrive. Your master will be looking forward to this battle, no doubt. What's his name?"

She bit her lip and tried hard thinking of any medieval names. "Sir Barnett...de Guy," she blurted out.

Brilliant. What kind of name was that?

Geoffrey cocked his head. "Never heard of him. But there are hundreds of knights that came, so I wouldn't know. It will take some time to find him, I think, in that camp. Must be close to the king's red pavilion."

"Oh, the king's red pavilion?" Her ears practically prickled with the knowledge she'd just gained. "Where is it?"

"In the northeastern quarter."

Ahead, at the end of the road, there was a castle, about five hundred feet away. If she didn't do anything now, Colum would be taken into the castle, and then...then she'd have a much harder time getting him out. She glanced back at Colum. He kept going, his jaw set, his eyes full of venom and concern —on her.

"You know, I saw a Scottish camp nearby. That's where this man is from. About fifty of them, on their way to join the Bruce's army. I think they're locals that switched to Bruce's side."

Geoffrey pulled back the reins and stopped his horse, his eyes like sharp daggers on Danielle. "Where?"

"I can show you."

"How far?" he asked.

"Not far. They're not as well armed as you. You can catch them by surprise."

Geoffrey nodded and cried out to his men, "We're going to spill some Scottish blood today! For the king!"

They all turned their horses and followed the road through the woods. She remembered the way to the swamp they had passed and turned the horse left, following the path she and Colum had come through. They'd ridden for about an hour when the swamp became visible. The air here became humid and rich with the rotten egg scent of marshy soil and decaying plants. Frogs and toads croaked, and a flock of ducks suddenly lifted into the sky.

"Where is the camp, boy?" asked Geoffrey. "I don't see anything but the swamp."

"It's over there." She pointed towards the middle of the swamp. "The ground is solid there so it's the perfect hiding spot. You'll be able to ambush them. They won't go far."

Geoffrey didn't look convinced. "Are you certain?"

"I am. Your last chance to catch them is now. They said they were leaving tomorrow."

Geoffrey clicked his tongue, and his horse moved. The rest of his men followed him. As they made their way through the marsh, slowly, Danielle got behind the party and closer to Colum. He stared at her with a question in his eyes but didn't say anything. Well done...

The sounds of water slurping under the horses' hooves and Colum's feet drowned out the croaking frogs.

The horses up front neighed and stumbled. She needed to act. She reached into one of the saddlebags and felt around, before finally pulling out a knife that Colum had used to skin fish and rabbits.

Straining, she reached between Colum and the horse leading him and cut the rope with the knife. In one large stride, he lunged past her and grabbed his sword from where the soldier had attached it to his saddle. The man yelped.

Geoffrey and the other Englishmen, who were deeper into the swamp now, cried out. Their horses stomped their feet, neighed, and shook their heads as they tried to get out of the deep swamp.

"Get them!" came Geoffrey's cry. "Don't let them get away!"

The Englishman drew his sword and spurred his horse forward. Steel flashed as he swung the blade and met Colum's sword with a *clang*. Danielle's heart wrenched as she watched him fight the horseman while he was on foot.

The man had a clear advantage, and it didn't help that the enemy was fully armored, but it was as though Colum had gained a second wind. He deflected the Englishman's hits from every direction. Then, finally, he got a window and slashed the warrior across his uncovered thigh. The man yelled as blood sprayed from his thigh. The horse neighed and staggered back and deeper into the swamp.

While the rest of the English band struggled to get out of the bog, Colum hurried towards Danielle and leaped into the saddle in front of her.

The wounded English warrior gained control of his horse and came back at them. They fought, steel clashing against steel, blades flashing in the gray light.

Danielle held on to the saddle and squeezed her thighs as hard as she could around the horse's body. It was like trying to hold on to a bucking bull. Colum's back tensed before her, and he swung a powerful thrust into the man's face. The solider raised his sword to block, but he didn't have enough swing because of the horse's head. Colum's sword sank deep into the man's skull.

Colum drew his sword back and spurred his horse, and it put on as much speed as it could, struggling through the shallow swamp until it reached firm ground. Behind them, Danielle could still hear the cries of outrage and helplessness, but they faded away.

She sighed in relief as Colum put his sword back into the

sheath. With their enemies gone, and only trees and bushes passing by on the left and the right, she wrapped her arms around Colum's hard body.

Her hands weren't shackled. She'd gotten Colum out of there alive.

She didn't know what would happen next, but for now, she pressed her cheek against his back as he rode and listened to his heartbeat drum along with the horse's hooves.

CHAPTER 16

COLUM PULLED on the reins and looked over his shoulder. They'd ridden for a long time, through the woods, making sure to change directions a few times in case of pursuit. He was currently headed west, even though it would lead them farther away from Berwick; it would also lead them farther away from Blackhaugh Castle and Geoffrey and his band.

He hurt all over, but, thanks to Danielle, they were all superficial bruises. They didn't matter to him.

The horse and the two of them needed to rest, and he needed to know what was going on. He was confused...astonished...in awe.

He jumped down from the horse and watched Danielle throw her long, graceful leg over the horse's back and leap to the ground. She still had her coif on, but he would never see her as a man now. In fact, he couldn't believe he'd ever thought her to be a man.

Those big blue eyes were so gorgeous he couldn't breathe. Her wide, sensual mouth with a lower lip slightly fuller than the upper one made him think of kissing. And her high cheekbones were elegant despite the smudges of dirt over them. It was her clothes that tricked everyone, combined with her confident posture and strong, slender body. And her low, melodic voice could sound like that of an adolescent lad if one was tricked by her clothes.

He tethered the horse to a nearby tree, letting it graze on the grass.

The woods were quiet, and gentle birdsong came from above. Bees droned in the flowers. He could smell raspberries and lilacs and a muddy pond. The trees weren't thick here, but there were enough bushes to cover them from a distance in case Geoffrey managed to track them by some miracle.

He traced the horse's head with his palm, feeling the rough, short, warm fur. "Why did ye do that, Danielle?" he asked. "Why did ye nae join yer people?"

She swallowed hard, her eyes avoiding his. She lifted the saddlebag from the horse and put it down on the ground. "All I wanted was to get freed. And they did that."

She rummaged in the bag and retrieved a horn flask, then drank some water from it. He watched her lips curve around it, her throat moving as she swallowed.

Those pink, sensual lips... What would it be like if they curved like that around his cock? Heat rushed through him in a hard, scorching wave....

God's bones, now that he knew she was a woman, even such a simple act as her drinking was doing this to him?

"'Tis nae what I asked, lass," he said. "Ye were free. Ye could have left. Why did ye stay, and why did ye risk yer freedom and yer life to save me?"

She said nothing, just stared at him, her chest rising and falling quickly.

"They are yer people. Are they nae?"

The silence was a live thing between them, filled with that gentle chirping and the hot summer air. He could brush it aside and go to her and kiss her.

"Ye're nae my enemy, are ye?"

Her eyes burned like polished aquamarine stones with light shining through them.

Only yesterday, she'd thrown herself at him. She'd lain under him, all hot and aroused. Like he had been aroused for her.

His heart pumped hard. Soft tingles went through his blood, making him feel like he was about to float up in the air. What an odd sensation...a sensation he hadn't had for years...

Was this how it felt to be alive?

He stepped forward, closer to her. "Ye like me."

Her face lit up as though scorched by the sun. "I do not!"

A crooked smile curved one corner of his lips.

"For someone who kept a pretense of being a man for days, ye're surprisingly easy to read right now. Ye like me, lass. And ye're nae my enemy, are ye?"

He took two more slow steps towards her, and only a few inches separated them. She was so feisty and incredibly strong. She'd defied ten warriors for him. She didn't lack courage.

And yet...she stood like a trembling bunny in front of him, vulnerable and raw and lost at a simple question.

She was on his side. Something melted and cracked open within him, unraveling. Freeing.

He stepped even closer, and their chests touched. He could smell her sweet scent, feminine and beautiful and delicious. Something fruity and very much her own.

He pulled down her coif, and her hair glistened in the small patches of sunlight that fell on them through the trees. His breath caught at the sight. She was golden, like a treasure, like something holy and healing. She was shining and not just on the outside.

"What do we do, then? Ye say ye dinna like me. I say ye do. Let's test it and see."

He leaned to her for a kiss, but the wee fox slid out of his embrace and put a few steps between them. "You're an idiot!" she said, her cheeks still blazing red. "Of course I'm not your enemy. I told you that several times. Had you believed me a while ago, we could have been spared all this drama. All these chases. I could have been on my way back home long ago."

He chuckled softly and stepped closer, taking the flask from her hand. "On whose side are ye, then, lass?"

"No one's. I told you, I'm from the future. And yes, I am a spy. I protect the United Kingdom—that's what England, Scotland, Wales, and Northern Ireland are called in my time—from external threats. I'm not fighting for King Edward. I'm from the future."

Colum studied her in disbelief. All those things sounded completely mad.

"And as for why I didn't leave...I just couldn't leave you alone like that. I...I knew you'd rather die than be imprisoned by the English again. I know you'd probably do the same for me had the situation been reversed. Still, you should be grateful I didn't leave you to die."

Future... United Kingdom... She was a spy protecting from external threats.... Those words whirred in his mind like a whirlpool.

"I would indeed do the same for ye," he muttered, surprising himself.

Because he liked her, too. Something he hadn't wanted to admit, something that was deeply disturbing to him because she was English.

He brought the waterskin to his mouth and drank thoughtfully. He needed to set camp and let them both rest and continue his way down to Berwick tomorrow.

She wasn't his enemy, but did he believe the nonsense she said about being from the future? No, that sounded too strange, too unreal.

Nevertheless, that would explain her odd speech, the shoes, the strange breeches.

"What about that man ye said ye were serving...Sir Barnett de Guy?"

"I made him up so that Geoffrey would believe me."

That could be true. The biggest proof was that she had saved him. And she had gained important information about the English camp in Berwick.

Wherever she was from, England of this time or the future, she hadn't come to Bruce's camp to spy for Edward II.

And she didn't belong to him.

He turned around and undid the sleeping roll from the horse and laid it on the ground.

"Ye may leave now, lass. I've kept ye captive long enough."

He straightened and shook twigs and leaves out of the blanket, but she still didn't say anything. She also didn't leave. Didn't walk away.

"Did ye hear me, lass?" he asked. "Ye're free to go. 'Tis my thanks for saving me from the English. I wilna keep ye captive nae more."

"I heard you."

He turned over his shoulder to look at her. She stood as though frozen, her chest rising and falling in quick breaths, her eyes as wide as moons.

"So?" he asked.

"You're an idiot. You're going alone into a camp of twenty thousand armed men. It's suicide."

Colum turned away from her and went to unsheathe his sword and clean it. His chest tensed. *Suicide...* Aye. Mayhap. But it wouldn't be the worst thing, to die protecting his clan and Scotland, would it? The tenth knuckle on his hand was still nameless. Maybe then his clan would know he didn't want to betray them.

"Say something," she insisted. "You must see it. You'll die if you go there alone."

He sat on a large fallen tree trunk and placed his claymore on his lap. He ran a piece of cloth up and down the blade. Without looking at her, he said, "Whether I live or die isna of consequence."

He felt her shock, heard a swift inhale, then leaves rustling and twigs snapping as she came and sank to her knees before him, her hands on his knees, burning his skin through the fabric of his braies.

"You want to die there," she said softly. "Don't you?"

His jaw muscles clenched and worked as he thought. "I dinna want to die there."

"But you wouldn't mind it, would you?"

How could she see it? How could she understand it so much better than even he understood himself? She could see right through into his soul. Into his corrupt, damaged soul.

"I wouldna mind it, lass," he said, surprising himself. "I'm half dead inside already."

Only, he wasn't, not really. Glimpses of life had shone through his soul ever since she appeared.

Her eyes glistened with moisture. "What happened to you, Colum? What happened when you were their prisoner?"

He slowly ran the cloth over the blade. "Doesna matter. What matters is to help my clan and my country."

She shook her head. "Stubborn, aren't we?"

He chuckled. "Havena met a Highlander before, have ye?"

She let out a deep sigh. "I will regret this. For sure. But it seems ever since I touched that rock, I'm quickly sliding down the slope of bad decision-making."

"What are ye talking about?"

She stood up, hands on hips. "I can't let you go alone and die out there. I'll come with you and help you. Someone has to make sure you come out of that camp alive."

CHAPTER 17

COLUM'S BREATH stalled in his chest.

She was coming with him? The creature he'd thought to be an enemy all this time?

After how he'd treated her for days, despite her relentless attempts to escape. She'd still saved his life, risking her chance to go home, wherever that was.

Showing him more loyalty than some people of his clan.

He didn't deserve her. And, aye, he knew where he was heading. He knew the danger of going alone into the camp of the most powerful invading army in Scottish history.

And there she was standing tall and proud, like the goddess of war in a man's clothes. Her beautiful face intense, her aquamarine eyes shining hard at him, lips firm, the blush she couldn't shake like the first color of the sunrise. Her hair was in disarray, like a halo around her head, the sun making each strand look like spun gold. She was like a Norse Valkyrie calling an army of seasoned warriors to battle.

The battle for him.

His throat tightened, and something stung his fingers hotly. He was clenching his claymore too hard. He cursed and looked at his hand. Blood oozed from shallow cuts on the inner sides of his fingers. He wiped the cloth over the blood, the cuts stinging.

"Ye're leaving," he said, his eyes firmly on the sword. "I wilna let ye come with me."

She sank to her knees in front of him again.

"Let me see," she said.

His breath stuck in his throat, he watched how she took his wounded hand and turned it to her.

"The cuts aren't deep, but they need to be disinfected. You can't touch an open wound with that dirty cloth again."

So authoritative. A female laird barking commands that bore no tolerance of impudence.

She looked up at him, and their eyes locked. He didn't deserve her care and her sacrifice and her courage.

"Do you happen to have any alcohol?" she asked, her voice low, as though she was affected by the contact as much as he was.

"*Uisge?*" he asked. "Aye. The farmers gave me a wee horn flask."

She nodded, still seemingly unable to look away. Her gaze swept softly over his face. "I'll get it and clean the cuts on your hand and face."

She left his proximity and went to the bag sitting on the ground.

He watched her thin back as she rummaged there. "I mean it, lass, dinna ye dare come with me. Ye may camp with me until the morn's morn, but nae way in hell will I let ye come with me."

She straightened with the horn flask and a piece of clean, dry cloth, and came to him, dropping to a crouch. She undid the cork and pressed the cloth to the mouth of the flask and tipped it over. She took his hand in hers, a wee bit more harshly than she had before, and pressed the wet cloth against the cuts on his three fingers. He suppressed a hiss at the sharp pain.

She was still not looking at him.

"Say ye wilna come. Say ye will return home."

"I will," she said as she wiped his hand gently. Blood stopped oozing from the cuts on his fingers, and disappointment mixed with relief washed through his body. "Once I know you are out of the camp and safe."

She stopped wiping his hand and looked at him, her eyes cool, her face impassive. She didn't meet his eyes, her gaze studying his face. "And you will help me get back to that stone. Then I'll go home."

She tilted the horn flask over the clean side of the cloth once again. Then she reached out to his cheekbone and pressed the cloth to the cut. It burned his face with a short, scalding sensation.

"'Tis nae safe for ye, lass," he said.

"Neither is it safe for you," she said, pressing the cloth a bit harder against his face than necessary.

"But 'tis nae yer fight. 'Tis nae yer war. It doesna concern ye."

She removed the cloth, cool air biting sharply at the raw cut.

She met his gaze then, and the ground moved under his feet.

"You concern me." It felt like the earth disappeared from under them, and he soared, high and free, surrounded by the aquamarine sky.

A slow smile spread on his lips. "Ye admit it. Ye like me."

She stood up and threw the wet cloth into his lap. "Go to hell."

He put his sword away and stood up quickly, clasping his hand around her biceps and turning her to him. "Ye like me, lass," he said softly. There her lips were, soft and pink and delicious. "Dinna deny it. I like ye, too. We can have tonight, but ye must leave after."

He could smell her, the scent of hibiscus and fruit and sin.

"I'm not leaving unless it's with you," she said. "You have dragged me for days, denying me my own will and my freedom. Now I'm without shackles and you keep doing it. You can't force me to leave."

He studied her, bewildered. How could she have any concern

for him when he had held her captive? The answer came simple and clear. He had felt it, too, in Berwick. The way his feelings had changed towards his captors. Understanding of their ways. Relating to his guards. After months of imprisonment, a shameful, impossible urge for them to like him, to accept him as their own.

The need to belong.

But he hadn't belonged anywhere since he'd sworn allegiance to England. Not to the MacDonalds. Not to Scotland.

Was that what Danielle was confused by? He'd held her captive, and she'd started to think she cared about him?

"Lass, ye're nae seeing things clearly."

"I believe I do. If you have someone else with you, you won't think of death. You'll think of how to keep that someone alive. And I believe that will keep you alive."

She hit him right in the heart with it. What an insightful woman he couldn't shake off.

"I think"—she traced her fingers gently over the side of his face—"it's the only thing that will keep you alive."

He swallowed hard. He felt their connection, as alive and as palpable as pain.

"Why do ye want to keep me alive at all?" All jests were unnecessary. As redundant as old rags. She'd stripped him bare with her care, with her questions, with her gaze that looked straight into his soul and knew more about him than he knew himself.

"It's not for you," she said, her voice trembling. "It's for me. Because if your death was on my hands... I'd live my life in regret and pain until the day I die. I'd be you."

He couldn't move, couldn't feel himself. He was an aching cloud around her, desperate to know.

"What happened, lass?"

He knew their pain was shared, their sorrow like a child of two regretful parents.

She didn't reply for a while. He saw the unshed tears, the

ache behind her eyes. She looked off somewhere beyond him, somewhere he couldn't see.

She moved away to sit on the fallen tree trunk, then put her elbows on her knees and stared into the space. Silence fell over them, filled only with the chirping of the birds and rustling of the leaves and the buzzing of the insects.

"I had this hearing," she said. "It was today."

He moved and sat on the tree next to her. "A hearing?"

"It's like a court where someone makes a ruling, but it's for my job."

She was keeping to her story about time travel. He looked into her eyes. Did he really believe her? Something deep in his gut told him she was telling the truth. At least the truth she believed in.

The thought of her being from another time made the ground sway under his feet. "All those things about the future..." he murmured. "'Tis true, is it nae?"

She nodded.

"Yer clothes." He looked over her braies and her shoes. "Yer words...'okay'...'job'...others... 'Tis why ye must return back so desperately, is it nae?"

She swallowed and nodded. "I have a family there. A job."

"What is a job?"

"It's what I'm paid for. The work I do. I told you I'm a spy, protecting my country from external threats."

"Aye. I understand."

She let out a sharp exhale.

"I have informants in other countries. People that spy for me. People I vow to protect. People—" Her voice caught. "People who put themselves in danger to work with me. With my government."

He ached to take her into his arms, protect her from any danger, take any harm meant for her, on himself.

"This one informant...in South America..." She glanced sharply at him. "It's a continent you don't know about yet. It will be discovered almost two hundred years from now. Anyway, there was a cyberthreat from a group in South America against my country. A cyberthreat is something that comes through computers...machines... In my time, machines store money, information, secrets."

Colum nodded, struggling to imagine massive mechanisms like modern clocks. He'd seen a clock in a monastery near Berwick once. It was a machine to show time. He imagined things like that somehow containing money and information and secrets. It sounded like magic.

"It was hard to track them," Danielle continued. "Hard to know anything. I...I recruited one of them to spy for me against the rest. That person...his name is Juan. He was supposed to deliver a major piece of the puzzle to stop the attack. But he disappeared. I was listening to him going into a meeting with the enemy, and then the last thing I heard was a gunshot. Then I lost the connection with him. Um. The attack happened, but we managed to contain it. They stole some intelligence against other countries. Thankfully, my colleagues managed to find Juan and save him. The hearing was today. I needed to be there."

He had a hard time understanding. Imagining everything. It sounded like she was talking of a land of faeries and elves.

He knew one thing.

She had a person she was responsible for disappear, and the threat she had to contain still happened.

"I am sorry ye missed yer trial, lass," he said. "What was it supposed to be about?"

"About me. My superiors were supposed to judge if I had committed an error. If I needed to be sacked."

"Are ye guilty, lass?" he asked. "Is the fault over Juan yer own?"

She gulped. "Yes. I should have never sent him to the meeting. I should have insisted we find another way. I knew how dangerous it was."

Her lips trembled ever so slightly. He ached to take her into his arms and kiss that tremor away.

"Did Juan also ken?" he asked.

She nodded. "He did. But the idea was my colleague Simon's."

He frowned. "Simon?"

"He's my boss. My direct supervisor. He has several missions like this he oversees. He suggested Juan go to meet this group of international hackers called the Gagas. They're from all over the world, boys and girls in their early twenties, but they established themselves in South America because it's harder to track them there."

He must have had the most bewildered look in his eyes because she smiled softly. "Sorry. Lots of words you probably have no idea about."

"Aye. All sounds like witchcraft."

She nodded. "I have the same thoughts about your time."

"But...why did ye listen to Simon?" he asked.

"He's my superior. Like Robert the Bruce is to you."

He narrowed his eyes. "Wouldna he have kent better than to send Juan on a dangerous mission where he could have been killed?"

She inhaled sharply, looking into space. "Yeah. I mean. Um. I haven't thought of it that way."

"Do ye nae blame Simon?"

She was silent for a while. "No. I know he never meant for Juan to get hurt."

"Is Simon getting a hearing, too?"

She frowned. "No."

"Shouldna he? He's yer Robert the Bruce."

She blinked. "Um... Maybe he is getting a hearing. I would know, had I been to my interviews."

"And what if he doesna? What does it tell ye?"

Her frown smoothed. "That they're looking for someone to pin the blame on. And it's not Simon."

He nodded. "'Tis ye."

"I should have known. I had this feeling in the pit of my gut. This feeling Juan shouldn't go there. But Simon was the voice of reason. Simon knew better. He has twenty more years of experience than me. I trust him..." She swallowed. "Like I trusted my neighbor. There was no logical reason not to trust him..."

She stared straight at him, and his throat tightened as though a fist squeezed it. "What did yer neighbor do?" he asked, his voice sounding like a bear's growl.

She let out a shaky breath. "I was sixteen years old. A shy, insecure girl with only a couple of friends and very little trust in myself. He had moved into the neighborhood a few months earlier, a man in his late twenties. An accountant. He had a nice car. He looked sharp and kind. He had a girlfriend we'd seen on the street. His parents and his sister came to visit. My mum invited him for tea, to be neighborly. He gave them advice on how to claim back part of their taxes. He invited me in one day, me alone."

Colum's heart dropped, and his hands clenched as he waited to hear what happened next.

Her face was a tense mask, and she looked at her clasped hands. "I thought it was odd, but he was so trustworthy. So wholesome. If anyone could be trusted, it was this man with kind eyes and a good job."

"What did he do?" Colum repeated softly.

She looked at him with tears in her eyes. "He locked me in his basement."

Colum's blood seared. "What?"

"He had a room set up. A bed. A desk. A toilet and a sink. A shower in the corner. There was a mirror on the wall, it looked like a regular mirror, but he could watch me from the other side."

His heart beat hard against his ears. "He held ye prisoner?"

She nodded, still staring at her hands. Colum was ready to

kill someone. Including himself. Because that was exactly what he'd done to her.

"Why?" he barked out.

"For his own pleasure. To watch me. To own me. Like some people collect insects. Put them on pins and watch them die. Then dry them and put them in glass boxes to look at them."

The growl that came out of Colum's throat surprised even him. "I'd tear the bastart's heart out of his chest with my bare hands."

She threw him an odd look. "I spent about a month there. He talked to me. He never touched me. Just asked me questions. Told me about his day. If I started to plead with him to let me go or cry, he just left. There was never any violence or anything sexual. I was, indeed, an object he had collected, and he wanted to study me and to know me and to own me."

"Fucking bastart."

"The police finally found me and arrested him."

"The police?"

"They're law enforcement. Making sure there's order. They arrest those who break the law. Protect those who need help. Investigate crimes. They were looking for me. And finally found me. When I got out..." Her voice wavered. "My parents were devastated. They'd both aged ten years. My dad has had heart problems ever since. My mom has depressive episodes. My sister still cringes at the mention of the name Sebastian. And I—"

She looked deep into his eyes. He was shaking inside. Torn between pure rage for her suffering and helplessness to not have been able to protect her from that man. And now he understood that she, too, knew what it was like to be kept against her will. And that he had been her captor.

"I can't trust people," she continued. "I never go out with men anymore. I don't have any friends. I don't want a relationship, don't want to be married, don't want to fall in love, don't want to be...intimate...um...sexually. All I had was my job. And I screwed even that up. I let harm come to Juan, who was an innocent victim that I could have helped had I listened to my gut and trusted myself instead of Simon. And now my gut is telling me I can't let you go there alone. I can't live with myself if I allow you to go to the English camp and get killed."

Sweet lass... His chest tightened for her.

"If they find out ye're a woman, they will rape ye. And if they try to—"

He couldn't say more. A spasm cut his words short. The horror, the memories of that night with the queen and the wee lass Marjorie, burned like hot coals.

"What happened, Colum?" She turned to him. The fallen tree was hard under his thighs, bark cutting sharply through the fabric of his braies.

"I told ye about my fellow warriors."

"Yes. But that's not all, is it?"

The need to tell someone was like weight on his shoulders. A weight he needed to shake off.

"Nae." He leaned forward, his elbows sharp against his kneecaps. He ran his fingers through his hair and let his head hang between his shoulders. He'd been running away from these dark memories for years. But now, he had someone to share them with. And he let them take him. "King Edward—he was a prince then—summoned me to a dark room in the dungeon. For months, they'd kept me prisoner. Kept me alive. Treated my wounds and kept insisting I would turn to the English side. I didna budge. I told them kill me, I wilna succumb."

He bit his lower lip till he tasted blood.

"But he kent how to convince me. There they were. The queen, Robert the Bruce's wife, bent over a table with her dress slashed and her arse bared, screaming and whimpering and crying with pain. And a man twice as large as her, ready to...to violate her in the worst way. My queen, Danielle!" he cried out. "My queen. The queen of the country that had barely stood on its legs like a wee newborn deer. The wife of a king that was a fugitive with nae men and nae land. And they were about to strip my queen of the last dignity she had left. The last honor. And all that in front of Robert the Bruce's daughter, Marjorie, who was nae but a wee lass then."

Danielle whimpered, and when he looked up, he saw she was crying silently.

"I couldna let him do it, lass," he said, his voice a rasp. "I couldna let Edward take the last thing that he could, that nae doubt kept my king alive and fighting. His queen and his daughter. Somewhere out there, he was hiding, mayhap hungry, mayhap wounded, mayhap holding on to the last remnants of hope and courage. I would have done it for any woman or lass. And he was my friend. The hero I looked up to. The man I fought for and was ready to give my life for. So I said aye. If Edward would let the queen and Marjorie go unharmed, I'd swear my allegiance to England. I'd betray my clan. I'd fight for the wrong king. And hope to fall to the next Scottish sword."

She was shaking. She leaned on him and wrapped her arms around his neck. He took her into his arms, feeling her tears wetting his skin.

"I wish I could have protected Juan somehow, Colum. I wish...someone would have protected me."

He swallowed. "Lass, I understand ye've been hurt by this bastart. But ye're robbing yerself of so much."

She scoffed. "Says the man that is going to the enemy's camp trying to get himself killed."

He swallowed, watching her full lips move. "I'm talking about the sex part."

She went completely still. "Oh. I...I never felt much...during the few times when I tried..."

If she let him, if she saw him as more than just another man who'd kept her prisoner, he'd show her what she'd been missing.

Something bloomed within him, in the place where the dead part of his soul resided. Something tingled and scratched and became alive.

"I admire ye, lass. I never thought it was possible to meet

someone like ye. I am sorry this happened to ye, and I am sorry I was another man that held ye prisoner. And despite all that, ye dinna wish me harm, and on the contrary, ye're risking yer life and yer...job back in yer time...for me. Ye show me what honor is once again. Ye show me what 'tis like to live again."

She inhaled sharply, and a single tear rolled down her cheek.

"Please, forgive me for taking ye prisoner," he said. "For entrapping ye once again. Can ye ever forgive me?"

She nodded. "You didn't do it to enjoy me like that sick bastard did. You did it to save your country. You thought I was a spy. Had I been on a mission and caught a foreign spy of an enemy state, I'd have done the same."

Relief lightened up his whole body. He had no idea why it was so important that she believed him. That she didn't think of him like she did about Sebastian.

"Good. Because I'm going to travel into yer time and kill that sick bastart if he still stops ye from living yer life and experiencing all that...a woman should."

He didn't know what he was saying. He had no right to talk to her like that, as if he were her betrothed or her husband.

"And you know what I should or shouldn't do?" she asked, her voice low and husky.

God's blood, he loved her voice. His whole body burned. He ached to show her what she'd been missing all those years because of some man whose life was not worth a drop of this woman's blood.

"I ken ye should stay away from me, lass. I ken ye should take the horse and take the bag and ride to Bannockburn and go to that rock and never look back. Because if ye dinna..."

He stopped talking, his heart drumming so loud he couldn't hear his own voice.

"What?" she asked. "If I don't, then what?"

His palms itched with the urge to touch her, to pick her up in his arms and carry her to a bed made for queens and worship her like the goddess she was. That was part why he wanted to hold off. He couldn't give her the experience she deserved in a rough forest camp.

He clenched his fists in a last attempt to stop himself.

He stood up and moved away from her. He had taken away her freedom and her home. He had no right to take more...

"Nothing, lass," he said. "I'm holding on to the last threads of my restraint. I want ye like I havena wanted a woman in my life. And I canna do this to ye."

She stood up and he felt her hot palm on his shoulder as she turned him to face her.

He met her burning gaze. She scoffed. "You think I'm some sort of a wallflower, a daisy that will crumble from a touch? You think he broke me?" Her voice jumped. "I haven't felt anything with anyone like I've felt every time you touch me. When we kissed...I didn't think my body was capable of singing like that. Your touch made me happy."

That was enough. There was no more hesitation, no more doubt, and no more remorse.

He curled his arm around her waist, brought her to him, and claimed what he'd craved for what felt like forever.

CHAPTER 18

HIS MOUTH WAS velvet and sin. He tasted like freedom, like the woods, and like a man.

Delicious. Sultry.

He didn't just kiss her. He demanded her. Craved her. Drank her in like a starving man. Like an addict.

He licked and curled his tongue around hers, stroking the tip along the roof of her mouth. A growl rumbled from his chest, and her inner walls clenched as the area between her thighs became hot and wet.

Where did this ache come from, for the next lick, the next fix of this drug?

She kept whimpering, purring like a sex-fueled kitten. She'd never heard herself make noises like that... Her fingers tangled in his long, silky hair.

Their tongues glided, entangled in a wild dance. Lips slid and joined together.

His arms around her were iron rods, but instead of feeling trapped and imprisoned, she felt safe...

She felt hot.

In fact, she burned to get closer to him, tighter, skin to skin. She hurled one leg over his hip and ground herself against a very long, hard erection. She had no idea if she was doing this right, or if he would enjoy it at all. The few times she'd had sex had been awkward, and she'd always waited for it to be over.

Not this time.

He cupped her bottom with both his hands and encouraged her, while he began rocking his hips in the same rhythm. She gasped into his mouth as the sweet friction created a delicious sensation, a pleasure like she'd never experienced before.

She knew one thing.

She never wanted this to stop. In fact, she wanted more.

It was strange. She wasn't a virgin. But all this was new. New and wonderful and thrilling.

"Please..." she whispered against his mouth. "Please..."

"Please what, lass?" he asked, his voice an aged-whiskey croon.

"Um...I don't know..." she panted. "Everything."

He growled, the low rumble of a satisfied wolf. "Do ye want me to touch ye, lass?"

She swallowed. Her sex clenched at the words. "Yes."

Even she could hear the throbbing ache in her voice. The growl repeated.

He lifted her up by her bottom, and she wrapped her legs around his waist. He walked with her wrapped around him like a koala and laid her on the sleeping roll. It was hard against her back. He pulled up her tunic and froze in bewilderment staring at her jeans.

"How do I...? What is this?"

She would have laughed if she wasn't this aroused. "A button," she said as she unfastened it. "And a zip."

She unzipped, and he looked at her. "The braies from the future?"

"Uh-huh..."

He chuckled with a lazy, playful crooked smile she'd never seen on him. She wondered if that was how he used to be before

Berwick. A carefree, self-confident, popular young man who knew how to please a woman.

She wondered how she was, before her own imprisonment... Did she have a smile then that she didn't have anymore? Would she have felt like this with every man she was intimate with if she hadn't gone through that trauma with Sebastian?

His grin thawed something deep inside her.

He tugged her jeans down her thighs and stared at her knickers. They were simple black knickers, and she wished she had something fancier on.

But the look on his face said he didn't wish that at all, and she stilled, stopped breathing as she found him slowly looking her over, his eyes black and liquid. He leaned over her stomach and came very close to the edge of her knickers. His breath scalded her.

"Ye're killing me, lass. Ye're so bonnie."

That had her holding her breath. Then he clenched the edge of her knickers between his teeth and dragged them down. The feel of his beard and his nose barely touching her skin was electrifying.

When the knickers were off, he slowly went up her legs, kissing the insides of them. She was shaking. Did his dark, molten eyes mean he liked what he saw? He'd just said she was bonnie...did he mean it?

She gasped, watching his head come closer and closer to the apex of her thighs. Her breath was so loud in her ears, it felt like her eardrums were clogged.

"Colum..."

No one had ever done this to her. Three times men had given her oral, but she hadn't felt anything. She just couldn't let go. Couldn't trust them. She'd felt the barrier between her body and her mind like a concrete wall.

Not now. Something was different about him. Or maybe she was different here with him. She'd never told anyone what she'd told him about Sebastian. About her private life. About sex.

How was it possible that she trusted this man more than anyone she'd ever met? This man who'd treated her like an enemy...

All her thoughts evaporated when he palmed the insides of her thighs and gently spread them open.

And there she was, lying naked and vulnerable for him to see. She felt like he'd peeled her open, like she'd let down her walls before him and had no more defenses. Like she could finally stop fighting.

"Ye're the most bonnie woman I've ever met, Danielle. And I dinna just mean yer body. I mean ye, inside. Body and soul."

Her throat contracted as she stared into his eyes. It was almost painful to hear. But so seductive to believe him. No one had ever said anything similar. No one had ever said they liked her, that they were falling in love with her or loved her. No one gave her compliments about her appearance or her character.

Maybe because she didn't let people get close enough to feel safe doing that.

He palmed her sex, the heat and the touch sending a lightning bolt of pleasure through her. Then he spread her folds and leaned down and licked up the length of her.

She gasped and arched her back, curling her fingers around the woolen blanket, the material coarse under her skin.

"Ye taste delicious, lass," he murmured.

More. More. More.

As though hearing her inner voice, he burrowed his mouth between her folds, his big hands holding her inner thighs, massaging them.

This is how it is supposed to feel. This incredible heat. These aching tugs. This need. This pleasure.

This was what it felt like to be in the arms of a man who knew what he was doing. Who had full control over her body, which she'd given him of her own free will.

And she loved it.

He lapped, sucked, and flicked. He feasted and teased and

nibbled. Pleasure built and intensified, and she wanted more and more.

He inserted one, then two fingers deep inside her. The invasion was absolute, her surrender irrevocable. Sensation blasted through her, and as he began circling his fingers around her and shoving them deeper, a wave of something exquisite began forming in her body like a hurricane.

"Oh, Colum..." she managed. "Oh, Colum!"

"Aye, lass," he murmured against her folds, "dinna fight this. Come for me. Come around my fingers, give it all to me."

"Ah!" The orgasm hit her like a wall of pleasure. Stars burst behind her eyes, the intense, sweet convulsions kept going and going.

"Och, lass, how ye're milking my fingers," Colum murmured, his voice raspy. "I'm about to burst thinking how ye're going to milk my cock."

When she lay quiet and still, relishing the aftershocks of the orgasm, Colum's dark eyes watched her.

"Lass, do ye even ken how bonnie ye are? Watching ye take yer pleasure, and knowing 'tis me that gave it to ye...that 'tis me that can worship ye and watch ye come back to life... 'Tis like I'm coming back to life, as well."

There was a knot in her chest that grew tighter and tighter. He stretched along her body and watched her, leaning on one elbow. He was so handsome he belonged in a movie. There were no men like him, they didn't exist—not in the real world.

"And had ye...had ye wished to stay in my world. Had I nae been on a suicide mission...had we had a chance for love..." She stopped breathing as she clung to every word. "I'd protect ye from any harm, from any disrespect. I'd shield ye with my body and defend ye with my sword."

His eyes were blazing, and for the first time she felt safe. Protected. He had trusted her enough to share his secret with her. And she had trusted him enough to share her pain and be vulnerable.

"But who's going to protect you?" she whispered.

There was one moment when the fury in his eyes dissolved and the walls that he had fortified for years cracked. And through those cracks, she saw pain and loneliness and fear, just like her own.

"You haven't told anyone what you went through, have you?" She reached out and cupped his face. He drew a sharp breath at her touch, but he didn't pull away. "Let me be your protector, too. You don't have to be strong all the time."

She fell in love with him a little more...a lot more...at that moment. Because he didn't pull away. He didn't lash out at her. He stayed in place, his anguish bare and open for her to see.

She rose on her elbow and kissed him. This was a different kiss. Slow and as gentle as the touch of a cloud. She gave him butterfly kisses. Kisses that said, *I like you. I got you. I want all of you.* Pain and anguish and dark thoughts—everything.

He groaned, and she grasped the collar of his tunic and pulled it up. He dragged it over his head, and there he was, his chest hard and broad, his biceps bulging like boulders, his narrow waist and ripped stomach. Silver battle scars lined his body, making her shiver thinking of the times he had been harmed.

She wrapped her arm around his neck and pulled him on top of her, kissing him. He was a large, pleasant weight, and just the feel of him, the taste of him, his muscular scent set her insides to simmering.

He kissed her in long, savoring strokes, like they had all the time in the world, and they were made for this moment right here, right now. There was just their ragged breath and the lavish, lazy slide of their tongues against each other, and the glide of his rough hands over her body.

His hand went under her tunic, and his calloused skin made her shudder. He pulled her tunic over her head and tossed it aside. Then off came her top. The air against her naked skin made her nipples harden and ache. The woods around them were like a castle. The trees like walls. The sun and the sky flickering between tree branches and leaves like a ceiling.

He looked over her naked body, his gaze scorching hot. "Lass, I-I've never felt like this before. Ever."

"Neither have I."

He leaned down and scooped one of her small breasts into his palm and took her nipple into his mouth, sucking. She arched her head back as pleasure ran through her, right into her crotch.

"Ah!"

"Aye, lass," he murmured between sucks. "Groan and scream and tell me how much ye like it."

"Oh, Colum." She dug her fingers into his hair.

He took her other breast with his palm while he continued to kiss and nibble and suck the nipple of the first. With his hand, he cupped her breast and massaged it, and circled the nipple with his thumb. She bit her lip. Then his hand left her breast and went down her body and over her stomach. A tremor went through her. He spread the lips of her sex and ran a finger through her slickness.

"Lass, ye are so wet... So ready for me..."

She clenched around him when he inserted a finger, simultaneously circling her clit and fucking her with his finger.

She was oversensitive there still, almost to the point of ache, and it made every stroke and every sensation that much more intense.

"Och, yer sweet pussy, lass," he murmured. "So sweet, so hot, so hungry."

"Ah..." She was hungry. Hungry for him. The finger was not enough. She wanted him deep inside, taking her, driving her over the edge. "I want you. Inside."

He stopped moving his fingers, and she met his gaze. "Are ye certain, lass? Ye can always say nae. Ye can always stop me."

She swallowed hard. "I'm a woman that is aroused and burning for you. But you'll have to pull out...I'm not on birth control. Can you?"

He gave a curt nod and growled. "Oh, lass, what are ye doing to me?"

He rose over her and palmed his erection. It was the first time she'd seen it, and she swallowed a gasp. It was huge, long, and thick. He positioned himself against her entrance, his eyes burning, his face looking pained. He stroked her with the tip of his cock, circling around her clit. She arched her back, pleasure swirling through her in a wild, primal dance.

Then he slid into her in one full thrust. They both arched, and he growled a curse. "Lass, how good ye feel. Oh Christ."

He filled her, stretched her. He never stopped looking into her eyes. His were so dark, she was sinking in them. He didn't move for a while, and she pulled at him to sink even deeper into her.

This connection between them wrapped around her like a warm blanket.

"Ye're mine now, lass," he whispered. "Mine."

How her heart ached to hear that...

And then he started moving, and she let out a long breath, arching her chest and tightening her legs around him. It felt delicious, and the harder and faster he thrust, the hotter it felt. She moaned, giving in to the rhythm, giving in to him.

Surrendering.

"Colum..." she heard herself groan.

He pulled one of her legs up to her chest and thrust into her so deep, she felt him stretch her to the very limit. She—the cold one, the frigid one—was all wet and hot and feeling all those things with this man that she'd thought she was incapable of.

"Lass, ye feel like heaven. I have been yearning for ye for days."

She couldn't reply; all she could do was meet his thrusts with her hips, wanting more of this silky, liquid, hot connection. Her throat kept making kittenish mewls of pleasure. They were sinking together. Sinking somewhere between past and present and future, into a place that couldn't exist but where he and she were meant to be.

And then the orgasm slammed into her like a lorry on full speed, and she cried out as intense waves of pleasure rocked her. Colum cursed and pulled out, palming his cock as he came on her stomach.

After a while, he collapsed onto her, then rolled to the side and pulled her head into the crease of his arm. They both panted, and Danielle felt like she was flying, like there were no more secrets and no more walls between them.

He'd just given her the most amazing and intense sexual experience of her life. From a frigid "stick" to this...this sex goddess who just had two orgasms...and was ready for more.

"Two orgasms in one night. Didn't know I was capable of that. I guess it was about being with the right man."

He brought her closer to him and kissed her forehead. "I am falling in love with ye, lass."

Her heart squeezed. She didn't dare to take her next breath. The knot in her chest tightened to the point of pain. And then it broke as though there was too much tension and something unraveled and warmed in her heart.

"I'm falling in love with you, too," she said softly.

And oh, how she was going to hurt when either he would die or she'd need to leave him forever and return to her own time.

CHAPTER 19

"So, what do you have in mind?" asked Danielle the next day, as she crouched in front of a wee bunch of wild strawberries. "For when you get to Berwick? Did you think it through?"

Colum struck his fire steel over some kindling. They had stopped in a well-hidden spot for the night. He hoped Geoffrey had given up the search, but Colum would not let down his guard. Nothing mattered more now than keeping Danielle safe. They were deep in the woods. Scottish pines grew dense here, their crowns shielding the light. A small brook gurgled nearby. It was quiet and dark and smelled like pine needles and mushrooms.

Colum blew on the embers in the kindling, and when the fire was burning well, he answered, "I'll go into the camp and find the red tent in the northeastern quarter."

"Right," she said as she stood and walked a few steps away, then sank to her knees again. "And have a twenty-thousand-man army stop you before you even manage to reach the king."

He'd been aware of her every movement, even as he'd constructed the pile of firewood and added the kindling. Truth be told, he hadn't thought much about his plans since they'd made love last night. And now he felt different. He wasn't the same man who had set out with an English spy to Berwick with a mission to kill the English king or die trying.

He had something to live for now. Someone...

Even if it was just for a few more days and not a lifetime.

Before he could reply, she inhaled sharply.

He jumped to his feet, his hand on the hilt of his claymore, his eyes darting among the tree trunks for any signs of danger. But there was nothing. She just stood between the trees thirty feet away, staring at something on the ground.

"What is it, lass?" he demanded.

"False morels."

"What?" He covered the space between them quickly. A handful of small wild strawberries clutched to her stomach, she stood over a large area where strange brown clumps grew out of the ground. He supposed those were mushrooms. He'd eaten some that looked similar, and they were quite good.

"False morels," she said in fascination. "I'm pretty sure. I'll need to check. Give me your knife."

He handed her his eating knife, and she handed him the strawberries. She sank to her knees and picked a rather large, clumpy brown mushroom that looked like an old, decomposed piece of brain. Its stem was white and thick. She studied it carefully.

"When my dad and I camped, that was one of the things we learned," she explained. "Foraging. Looking for good mushrooms —like true morels—and poisonous ones. With true morels, their caps should remind you of a honeycomb, and their insides"—she cut the mushroom in her hand in two. It was full, the white stalk of the mushroom going all the way up to the brown top— "should be hollow. Empty. This is the false morel."

Colum frowned at the clearing full of brown caps hiding among the green grass. "All right. And?"

"And," she said, her eyes bright, "it's poisonous. It causes vomiting, abdominal pain, diarrhea, dizziness, headache...all those symptoms typical of poisoning."

He frowned even harder. "Then you shouldna hold it in yer hands!"

She chuckled. "You're absolutely right! Even inhaling the spores is dangerous. I read it has this toxin...monomethylhydrazine..."

"Mono...what?"

"Monomethylhydrazine. It's one of the components of rocket fuel in my time."

He frowned in confusion. What was she talking about?

"Doesn't matter," she said, no doubt seeing his reaction.

He hit her hands, and the mushroom fell to the ground. "Danielle, I am serious. Dinna ye dare take this in yer hands again!"

She sighed and grinned at him. "Holding it in the open air is perfectly fine as long as we wash our hands after. But eating it is very dangerous and can even be deadly..."

He cocked his head, watching an idea form behind her eyes. "What do ye have in mind, lass?" he asked.

She chuckled. "You want to stop the English army? Instead of trying to kill the king, just slip these bad boys into the cauldrons across the camp."

CHAPTER 20

"OH, BLOODY HELL, THERE IT IS," muttered Danielle two days later as she peered from behind the hill.

Colum's stomach dropped as he followed her gaze. Through the bushes and grasses, a spectacular view lay before them.

Tents, horses, carts, and armed men—a mass of people—spread over the hills near Berwick like a swarming blanket of ants. Ants armed with spears, swords, longbows, and the best warhorses gold could buy. Banners with English colors, Welsh, and also some that Colum didn't recognize waved in the wind here and there. He wondered if those were the knights that had traveled here from France, Germany, and Eastern European kingdoms. They had been hired for money and promised land and glory.

He narrowed his eyes, scanning surroundings that he knew well from his time at Berwick Castle.

The castle itself loomed in the far distance on the hill right by the river. It had three rows of walls and large inner baileys. On the other side was the North Sea and the cliffs that ensured the castle was impenetrable.

On this side, the village of Berwick flanked the castle, a steep hill sloping up towards it. Several towers shot into the sky at the corners of the walls. A huge gatehouse with two round towers on both sides of the doors rose high above the drawbridge leading into the castle.

His prison. The place of his shame, where he'd been broken in more ways than he could count.

He had spoken about it with Danielle for the past three days. He had told her more than he had told any living being. It made it easier knowing that she understood what he had gone through, but it was more than that. It was how similar they were, deep down. She was as much a woman of honor as he was a man of honor. She had a kind heart, and she wanted to make peoples' lives better and protect them from threats.

She'd taught him a new game—the game of chess. At one of their stops, they'd created a chess set using pine cones, twigs, and pebbles and played right on the ground. She usually beat him, wee minx, but he'd also won at least once.

Despite their differences, they complemented each other. She told him she was naturally more reserved and quiet around people. He'd always felt he needed the company of others. That was, perhaps, why she had been fine working alone or with a few informants as a spy while he felt the absence of his clan's support and friendship like a huge hole at the core of his soul. Most of his true friends had been killed after Methven, and those who didn't know what had happened to him—everyone but the Bruce and Uncle Aulay—still treated him like a traitor. The silent treatment and the coolness were quiet demonstrations of their opinions and distrust.

They treated him as if he were a snake that might strike and kill at any moment.

He missed the friendly banter. The brotherly support. The unspoken trust.

He needed to talk to people daily. He missed being at the center of a party, laughing and jesting and making everyone feel jolly.

And she...she showed him it was perfectly all right to be

alone and still feel that joy, that laughter, that sense of being fully alive.

But he had never felt more alive than when he made love to her. They had made love every night and whenever they stopped to eat or rest the horse. Even one time right on the horse, when she was in front of him, and he could slip his hand into the tight space between her braies and her flesh and make her come while they rode.

The few birds and trees didn't mind.

She was his friend, a warrior at his side, and the woman he was falling in love with.

The woman who didn't belong in this time. The woman who would never be his wife because either he'd be dead or she'd leave him and return to her time.

She bit her plush lip that he wished he could bite. "How are we ever going to give them enough mushrooms?"

"The king and the commanders will eat meals together and make their plan of attack," he said. "Mayhap we should poison that meal. The regular warriors wilna go on without their commanders."

Edward II would wriggle and crawl clenching at his stomach like Queen Elizabeth had wriggled and crawled in desperation to escape her assailant. While he did that, Colum would cleave his head from his neck.

The man had destroyed his very soul—until Danielle had come along and shown him it may not be as dead as he had thought.

"Yes. So we look for the red tent."

"Aye, lass."

She turned away from the camp and leaned against the steep slope of the grassy field. Their horse grazed twenty feet down the hill. The scent of warm earth and wet grass was thick and moist inside his nostrils.

"We will need to hide any signs you're a Scot," she said, and he got distracted by her luscious mouth again.

"My sword," he said, swallowing his lust. "'Tis a claymore. My léine-chròich. My accent, of course. But if I dinna have to speak…"

She nodded. "Good. Let's watch the camp for a bit to see where there are weaknesses."

He leaned down and kissed her, a reminder of what he had to fight for.

"Lass, I ken an English camp—like a Scottish camp—inside and out." He pointed at three small figures carrying timber from the woods towards the camp.

"We need to appear as though we're carrying something. We need to make ourselves invisible. The army may be twenty thousand souls, but thousands are those that serve it. Peasants. Cooks." He pointed around the camp where men and women were preparing food. "Hunters." He indicated a man with rabbits hanging over his shoulder. "Provisioners going into the village of Berwick and buying every single fish and head of cheese and loaf of bread that has been made in the past couple of days. Servants that go to the streams and wash the dirty laundry of their masters."

She grinned. "Yes. Servants appear to be invisible. That's how we'll hide. What are the most common jobs?"

"Chopping wood to heat in the cauldrons." He nodded to another side of the camp where a herd of horses grazed surrounded by a fence. "Tending to the horses." He nodded to the depths of the camp, where men sparred and shot arrows into targets in the middle of a clear field. "Cleaning and sharpening of tools and arrows."

She nodded. "Okay. When do you want to do this?"

He narrowed his eyes. "Tonight."

"We'll hide your sword under your cloak. I'm sure you will need it in the camp. No way I'd let you go into a twenty-thousand-man camp without a weapon to protect yourself."

He chuckled. "Lass, ye're nae in charge of my safety here."

She shook her head. "Sure, you big, sexy Highlander. Whatever you say."

And why did it feel like the opposite of what she said?

But he didn't have a chance to respond to her sarcasm because she continued. "We move through the camp at night as though we're carrying something. Maybe firewood would be the easiest. Everyone needs firewood. Don't forget your accent. Try not to say anything. If you have to, can you do a good accent when you speak English?"

"I dinna think I can," he admitted. "I may try to do a Lowland one. Nae doubt there are plenty of Lowland clans out here."

"Right. That will work. Good."

But Colum knew better than she did. It wasn't good. He needed to talk her out of this.

"Lass, I implore ye to stay here. Dinna come!"

"But we agreed—"

"'Tis one thing to go on this suicide mission when I was alone and ready for death..."

It was another when he was going with the woman he was falling for.

"Ready for death?" she asked. "You don't mean it still...do you?"

A cold shiver ran through him as he realized it was exactly what he had wanted. The memories of his friends' necks severed, their limbs torn from their bodies, their guts spread over the land.

He should have been among them. He still didn't think he should have been allowed to live when better people had died.

He locked his eyes with hers. "For the first time, lass," he said, "there's something to live for."

Her glacier-blue eyes warmed to a gorgeous turquoise. "Yes. You do." She cupped his face with both hands. "For me."

The kiss was slow and soft and as delicious as a last feast.

When he let her go, he looked deep into her eyes. "I'll save ye, lass, if anyone tries to harm ye."

Even if it meant he'd be distracted and watching her more than watching his own back. She was more important than keeping his own life.

"But I'll tell ye one thing," he said as he glanced over the edge of the hill at the camp. "I'm nae going to be a prisoner again. If they catch me, consider me a dead man."

"Colum, you don't mean it."

His soul ached as he remembered the haunting months he'd spent in Berwick. His skin became clammy, and his pulse raced. His jaw clenched and his legs went weak. "The last time, they broke me. If they catch me again, I'll find a way to get killed."

"Then I'll have to get you out of there," she said. "Because I'm not ready to give you up."

CHAPTER 21

THE CAMP WAS a sea of orange campfires in the darkness as Danielle walked down the hill between sparse trees, rocks, and bushes. Colum moved by her side, as silent as a puma, his hand on the hilt of his sword, his shoulders rounded, his dark eyes alert. They'd gathered sticks for firewood in the woods and now carried the heaps in their arms.

The scents of woodsmoke, wet grass, and herbs hung in the air. An owl hooted somewhere behind them. Dark clouds passed over the moon and colored the sky silvery gray.

Danielle's heart drummed in her ears. Was she really doing the best thing by staying? She had no doubt she needed to help Colum, but what if she got stuck? Or hurt? Or killed?

And risking her life for a man from another time, whom she hadn't known long... He didn't feel like a stranger to her, though.

And she couldn't bring herself to leave him.

She was falling for this man. He'd unraveled her body. He'd brought back to life the part of her she'd thought was dead. The part she'd thought needed protecting.

She'd been keeping people away so that no one would betray her trust and hurt her. Her job was a perfect excuse to steer clear of relationships. Only close people were supposed to know what she did for a living, and she'd told herself it was better that way. If she didn't let people into her life, she didn't have to lie.

If their mission ended well, and she returned to her time only to be sacked, then what? She wouldn't be able to use her job as an excuse to keep people away anymore.

She had no answer. This thing with Colum had no future, no matter how convinced Sìneag was that he was the man destined for her. She would just remember it as a vacation fling and would forever be thankful to him for making her feel the way he did.

But for now, she had to protect him. When Sir Geoffrey and his men had taken Colum, she'd seen how terrified he was of going back into English hands—the panic of a trapped animal. For him, being imprisoned was a fate worse than death.

When they reached the camp, her pulse beat fast in her palms.

Danielle covered her head with the coif, hiding her hair.

Colum glanced over the camp quickly. The nearest tent was quiet. The next campfire was about twenty feet away. Tents had been erected with rows between them so that people could walk through the camp. Wood, baskets, and chests lay between them. Hidden by the darkness, Colum wrapped his arm around Danielle's waist and planted a long kiss on her lips that left her reeling and her knees weak.

"Be careful, lass," he said, scalding her face with his hot, dark gaze.

"You, too," she whispered.

Then he let her go.

A large pouch of false morels was attached to the girdle at Danielle's waist. Colum had one, as well.

They walked through the camp about one tent away from each other, separate but still close enough. They passed by a few campfires. Most men were asleep, only one or two sentinels were awake and threw lazy gazes at her as she passed by. She nodded to everyone who made eye contact with her, appearing friendly, while her feet were cold and her back sweaty.

It must have been the fifth campfire that she passed when one of the sentinels called, "Boy! Hey, boy!"

She froze and slowly turned to him. Behind the tent, Colum's figure went completely still. "What is it?" she asked.

The man's face was dark under the shadow of his coif. "Boy, put some wood into my campfire."

She swallowed and threw some branches into the fire, causing sparks to fly into the air.

The man nodded and waved her off. With her chest rising and falling quickly, she resumed her walk.

It must have taken ten minutes before she saw the king's pavilion about a hundred feet away. Large and red, it was impossible to miss.

Passing by the next campfire, Danielle gathered a handful of morels, which they'd ground up as finely as they could using rocks, and nodded to the men sitting around it.

Lowering her voice, she said, "Some wood for your fire."

She stood with her back to them and put the sticks into the fire. Then, with her heart drumming hard, she subtly tossed the morels from her hand into the cauldron.

The men didn't say anything, just nodded, and she went on. As she progressed, she kept throwing glances towards Colum, but she couldn't see him anymore. She continued putting wood in the campfires and throwing false morels into the cauldrons.

Because of the darkness and the sleepiness of the sentinels, she was sure, no one stopped her or noticed anything. But she'd also lost sight of Colum. She needed to make sure he was all right. Her whole reason for coming along was to ensure he would leave here alive. Worry for him twisted her gut.

She made her way to her right, in the direction where she'd last seen him. She passed by quiet tents and more campfires and came upon him very suddenly.

He sat at a campfire with the English soldiers, his back rounded, a wooden bowl with food steaming in his hands. He met her eyes, a panicked expression in his gaze.

"Where did you say you were from?" asked one of the soldiers.

"Here. Nearby," said Colum with his best imitation of a Lowland accent.

"Why haven't I seen you before?" asked the second one.

"I'm new," said Colum.

Danielle's mind raced. She needed to figure something out and help him.

"Got some firewood," she said and put the last of her sticks into the fire. "And where've you been?" she said, addressing Colum. "You had the ax, and I can't find it. I need to keep cutting firewood."

"Oh, aye." Colum stood up. "Let me show ye where it is. Thanks, lads." He put the bowl on the ground.

As he and Danielle walked away from the campfire, she had to restrain herself from breaking into a run. Her heart beat in her ears as she expected the knights to call after them.

But step after step, they moved farther and farther away. And once she could see the red roof of the king's pavilion again, she sighed with relief.

"The fucking bastarts are already dividing my land between themselves," Colum growled in a low voice. "One of them is Gilbert de Clare, Earl of Gloucester. A fucking lad of twenty-three. Nephew of the king. Ye ken what he brought with him? Half of his household. Servants. Plates. Chairs. Tables. He's sure he'll get Inverlochy Castle and is thinking how to furnish it!"

He scoffed in disgust.

Danielle sighed out a long breath.

"Well, he won't get it. You guys will win the Battle of Bannockburn. But we must play our role, too. Come on, Colum," she said. "You see the red roof? That's Edward's pavilion. Let's go."

CHAPTER 22

As they got closer to the pavilion, Colum laid his hand on her arm and pointed at another large tent.

"Lass, do ye see that banner?"

She squinted to see through the darkness. "Blue and white stripes, red birds along the edge?" she asked.

"Aye. 'Tis Aymer de Valence's, Earl of Pembroke. He's Edward's right hand. Let me get over there and put some morels in their stew."

"Okay," she said and squeezed his hand. "Be careful. I'll go and snoop around the king's pavilion."

She went on by herself and lingered in the shadows behind the next tent, watching. There was no one in the king's pavilion. The four sentinels still sat around the campfire, talking in low voices. In the shadows next to the entrance of the pavilion stood a tray of food—a bowl of steaming stew, a plate with apples, and a piece of grilled meat. Rich and untouched. It must have been prepared for the king and no one had brought it to him yet.

She looked around. Besides the four sentinels, everything was quiet. The only sounds were campfires crackling, quiet voices murmuring, and people snoring peacefully inside the tents. She quickly made her way towards the tray and poured a whole handful of ground morels into the bowl, then picked up the spoon and stirred it.

A shadow blotted out the light of the fire behind her, and her stomach dropped.

"What are you doing, boy?" asked a man's voice.

She turned around, her heart in her feet. A richly dressed nobleman, he had a crimson tunic with golden patterns of flowers and leaves. He was in his thirties, with dark blond hair in a jaw-length, wavy style. He had a short, well-trimmed beard and gray eyes that looked her over with a glistening interest. There was an air of arrogance and entitlement about him with his nose high and his straight back.

A little behind him followed two men-at-arms, fully armored and bearing swords and shields that shone in the firelight.

This must be the king.

Danielle's feet as heavy as lead, she thought hard. How much had he seen? An idea struck her. She picked up the tray and took a step towards the king. "I was just going to bring this to you, Your Grace."

He looked her over, and there was something odd in his eyes. A look she didn't like. As though she was a curious little specimen he wanted to inspect more closely.

He nodded and took one step closer to the pavilion's entrance, pulling the drape aside. "Then come in."

Heart in her throat, she stepped in. Inside, it was rich and beautiful. A large carved bed was at the other side of the tent, and a brazier illuminated the space. There were swords and axes and shields stacked next to a beautifully carved chair. A large table with empty silver and golden plates stood in the middle of the room, with several chairs around it. Furs covered the floor and the bed, and at least a dozen chests stood along the walls.

When Danielle put the tray on the table and turned around, she noticed they were alone. The guards hadn't followed them.

Danielle nodded to King Edward, pressing out a polite smile, and walked to the exit. But the king took a step to the side and blocked her way.

She stopped breathing. He stood close, an inch away. She could smell him—light sweat and alcohol on his breath and the scent of dust.

"Where are you from, boy?" Edward asked.

"South, Your Grace."

"Hmm," Edward said, narrowing his eyes. "There's something…different about you."

She met his gray gaze. There was interest in it. Interest that went beyond curiosity. Interest that she saw in the eyes of men who liked her.

God…did he realize she was a woman?

Or was he interested in the boy she appeared to be?

Danielle wasn't a history connoisseur like Jamie, but she did remember Edward II had been married and had a son. He was married to one of the most notorious femme fatales in history, Queen Isabella, the She-Wolf of France. Edward III was his son and considered to be the most perfect king.

"Different?" she asked, wondering if that was a code word for him checking if she—he—was gay.

"Yes, boy. Some men prefer the company of other men. Especially when they're as young and handsome as you are."

Panic ripped through her.

This was going to be a disaster. She needed to leave, quick.

She must think of something smart and yet diplomatic to get out of this. But her brain was numb.

"Forgive me, Your Grace." She stepped aside in an attempt to walk around him, but the king caught her by the arm.

His gaze was hard. The glare of an angry king. A king who had told someone to rape the Queen of Scotland in front of her stepdaughter so that Colum would switch to his side.

What was he capable of? Danielle's breath caught in her throat.

"No one says no to me, boy. I always get what I want. On John the Baptist, I will get Scotland. And tonight, I get you."

He pulled Danielle against his chest and looked her over with lusty, hungry eyes.

"Look at you. So sweet. Innocent. Almost delicate. And I know you're like me. Will you give in to me, sweet boy? Will you allow me to have my release before we march to the greatest battle of my life?"

Danielle couldn't feel her feet, couldn't feel her hands. "Your Grace, I'm not what you think I am."

His face went from longing to threatening. "You are. Even if you don't know it yet, even if you deny it, you are exactly what I think you are. I'll show you. Tomorrow, you'll be grateful to have been taken by your king."

He grasped her hard and pushed her down onto the table. One strong arm held her down while with his other hand, he yanked her jeans down painfully over her hips and her bare bottom was pressed against his hard erection.

CHAPTER 23

Colum peered from behind the tent's edge. The sounds coming from the king's pavilion made his stomach twist and his throat fill with acid.

After he had thrown a good handful of morels into Aymer de Valence's cauldron, he'd come back to the king's tent. With a horror spilling through his blood like ice water, he'd watched Danielle go inside.

Carefully, he'd approached. The two king's guards had joined the four sentinels at the king's campfire, but they would see him if he tried to enter the pavilion. He'd hidden in the shadow of the nearest tent and watched the red pavilion, praying she would come out.

But moments had passed by, and no one had come out of the pavilion. With his legs barely moving from panic, he'd quietly sprinted towards the other side of the structure. Behind the thick, canvas wall, he'd heard their muffled voices but couldn't tell what they were saying.

Then there were the sounds of struggle.

When he recognized Danielle's panicked whimpering and crying, he got his claymore out of the sheath and cut the canvas open. The sound of fabric ripping was like thunder.

What he saw made cold sweat break across his body. It was like he was sucked back in time into the night in Berwick Castle with the queen spread over the table and Sir Henry de Bohun leaning over her and about to rape her.

Only, it wasn't the Queen of Scotland, and it wasn't Sir Henry.

Danielle was spread on the table, with her bottom bared, and Edward held her down with one arm while trying to shove his stiff erection into her. Her face was red, straining. The king's head was turned to him, his mouth opened in quiet shock.

Rage thundered in his blood, deadly and hot. He raised his claymore and sprinted towards Edward. "Get away from her!"

The king, his braies still down, scrambled away from Colum and picked up a sword from his armory. His eyes darted to Danielle. "Her?" he asked.

But Colum didn't pay attention. He was going to murder the bastard. His claymore came down onto the king's sword with a loud crash. From the corner of his eye, he saw Danielle scramble to her feet and pull up her odd blue braies.

The king saw that, too. And he must have seen what was between her legs. His face went ashen.

"He thought I was a man," Danielle spat out bitterly.

The king's face turned livid as he recognized Colum.

"You," he said, his teeth bared. "Colum MacDonald. A traitor. Guards!" he yelled. "Guards!"

Colum needed to act. With a furious roar, he raised his claymore above his head and swung it again and again against Edward's sword. The pavilion filled with the clang of metal.

"Ye changed who I was, ye raping bastart!" Colum yelled between grunts. "Ye made me a traitor. But nae to ye, ye shite. To my clan!"

Edward laughed forcefully, loudly. "I didn't make you anything you weren't already."

Colum thrust the sword from below and from the side but always met the king's blade. "Go to hell!"

"And who is this woman?" Edward asked. "Did you send her to pretend to be a boy? To distract me?"

"She isna of yer concern. Dinna talk about her."

"She's English? So she's a traitor, too, if she's with you!"

Colum threw a quick glance at Danielle. She should run. She should leave before the guards arrived. "Run, Danielle!"

But she wasn't running. She was watching Colum with wide, panicked eyes. Using Colum's moment of hesitation, the king went on the attack, and Colum had to take a step back to block his swing. Edward was, unfortunately, a good swordsman.

"What were you doing near my tent, with my food?" Edward asked, and sudden realization made the muscles of his face go limp. "You wanted to poison me. Guards!" he yelled with all his might.

Then there were worried cries and yells from outside and the shuffle of many feet. The curtain at the entrance to the tent was lifted. The two king's guards and the four sentinels barged in, their swords drawn.

His only chance now was to take the king hostage. He pretended he was about to make a movement to one side, but instead he lunged to the other side, which was unprotected. He managed to put the tip of his sword against the king's neck.

"Drop yer sword," he said, "or I will slit yer throat."

Edward threw a hateful glare at him and panted heavily.

"Your Grace?" asked one of the guards.

The king's eyes darted to Danielle.

"The sword!" roared Colum.

Edward dropped the sword, and it thumped softly against the furs that covered the floor. Triumph blasted through Colum. If he could just reach out and grab the man—

But there was a movement behind him, and when he looked, his heart dropped to his feet. One of the guards held Danielle, a sword at her throat.

"Let the king go," the sentinel said slowly, "or the lad dies."

Colum growled.

Danielle shook her head, tears rolling down her cheeks. "No, Colum."

"It's not a lad, by the way," said Edward. "It's a woman that is as much a traitor as this man. She has no value other than, apparently, that Colum cares about her. So yes, MacDonald. He will kill her if you don't let me go."

He had been so close. He could have murdered the man. Gotten his revenge. Helped win this war, win this battle. Left England without a head of state.

But nothing was worth Danielle's life. If he cut the king's throat, they'd kill her. They'd also kill Colum, but he was ready for that.

Danielle didn't deserve it.

He lowered his sword, and the next moment, several pairs of hands grabbed him and held him. They shoved him close to Danielle. Edward finally pulled up his braies and tied the girdle.

He looked at Colum and Danielle with eyes full of contempt. "The Scot will be beheaded tomorrow together with this traitorous Englishwoman. Now, take them to the cage."

CHAPTER 24

DANIELLE WAS SHAKING. The wooden cage she and Colum sat in was suffocating her. She'd thought she was finally free, only to end up in another cage. The camp was still quiet around them. It was hard to believe everyone was sleeping peacefully while Danielle and Colum would die tomorrow... One guard sat next to their cage, leaning against the grating, his back rounded.

"A beheading..." she murmured.

Colum sat next to her, his arms around his bent knees. His jaw was tense, his gaze jumping around the camp, his expression thoughtful.

He looked at her, and his eyes softened. "I am sorry. I should have never taken ye with me."

Danielle shook her head. "No, I should have never let you do this stupid thing anyway. It was clear it would be a disaster."

"Are ye all right? I mean, after that bastart tried to...take ye like that?"

A shudder of disgust ran through her. She understood now some of what rape victims must have gone through. The humiliation, the helplessness, the incredible rage at the bastard. That feeling that she was just a piece of meat to him, with no will of her own.

She knew Colum had been worrying about her. He could have killed the king, but he'd chosen her. The warmth of realizing they were a team, that they had each other's backs, washed over her. She smiled.

"I'm fine. What a tosser that man is. But it would take more than that to break me. Thank you for choosing me... You gave me back what I lost when Sebastian held me captive. The belief that I can trust people. That I can let them get close to me. That I might...might find love and happiness."

Their eyes locked. Even sitting now in this cage, simply looking into his eyes made her breathe easier. Calmed her down. Gave her back hope.

"Lass, 'tis the very same for me. Love and women werena even on my mind after Berwick. I thought I'd die alone. I had a betrothed before Berwick, but while I was gone, the engagement fell apart. I liked her. I may have been infatuated with her. But I didna think I would ever meet a woman like ye."

She smiled and kissed him. His lips were soft, and the kiss was more tender and slow than passionate. She inhaled his scent, reveled in his taste. Then she put her forehead against his. "If we do die tomorrow," she said, "I want you to know it was all worth it because I met you. I'd do it all over again."

"My heart is full with ye, lass."

She kissed him again. If she died tomorrow, at least she would die knowing what true love was. What it was like to trust someone, to love someone, to have them love her back.

She'd been sacked by now, for sure. But the funny thing was, it didn't seem so significant anymore. Not after how this man had changed her perspective on herself. She was no longer a frigid woman who needed to use her work to keep herself at a distance. She was a regular woman who could have a hunky man like Colum love her. Who melted from his touch.

And who could, after all, love with her whole heart.

This adventure had taught her she was more resilient than

she had thought. No matter who had bound her, she'd never stopped fighting, never stopped trying to get out.

"You know," she said, "you didn't give up after that horrific thing Edward put you through. You're still fighting to reclaim your honor, to get back in the good graces of your clan. So we shouldn't give up now, either."

"But how will we get out?"

"I don't know yet."

The guard at the door of their cage gave a long, pained groan and held on to his stomach. Danielle and Colum exchanged a puzzled look.

"Oh, God's blood," the guard moaned. "What—"

Then there was the sound of growling guts and a long, loud fart.

"Ahhh..." the man groaned.

"You all right, mate?" Danielle asked, moving closer despite the foul odor.

"Go to he—" He bent over to his side and vomited.

Danielle pulled back and watched him retch and empty his stomach. She looked at Colum. "How many cauldrons did you manage to poison?" she asked quietly.

"Mayhap a dozen...mayhap fifteen. I almost emptied my pouch."

"Oh!" she said in surprise. "I managed maybe seven or eight. Well done! Could he have eaten from one of them, do you think?"

"Ahhh!" The man clutched his stomach. "Ahhh! Is there a beast inside feasting on my guts...? Oh God!"

Then there was another long fart followed by the liquid sound of diarrhea.

Danielle and Colum pulled back, their faces disgusted.

"Oh no!" cried the guard as he pulled down his trousers and sat in a crouch and proceeded to empty his guts right next to the cage.

At the same time, more groans and cries came from all

around them. And then three men ran past the cage, clutching at their behinds. Someone else a few steps away kept vomiting. The scent of woodsmoke was replaced by the horrible stench of diarrhea and vomit.

Danielle and Colum looked at each other. "Ye were right. We shouldna give up." The guard's trousers lay in a heap right next to the wall of the cage. And at their edge was a key chain.

"Oh my God," Danielle said. "You think it got dirty in his...poop?"

"I dinna give a shite," Colum said as he crawled towards the trousers. "Forgive the expression," he said as he threw a sideways glance at the poor man who squirmed on the ground while his body struggled to get rid of the poison.

"Ahhh!" the man cried again.

She moved to the door as Colum put his hand through the gap in the wooden grating and grabbed the trousers. Careful not to touch the soiled parts, he took the key chain and rushed to Danielle. The clang of the metal keys seemed deafening, and the guard looked at them, his face a grimace of pain.

"What are you doing?" he demanded.

"Sorry, man," said Colum as he put his arm through the grating of the door and inserted the key into the lock.

When it turned and the lock fell, the door opened with a loud *clang*. Danielle's throat caught at the sight of freedom.

Then they were off.

CHAPTER 25

As Colum ran next to Danielle, dodging tents, barrels, and sacks, the chase after them was like a tidal wave. Those who didn't get sick had been awoken by the noise and were quick to take up arms in pursuit of the runaway prisoners. But the mayhem helped their cause, and Colum and Danielle ran as hard as they could. His lungs hurt, his stomach was tight, and his legs and arms were tired and aching as he kept pumping them. He never let his attention slip away from Danielle, always on the lookout for her.

Finally, they were out of the light of campfires and in the darkness beyond the camp. They ran up the hill, using clumps of grass, bushes, branches, and roots to pull themselves up. When Colum looked back, there were people with torches running in all directions. They didn't know where Colum and Danielle were, but they were searching, and some lights were moving up the hill after them.

Once they reached the top and started descending the other side, it was easier. When he heard the soft neighing of his horse, a flame of hope lit in his chest. He helped Danielle up, then swung himself into the saddle, as well. As he lifted the reins, he saw the first torches reach the top of the hill.

With Danielle safely between his thighs, he spurred the horse, knowing it would probably alert their pursuers, but they were on foot. The horse set off in a gallop, and he spurred it harder. Even in the darkness, it moved as fast as it could between the trees and the bushes.

Only at dawn, when he knew the English had been left far behind, could they rest. They stopped in the deep woods near a brook, and once they both dismounted, he led the horse down to the water to drink.

He and Danielle drank, too, standing over the softly burbling water, their eyes locked.

"You're safe…" she whispered. "You did what you came to do…almost. I got you out. We did it."

Something tightened in his chest. She meant it. She cared about him. She cared that he was safe.

"I got us out, lass," he said. "I picked up those shitty braies."

The tension of the previous hours…nae, the previous few days…burst within him in an explosion of laughter. She giggled. Then their shared laughter turned into full-blown hysterics. And they laughed and laughed and laughed.

He didn't think he'd laughed like that since he was a lad.

Then the laughter died down. He felt a lightness in his stomach when he looked at her. This woman, not of his clan, not of his time, not anyone to him…had come to his rescue. Had come with him to face his worst enemy. And risked everything for him.

This woman, who knew intimately what his pain was like.

He didn't laugh anymore. Neither did she. Her eyes glistened hotly in the semidarkness. The gurgling of the brook was deafening in his ears. He was barely aware when the horse moved a few feet away and grazed on the grasses growing in abundance between the trees.

All he could concentrate on was Danielle's eyes. Those gorgeous eyes were as dark as sapphires.

And they were on him, asking, glowing, wanting.

They came together like two animals. She wrapped her arms around his neck. Her lips were soft against his. His tongue swept and danced with hers, stroking, plunging, worshipping. She tasted like a feast made just for him, and he had been hungry for a hundred years.

His cock throbbed for her, at the silky, warm feel of her. His senses were heightened, the aching, sweet, insatiable desire for her stronger. And then, maybe because of the danger they'd been in for the past days, or because he'd gone to what should have been his death but come back alive, he couldn't contain the words.

"I love ye, lass. I love ye."

Because that was what his goddamn, stupid, silly heart was telling him.

"I love ye," he kept saying through the kisses, through the brushes of hands and the smell of her hair that was in his face.

"I love you," she echoed, and his heart welded together in his chest, melting from the heat of her body, healed by the warmth of her words. "I love you."

He undressed her and laid her down on the sleeping roll. There were her soft lips and her delicate breasts that he adored, so sweet, the nipples tasting like butter and strawberries. She wriggled and writhed under him, so sensual he could come just from hearing her moan.

"Danielle..." He whispered her name like it was his undoing, finally feeling like he had permission to be himself.

"Colum..." she echoed, as though saying his name was a spell that could break her into a new realm.

A realm where they both were free to love and be loved.

He watched her face as he caressed her bonnie breasts. She gasped out and arched her torso into his hands. God's bones, he loved it. He took one nipple into his mouth, and when it puckered and hardened, he clung to her breasts, alternating between sucking them and caressing them with his fingers.

"Oh God," she whispered. "Oh, Colum..."

He looked at her, continuing to caress her nipples. "Och, lass. I could come just by hearing ye say my name like that."

She pulled his tunic higher, and he dragged it off over his head. She brushed his chest with her fingers, tracing the battle scars, making the blood simmer in his veins. As her fingers moved down his stomach and stopped at the line of his braies, he was throbbing for her so hard that he ached. The need to dive deep inside her wet heat was a constant pull in his blood.

"Lass..." he groaned.

"You like that?" she asked, breathless. Her eyes were wide and dark staring at his stomach. "You're magnificent, Colum. I could get lost in the valleys between your six-pack."

"I have nae idea what a six-pack is, lass, but I wish ye'd get lost a wee bit lower than that." He chuckled.

She grinned and bit her full lower lip, the color of wine from his kisses. She undid the girdle holding his braies and pulled them down. His erection sprang free, and she gave a wee appreciative whimper watching it.

"You're so big, Colum..."

She was ready. He knew she was. He was still careful with her, even after days of sleeping together, knowing she hadn't enjoyed coupling as much as she could have before. But with him, she was a wildcat. A lustful siren, calling him, inviting him for pleasure until he forgot himself and crashed on the rocks.

"Yeah," she whispered and pushed him so that he lay on his back.

She undid the odd opening of her blue braies. As he helped her pull them down her gorgeous, long legs, he felt he was burning. His fingers shook as he watched her remove the small undergarment she'd called "knickers," and then she was completely and gloriously naked sitting over him. His erection jerked and twitched nestled against the apex of her thighs, the wee soft hairs of her sex tickling him.

"Ride me, lass," he croaked. "Use me for yer pleasure. Use my cock and my body to make yerself come."

She nodded, flushed. Did she have any idea how magnificent she looked, being aroused like that? How her long, willowy body was worthy of a minstrel's song, and every red-blooded man's dream?

As she rose slightly over him and took his cock in her soft palm, he stifled a groan of pleasure. She palmed him in her tight fist and moved her fingers up and down his length, making pleasure burst through him. He swallowed hard, his heart racing, watching her, afraid to miss a moment.

When she took his tip and rose and placed it against her folds, he couldn't stop a groan. "Like that, lass."

She used him to circle the wee bud of her clitoris between the lips of her pussy. She arched her back, closed her eyes, and her head dropped back as she gave a long moan of pleasure. He took her hips into his palms but didn't move them. He just wanted to feel her everywhere. When she started to move her hips in circles, unapologetically chasing her pleasure, he loved it.

He wanted more of her doing that. He loved that she was so free with him. That she was herself.

Because he was himself with her, too.

Soon, his cock was harder than it had ever been and was dripping with her arousal.

"I want you inside, Colum," she said.

"Aye, lass. Use me."

She put her arms on his chest and put her weight on him. When she lowered herself onto his cock, he thought he would burst. Her tight, hot, sleek core took him in like a fist. She arched her torso, and her fingers dug into the muscles of his chest. He had to restrain himself from thrusting inside her, from plundering her and fucking her until she forgot where she was and who she was.

But it was all about her. He wanted to know more about what she liked and how she liked it, because he wanted to bring her to her climax many, many times.

Only, he probably wouldn't get many, many times.

But he couldn't allow himself to think about that now. And when she started to move up and down his erection, all those thoughts evaporated.

All thoughts disappeared, period. He watched her beautiful breasts bounce as she moved, saw her nipples harden and darken. Her eyes were closed, and whimpers of pleasure kept escaping her mouth. Those sounds... God's blood, she was driving him mad with those sounds.

Very soon, he was delirious with lust himself, and he couldn't stop from thrusting back at her, meeting her movements. He placed his thumb on her clit and rubbed her there.

"Oh, yes, Colum," she gasped, opening her eyes to meet his gaze.

He watched her heavy-lidded eyes haze up with pleasure, and as a red blush covered her neck and her upper chest, and her whimpers became urgent and fast, he knew she was close...so close...

So was he.

"Come for me, lass," he growled out. "Come for me."

Still looking into his eyes, she fell apart. Her inner muscles tightened around him, and she froze, her mouth open, the most beautiful expression of tortured pleasure on her face. Then her eyes rolled back, and a whole-body shudder shook her. She cried out, and that was his undoing.

He pulled out of her, and the world shrank and expanded as he came and came and came on her stomach, still holding her hips in his palms.

He held her in his arms for a long time, and they talked and laughed lazily, both pushing away the thoughts of the chase and of the war and of the future. Then they ate and slept.

He woke to the rumble of many hooves against the ground. He jerked up and his hand found his claymore. Danielle was still sleeping on the bedroll.

He couldn't see anyone and couldn't hear anything. But when

he pressed his ear against the ground, he could hear it and feel it. A deep rumble, like a distant earthquake.

That meant one thing. The English army was on the move. Their diversion hadn't worked...or not fully, at least.

He cursed and gently stroked Danielle's head. She turned and looked at him sleepily. "Everything all right?" she asked.

God he loved her in the mornings. Sweet and vulnerable and delicious.

His.

But not for long. Their wee bit of heaven was over.

"We must leave now, lass, and we must hurry. The English are on the move. We must warn the Bruce before they get to him."

CHAPTER 26

THEY ARRIVED at Bruce's camp three days later. Without hiding in the woods, being chased, or stopping to save anyone, they'd saved a lot of time. They'd gone straight down the Falkirk road and ridden like hell, barely giving the horse time to rest.

Danielle's knees were wobbly and weak from exhaustion. Her thighs and her bottom ached from riding so long.

As they rode towards the camp, she took in the landscape, which was so different from how it would look by 2022. The forest hiding the Scottish camp was ahead of them as they crossed the stream called Bannock Burn. To her right, she saw a field, which was circled in a large U shape by the Burn. She remembered Jamie telling her something about the Bruce's men digging several pits on both sides of the road and covering them with branches. That was the key to the Bruce's victory on the first day of the battle, because the English couldn't flank Bruce's forces when they tried to attack them from the sides. The cavalry kept sinking into those pits. The horses fell and broke their legs. So Edward's army had been forced to attack them head-on.

And they couldn't break through Bruce's military formations. What was the name that Jamie had mentioned? Danielle didn't remember, but it was something about tight squares of men with pikes. Like hedgehogs, Jamie had said.

Danielle couldn't see any branches around the road, just grass and a marshy sort of area. Maybe Bruce was still planning to dig them. Or maybe they already had been dug and were so well hidden Danielle couldn't see them.

That was none of her business. She looked at the hill where the ruins lay. The way back home. Heavy stones weighed on her chest. She needed to return to her time, but how could she leave Colum? How could she ever imagine a life without him?

What had she expected? She'd known she'd get hurt if she fell in love with him. She'd known there wouldn't be a future for them. And now the day had come when she could finally return home.

Colum followed her gaze, and his eyes darkened. "When are ye leaving?"

She couldn't stand the ache in his voice that echoed the pain in her own chest. "I'm not certain. But I need to go as soon as possible."

He nodded. "Please stay a wee bit longer, lass, if ye can spare the time."

She smiled. "Just a little longer."

When they entered the camp, the king was on his horse, barking orders at ten square formations of Highlanders holding pikes. From far away, they looked like a strange, magnificent beast with huge quills, the men moving and breathing as one.

They rode closer to the king and dismounted. Colum brought the horse to the enclosed area where the rest of the cavalry horses grazed, drank, and rested. Then he and Danielle approached the Bruce. He sat with his back straight and his face dark and tense and cut the air with his arm, yelling, "Schiltrons, back, back, back!"

Schiltrons. That was what those formations were called. Like loyal, disciplined dogs, the schiltrons moved back, the shoulders of the men never separating from each other.

"Yer Grace," Colum said as they drew closer to the king.

Bruce threw a glare in his direction, then momentarily, his face relaxed. "Colum. Ye're alive."

He turned to the man on the horse next to his. "James, keep this up. I need to have a word with MacDonald."

"Aye, Yer Grace," said the man whom Danielle recognized was James "Black" Douglas.

Bruce dismounted, and when he stood on the firm ground, he hugged Colum. "Ye gave me such a fright, lad. Did ye go to the English camp?"

Then the Bruce's eyes fell on Danielle, and all friendliness left his face. He stepped back, unsheathed his sword, and pressed the point against her ribs.

"Yer Grace!" Colum said as he stepped between the king and Danielle and put his hand on the sword. "She's on our side."

Bruce's eyes bulged as he looked her over. "She?!"

"Aye. Danielle. She's a woman."

"Nae. She or he, or whoever this is, isna on our side. 'Tis a spy!"

"Nae, Yer Grace. She saved my life. She helped me create a diversion in the English camp. She isna a spy...well, nae like ye think."

Danielle's back grew damp with sweat. Now she'd angered two kings in this time, the English one and the Scottish one.

"I'm on your side, Your Grace," she said, raising her hands in submission.

"There's a bigger worry, Yer Grace," Colum said. "We rode as fast we could. We went to the English camp, to sabotage them and postpone their march, but it didn't work, and now they're marching. They're on their way."

Bruce lowered his sword a little and studied Colum. "They are? Well, 'tis to be expected. They need to be here in three days at the very least if they want to honor the agreement and reclaim Stirling."

"Aye," Colum said. "But ye need to ken that they are an enormous army. Six thousand cavalry, including famous knights from Germany, France, and Eastern Europe. Men-at-arms. Thirteen thousand infantry and Welsh archers with their longbows. There are about three times more of them than of us."

Bruce's face grew paler and paler. He still held Danielle at a swordpoint as he listened. "Dinna ye dare say this to anyone else. Morale is good so far, and this information might break the men's spirits. They dinna deserve this."

"Aye, Yer Grace, of course."

"And what did ye do there? What sort of sabotage did ye do?"

While Colum told him, Bruce's eyes flicked between Danielle and Colum. When he finished, Bruce shook his head and his face showed rage. He looked at Danielle. "I am appalled that ye are so deceptive. Ye seduced Colum into betraying his people and going to the English camp. He could have died."

"Nae, 'tis I who dragged her from her imprisonment, thinking she may ken her way around the English camp. Well, back then I had thought she was a man. But she helped me, and she can be trusted. She truly saved my life."

Danielle was in turmoil. There was no way she could prove that she wasn't the enemy.

Bruce shook his head. "Ye're a fool to trust a woman who would sneak into the camp like that. She should be locked up. Who kens if she will set a diversion among us. Edward could use her to attack and destroy us."

Colum opened his mouth to contradict his king again, but Danielle spoke first. "Look, Your Grace, your mistrust is very understandable. If you'll allow me to leave, I'll be on my way home, and you'll never see me again. I can go right now..."

The look of heartbreak on Colum's face almost killed her. She'd just told him she would stay a bit longer, and now she was saying she would leave right away. But she couldn't bear to be locked up again, and she also didn't want to get Colum in worse trouble.

"Ye dinna mean it, lass, surely..." he said in a low voice.

Someone was coming towards them—three men and a woman. One of them was young, maybe early twenties, with dark blond hair. The woman was Black, which, Danielle thought, must have been unusual for these times in Scotland. She was dressed in Scottish armor—léine-chròich—and had a sword at her back. She was tall and absolutely stunning. At her side walked a tall, blond man with chin-length hair and a short beard. Next to him strode a man whose dark hair was short-cropped, also strange for the Middle Ages.

He reminded her of a modern man.

"What is going on, Yer Grace?" asked the blond warrior.

"Owen Cambel, we have ourselves an English spy," said the king. "She wrapped her wee bonnie charm around Colum's head, and he canna see clearly."

The four people looked her over from head to toe with frowns. When their eyes fell on her jeans and shoes, their expressions changed to astonishment. They exchanged a look with one another.

"Your Grace," said the woman, her accent oddly familiar. It couldn't be American! "I believe Colum. She's not a spy. Trust me. She's not working for Edward."

"I agree with Amber," said the young man, his accent similar to the woman's.

Doubt registered on Bruce's face, but he was still not lowering his sword. "David, ye, too? But how do ye all ken that?"

Colum watched them with an open mouth and a confused frown.

The man with a modern-day haircut cleared his throat. "We know that because I know her from back home. From Oxford. In fact, she's my distant relative. I'm English, and yet you don't suspect me of being a spy, do you?"

Bruce studied him. "Of course I dinna suspect ye. We fought together. Ye belong to clan Mackenzie, James. And I dinna ken that woman. She was caught more than a sennight ago listening near my tent. We all thought she was a man, and then she said there was an assassin in the camp that came for me. Based on her accent and the fact that she was caught spying, we all had nae doubt that she's a spy for Edward."

Danielle couldn't believe her ears. Why were all these people protecting her like that?

"Yes," said James, "she was looking for me. We got separated over the years, and when she contacted me, I invited her to join me here and then later to come to Eilean Donan. She was on her way and looking for me. Weren't you, um..."

"Danielle," said Colum helpfully. "The lass did mention Jamie when we caught her, as ye'll recall, Yer Grace."

"Well, there we are," James said, hiding any shock behind a poker face.

Bruce took a long breath in as he studied them all. Then he reluctantly lowered his sword.

"I trust ye, James," Bruce said and looked at Danielle. "I just dinna understand why ye didna tell me earlier ye were James's relative. We wouldna have needed to put ye into the cage. And why did ye let us believe ye were a man?"

Danielle cleared her throat nervously. She couldn't believe this was it. She still needed to understand why they'd all helped her.

"It was a misunderstanding," she said. "I wish I had been clearer on who I was. But could you blame me? It's not exactly the safest place for a woman."

"Aye. Well," Bruce said. "I'll let ye talk to yer relative, then."

He turned and started to walk away when Danielle called after him. "Your Grace...did you plan to dig traps around the road?"

He frowned. "What traps?"

She looked back in the direction from which she and Colum had come. "Have your people dig some pits in the ground around the road near the entrance at the forest, between the burn and the forest. Cover them with branches and leaves. When the English army comes, they will be forced to meet you from only one direction. Use that to your advantage to reinforce your anti-cavalry strength. The English may have higher numbers, but that doesn't mean they will win."

Amber turned to Bruce. "I like that. It's a smart plan, Your Grace."

The king looked at her thoughtfully. "I will take this under consideration."

As Danielle watched his broad back recede into the distance, the realization settled into her bones. She was free to go.

CHAPTER 27

THE FOUR PEOPLE who had protected Danielle surrounded her and Colum. Their eyes were bright and joyful as they watched her.

"Why did you protect me?" she asked as she looked around at their faces.

"Why do you think?" said James in perfect, modern English.

She frowned. Modern English? There had been some sort of recognition when they'd seen her jeans and shoes.

"Yes, Danielle," said Amber with a soft chuckle. "I think you already know, even if it's hard to believe."

And Amber and David had American accents, she was sure now.

She swallowed hard. "Did you all go through the rock?" She looked at the hill visible above the tops of the trees.

"Rocks," said David. "There are several."

Colum's face went blank. "David...ye are from the future, too?"

David nodded. "I am. My sister, Rogene, too."

Danielle swallowed. "There are more of us?"

"Yes," James said. "We're like a small, secret society here. Now you, Colum, are a member of it, as well."

"Oh my God," whispered Danielle. "I *can* go back, right?"

"Yes, you can," said Amber with a smile and looked at Owen with so much love, it stole Danielle's breath. "We chose to stay here for those we love."

James crossed his arms over his chest. "I am...well, I was a police detective from Oxford. I'm married to Catrìona Mackenzie of Eilean Donan."

David chuckled. "He was investigating my disappearance—mine and Rogene's."

A slight shiver went through Danielle. "I remember that. A student and her brother disappeared in Eilean Donan. That was all over the news what...a year ago?"

"Yes, that's us. Only, for us it's been four years. Rogene traveled in time and fell in love with Angus Mackenzie. I tried to stop her from returning to him and fell through time with her. Now I'm married to Anna MacDonald, who's Colum's cousin and Robert the Bruce's daughter."

Danielle opened her mouth. "No, really?"

He nodded, proud.

"What about you, Amber?" Danielle asked.

"I was a US Army officer. I actually was on the run for a crime I hadn't committed and fell through time...and fell in love with this hunk." She winked at Owen, and he wrapped one large arm around her waist and brought her to him, planting a long, passionate kiss on her lips.

"Get a room," said David, and everyone chuckled.

Colum watched them, shaking his head. "I didna ken any of that. I thought there was something different about ye, David... But I didna ken. And ye all stayed here for love?"

The three time travelers nodded. When Colum looked at Danielle, his gaze was full of longing, and her throat clenched. She knew what he was thinking. She was thinking the same.

If there were people who had stayed back in time for love... could Danielle stay for him?

She swallowed hard as her heart drummed heavily in her

chest. She had no idea if she could. Actually, she knew she couldn't. Her life was in the future. Her family. Her job—if she could somehow get it back. How could she uproot her life for a man she had met less than two weeks ago...a man who had kept her tied up for half of that time?

She was in love with him, yes, but it was a fling, wasn't it? The thought of committing to him and leaving behind everything she knew filled her whole being with fear. The same fear she'd felt after what had happened with Sebastian—the reason she'd never had a boyfriend and had avoided dating.

Because she couldn't trust people. She couldn't even fully trust herself.

"How did you get here, Danielle?" asked Amber.

She told the story about visiting her sister, Jamie, who was a coordinator at the Bannockburn reenactment. That got a lot of excited nods. She told the story about Sìneag and her little chat with her. Then how she'd traveled in time and thought at first she was still at the reenactment. Then how Colum had caught her eavesdropping and thought she was a spy. And as Colum stepped in and told them how he'd dragged her to the English camp and then how she'd saved his life after the English had caught them and how they'd gotten into the king's camp and escaped a beheading, the time travelers and Owen exchanged meaningful glances with one another.

"And now," said Amber, "you two are part of the club."

Danielle wanted to tell her there was no "you two," but she didn't want to hurt Colum's feelings.

"Maybe," Danielle said. "Only, I'm not staying. I'm positively shell-shocked that you, modern-day people, chose to stay in this time and make a life here. That you left important jobs and good lives and people you love."

"To be happy with the ones that we love," said Amber. "I've never once regretted my choice."

"Nor have I," echoed James.

"Neither have I," said David. "Well, I did regret it for the first three years. But not since Anna agreed to marry me."

"What are you going to do, Danielle?" Amber asked.

Danielle looked at Colum. She knew she wouldn't stay, but also couldn't bring herself to leave yet, knowing she'd never see him again. As he stared back into her eyes, it felt like they weren't finished yet. There were words unspoken, decisions not made, important things not discussed.

"I don't know. But I know the Scots need all the help they can get, and so I can at the very least lend a pair of working hands."

Amber clapped her on the shoulder. "Okay. Thank you for that. There are more of us time travelers in this camp. Find us later. I feel like you two have some stuff to talk about."

She turned the men around and they walked away.

When Danielle and Colum were left alone, the silence between them was a living thing. "Let's go find something for ye to eat, lass," Colum said. "Ye're exhausted."

Even now he was caring about her, making sure she was all right. Her heart melted as they walked towards a campfire together.

"Would ye stay until the morrow, lass?" he asked. "I canna bear the thought of never seeing ye again."

She thawed as he took her hand in his and squeezed it. "I will, until tomorrow. I'll help however I can. And...I also can't bear the thought of never seeing you again."

There was great sadness in Colum's eyes as they sat at the campfire and Colum checked a boiling cauldron. There was no one near, and the food in the camp was communal, so he took two clean bowls and poured some stew into them. He gave a hot bowl to Danielle, and as she blew on the steaming food, she murmured, "Oh yum. I'm only now realizing how hungry I am for a real, hot meal. We did the right thing by saving time and only eating what we had in the packs on our way back. But I'm so happy to eat this."

Colum chuckled and opened a horn flask of uisge. "Sláinte."

As he drank, there was so much sadness in his eyes, her heart broke.

"Ye may stay for a few more days, lass," he said. "As long as ye can afford to. But as much as it breaks my heart, 'tis a good thing ye're leaving. I wouldna want ye to stay for the battle and risk yer life. 'Tis better that ye're away and alive than by my side and dead."

CHAPTER 28

"Where do ye think ye're going?"

The voice came from behind Danielle's back. She was headed towards the road with a shovel in her hand. Several Highland men and women went that way, as well. It was the day after Colum and she had arrived at the camp. Just this morning, Bruce had announced that pits should be dug in the fields on both sides of the Falkirk road right before it went into New Park forest. The area that needed to be dug out was hundreds of square feet. Colum had been commanded to form a unit that would dig the pits, and she had volunteered to help.

The woods ended about ten feet away, and the Falkirk road spread before her. It was dark under the shadows of pine, birch, and aspen trees, with sunlight shooting through gaps in the canopy here and there like laser beams. Around the forest spread a field of tall grasses and weeds, occasional bushes, and clumps of wildflowers.

Danielle turned around. The voice sounded like it was directed at her, even though she was pretty sure she had done nothing wrong.

She could see the hill with the time-traveling stone about six hundred feet to her right. If she ran, she could reach it in a few minutes. But she couldn't leave Colum. Not yet.

"Yeah." She turned back, her gut clenching. The voice hadn't sounded friendly. Anytime she'd spoken to anyone besides the time travelers in the camp, she'd faced animosity. Upon hearing her accent, the person would freeze like an animal waiting to see if it should fight or flee.

This voice sounded like that of someone who'd decided "fight" was the answer.

The man who stood before her had a shovel in his hand, as well. He was a tall man, in his late thirties or early forties. His beard was dark, like most Mackenzie beards were, Danielle had learned in the past twelve hours. Was this man a Mackenzie?

He scrutinized her with a cautious, antagonistic gaze.

"I'm going to dig the pits like the king commanded," she said.

"Ye're doing nae such thing," said the man and headed towards her, his gait broad, his scowl hard. "Ye shouldna even be here at all."

He came to her and unceremoniously grabbed the shovel out of her hands.

"Excuse me!" she said. The other men and women who carried shovels towards the fields glanced back curiously.

"Ye think ye're allowed to go in there and do yer things?" the angry Scot demanded.

"What things?"

"Yer...Sassenach things."

"Aye, Marcas," another man chimed in, stepping up beside the first. He held his own shovel menacingly and looked at her with dark eyes under dark, bushy eyebrows. "What do ye think ye're doing?"

Outraged, Danielle reached out to take her shovel from the first man, but he jerked his arms, keeping it just out of her grasp.

Danielle slowly became aware of several other men and

women stopping and turning to her. She felt their gazes burning into her like torches.

This was exactly the wrong thing to happen to someone who wanted to blend in and befriend people.

"I must go and dig those pits," she said.

"I dinna think ye will," said Marcas.

Danielle's heart raced. His dark eyes glittered with obvious menace.

"Why's that?"

She wondered if she had done something to offend this man, besides being English. But since she had talked to Bruce yesterday, she'd only helped Colum to set up his tent, gone foraging, and found some useful herbs for Catrìona and some mushrooms and berries for Kate. Then she'd cooked with the time traveler women, and they'd made enough to feed at least thirty men.

Then she had spent the night with Colum, kissing, giving each other sponge baths, and letting him have his way with her... or was it the other way around? After which, she'd fallen asleep in his arms, her body fully satisfied, her mind refusing to think about the stone up the hill. Refusing to think about her parents and her sister going mad with worry.

Shoving aside the distracting thoughts, Danielle made an effort to sound nice and civil. "Please, give me back my shovel."

She wasn't afraid of these men. She could already see Marcas had a bad left leg and knew she could inflict a lot of pain with one kick. The second man was shorter and leaner—she'd be able to knock him down if she had to.

Would those surrounding them attack her if she tried to fight her way past the two men, though? In the camp, many had given her dark glances and even made comments loud enough that she could hear them: *Sassenach pigs... Nae Sassenachs are welcome here... Sassenachs should just go home...* They were never directed towards James Murray, who was also English. He had earned their trust already.

"Look," she said, "you two seem like reasonable people—"

"Give the lass back her shovel."

The voice was harsh, masculine, and had an unapologetic authority about it.

She looked around. It was Colum, his shoulders straight, his scowl like a declaration.

"Of course ye would defend her," scoffed Marcas, still holding Danielle's shovel. "She's the only one spreading her legs for ye. All the MacDonald lasses ken better."

The veins on Colum's reddening neck bulged. A flush crept onto his cheekbones. In one large step, he reached Marcas and grabbed his collar.

"Dinna ye dare insult her," Colum spat. "What she's doing is nae concern of yers."

Danielle's stomach clenched. He was going against his own clan for her, protecting her honor... No one had ever done anything like that for her.

Marcas bared his teeth. "If there's a traitor going around the camp who may betray us during the battle, it definitely concerns me. And most importantly, it concerns my clan and my king."

Colum kept scowling at Marcas. "Apologize to her."

Danielle stood close to them. "Colum, there's really no need..."

But Colum didn't budge. He stood like a bear, ready to tear Marcas apart.

Marcas scoffed. "Ye think the clan will accept her? A Sassenach woman? From ye, the traitor?"

Danielle's heart broke in two. "Colum, please don't try to—"

"No, Danielle. Marcas hasna trusted me for eight years."

"'Tis because I was one of the first ones to come and fetch ye from Berwick. Imagine my surprise when I saw ye almost cut Aulay's head off. Yer own uncle that had always been yer champion."

Colum's face lost all his anger. He let go of Marcas and pushed him away, taking several steps back. "Aye. Uncle Aulay has always stood for me because he kens..."

"Kens what?" Marcas demanded.

Colum's jaw worked. "Doesna matter. Leave Danielle alone."

"She's the enemy. She'll never have a place with the MacDonalds." Marcas threw Danielle's shovel into the bushes and walked away.

Danielle felt her heart soar, knowing that Colum had protected her. Her blood was like warm honey flowing through her. As people dispersed around them and kept going, Colum came closer and stood before her, just one step away.

His eyes locked with hers, dark and liquid and hot. "Lass, dinna fash about him—"

"He's right, though, isn't he?" she asked. "They'd never accept me. Maybe they wouldn't accept you because of me, as well. And being accepted and forgiven is all you've wanted since you returned to your clan."

Colum's jaw muscles hardened, and his already sharp angles became sharper. "Lass, dinna—"

"But I am something that would always hold you back, aren't I?"

"Nae, lass—"

She nodded. She hadn't really thought about how devastating her and Colum's differences were for a couple in this time. Back in her century, a Scottish man and an English woman wouldn't make a splash. In this century, Colum was seen as sleeping with the enemy simply because of her birthplace and accent.

Given the history that Colum was trying to overcome, she would never be an advantage for him.

She'd always be a burden. An obstacle to getting what he wanted most.

She found her shovel and spent the whole day helping dig the pits around the road, then putting grasses and branches over them.

Despite the long, hard day, she and Colum still made love, and he made her come twice. Then she fell asleep in his arms. It was early morning when she woke to find him watching her. His face was completely relaxed, with a smile of pleasure and admiration. He stroked her hair gently.

"Did you watch me sleep?" Danielle asked, her voice hoarse.

"Aye," he said. "Ye'll leave me soon. I didna want to miss a moment with ye."

She nestled deeper into his embrace. Through the canvas of the tiny tent, sunlight played through the branches. The sounds of a waking camp came through: the clanking of utensils against iron cauldrons, the cutting of food against wooden boards, conversations and orders being called out, horses neighing, feet shuffling. Someone put on a cauldron of something delicious-smelling to boil, and Danielle's stomach growled.

"Colum—" she said.

"Nae, lass," he said and planted a soft kiss on her lips. "We only have a short time together. Let's pretend that this time is all we have in the world."

He had broken her walls down. He'd been there for her—protecting her, unraveling her, introducing her to how she was always supposed to be.

How could she pretend all they had was this moment, when what she wanted was eternity?

CHAPTER 29

ONE DAY LATER...

"THE ENGLISH ARE COMING!" THE CRY CAME IN THE EARLY hours of the morning, and Colum scrambled to his feet.

The whole camp froze and stared at the sentinel who'd just ridden in through the trees, panting, his horse wildly shaking its head.

The camp had grown and expanded a bit since the day Colum had caught Danielle spying. More men had come to join Bruce's camp and trained vigorously.

Today was the Eve of John the Baptist—that was the last day the English could arrive to fight, or Stirling would be given over to Scotland. Since the camp had first stirred to life this morning, the mood had been tense. Agitated. They knew the battle could be only hours away.

And yet, the news came almost like a shock. Schiltron formations stopped moving. Those sparring on swords stopped midswing. Men checking and polishing their claymores and Lochaber axes halted with cloths in their hands.

It was quiet. So quiet, Colum could hear the combined breaths of six thousand men, the cracks of finger joints as warriors tightened their fists around their sword hilts, the booming of their hearts as they knew...

Here it was. The day they'd been preparing for this past year, but also in every battle they'd ever had, with every warrior they'd lost and every castle they'd retaken from the English. This would be the battle that defined what it was to be a Highlander, to fight for independence, for freedom.

And in the next moment, they all moved. Everyone knew their place, the schiltron they belonged to. The commander they followed. Their place on the battlefield. The sounds returned— the pounding of feet, the urgent grunts of men as they hurried to put on their armor and grab their weapons. Armorers handed out pikes to those who didn't have them.

Colum had spent the past three days training with his clan and the rest of the men holding schiltron formations and practicing quick echelons—diagonal formations of the schiltrons. Bruce and his commanders—Aulay MacDonald, James "Black" Douglas, and Thomas Randolph—had relentlessly trained them to make quick movements across fields while maintaining the shoulder-tight schiltrons.

At nights, he'd come back to Danielle and made desperate, sweet love to her. He was just thankful she was still here, that she still hadn't left. He was grateful to have as much of her as she would give him.

He turned to her. She was on her feet already, the bowl of porridge in her hands forgotten. "Colum..." she said, her voice urgent.

She still wore a man's clothes, and he sometimes imagined how beautiful she would look if she wore a lady's dress, one that hugged her willowy figure, with her golden hair spilling over her shoulders.

But she'd needed the man's clothes to dig the pits in the

fields on the sides of the road leading to New Park forest—she'd insisted on helping and he couldn't stop her. He'd even seen her training on swords with Owen. And he loved her in any clothes. He loved that she was spending as much time with him as possible. He loved that she was doing all that she could to help the Scots.

And yet, the end had always been in sight. And it came now.

He picked up his sword belt and sheath.

"Danielle, lass." He took her face in his hands, and her eyes were wet. "Ye must leave now."

She opened and closed her mouth. "Colum, I..."

"Ye what?"

To his surprise, she wrapped her arms around him and clung to him like a crab. He pulled her into his embrace so tightly, he thought he heard her squeak. He buried his face in her hair, shamelessly sucking in her scent.

Around them, the controlled panic that always came before a battle started to settle in. The cries of commanders, the sound of swords being put into the sheaths, the drumming of feet against the ground.

Sweat broke through his skin. He needed to go. His clan needed him. His king needed him.

"I need to let you go," he rasped against her neck, then pulled back and looked deep into her eyes. It was the last time he'd see that aquamarine blue of a heavenly sky. The only color he wanted to see for the rest of his life. "Go, Danielle, or I wilna be able to let ye leave."

She nodded. "I'll always love you, Colum." She sobbed softly.

He cupped her face with both his hands. "Be well. Be happy. I love ye, lass."

But she wasn't letting him go. Her wee fists held the collar of his tunic, and as tears streamed down her cheeks, he kissed them away.

"Don't die, do you hear me?" she whisper-yelled into his face. "Don't you dare die!"

Die...

"Lass."

"Promise me you won't die!"

It hurt him too much. How could she care if he lived or died if she wasn't going to be here anyway? And what did he have to live for without her?

His clan. That's what. As much as he didn't want to admit it, she was right—his clan would never accept her. They would always think he was a traitor fraternizing with the enemy.

It hurt too much. He couldn't wait another moment. He planted a quick kiss and tore away from her. "Goodbye, lass," he said.

He saw other MacDonalds taking their Lochaber axes with them. Lochaber axes were excellent weapons against cavalry and proudly used by several Highland clans. They were as tall as pikes and had a long, narrow blade with a sharp point attached to the top.

"You're not asking me to stay anymore," she whispered.

He put on the chain mail coif, its weight cool and heavy on his shoulders. "'Tis what we both understood, is it nae?"

He put his sword into the sheath, then picked up the Lochaber ax and ran to take his place.

Bruce was on his horse and yelling commands for two schiltrons forming at the south end of New Park forest, where the Falkirk road led into a clear space between the burn and the woods.

He joined the Cambel schiltron that was forming at the edge of the forest. He knew his uncle Aulay was responsible for the MacDonald schiltron—where Colum should have gone.

But Aulay's task was to hold on and protect the back of the camp that was facing north, towards Stirling Castle.

And now that Danielle was leaving, Colum needed to move. He needed to do something to distract himself from running after her and stopping her.

He needed to fight. To be useful.

As he stood shoulder to shoulder, squeezed between Craig and Ian Cambel, he exchanged a look with them. They both held a pike in their hands. Craig was in his forties now; so was Ian. But they were both still huge and powerful warriors.

"Colum MacDonald," said Craig. "Are ye lost, lad?"

"'Tis Danielle," said Colum, his throat tight. "She's leaving."

The two knew what it meant. Amy and Kate were both here, and they'd already met Danielle.

"Sorry to hear that," said Craig.

But that was all he could say. Colum and the Cambels were in the front line of the schiltron. Behind them were man after man, each with a pike. Colum felt shoulders, backs, chests of his countrymen supporting him. They needed to be as one. One being, tied by loyalty and honor, fighting for its life.

Before them was the Falkirk road. Around it, on both sides of the fields, Danielle and dozens of others had dug pits and covered them with branches and grasses.

"Advance!" came Bruce's powerful cry, and the schiltron moved forward.

They marched in their tight formation, feet and elbows scraping against Colum. Their pikes were up, shooting high into the sky like the trees they were passing. The pungent scent of sweat was sharp in Colum's nostrils. Then the trees gave way to an open area, and they marched farther south down the road. Bruce was in front of them. Three more schiltrons—one to their left and two to their right—followed in the same, tight, hedge-hog-like rectangles.

When Bruce held his arm up and gestured for them to halt, Colum watched the English army approach. The glare of the sun reflected from the armor of hundreds of knights blinded Colum, and he squinted, trying to see. Their swords glistened like slashes of light, hurting his eyes. He could feel the rumble of the thousands of hooves against the ground, thousands of feet marching to bring death.

Then the banners appeared—red with three golden lions.

The King of England sat up front on his huge, white warhorse, countless warriors marching and riding behind. Proud, powerful cavalry with hundreds of mounted knights wearing expensive, solid iron armor. But their horses looked tired, sweaty, uncared for. They tossed their heads and stumbled a bit. The somber faces staring at the Scotsmen from under the helmets weren't full of battle rage. They were tired, too.

Still. Exhausted or not, they outnumbered the Scots about four to one. And they were cavalry.

"They expect us to back down into the forest!" yelled the Bruce as he watched the approaching army. "But we wilna, will we, lads! They dinna ken what is waiting for them once they try to flank us." He opened his mouth wide and glanced back at them. "Hold, lads! Hooooold!"

This was the moment they had been preparing for—training in the damned woods for moons, fighting smaller battles for years. The moment when the woman he loved was on her way back home and he'd never see her again.

Behind King Edward II flew the banners of several important noblemen who, no doubt, commanded their own units. All of them were mounted on warhorses, which were very different beasts than palfreys—regular horses used for riding long distances. A warhorse cost eight times as much as an ordinary horse, the yearly wages of four knights.

And then Colum saw the man who'd been in that dungeon eight years ago, menacing and huge over the Queen of Scotland, about to rape her.

Sir Henry de Bohun.

He approached from behind Edward on his horse and then leaned down to him and said something into his ear. He was in full armor—the most expensive armor Colum had ever seen. The breastplates and arming points were heavy and as shiny as new silver coins. He wore a heavy helmet with feathers in his colors—blue and yellow—at the back of his head.

Edward nodded, his eyes heavy on the Bruce. Then Henry

lowered his helmet and steered his fully armored beast of a warhorse out of the way of the approaching English cavalry. He pointed his lance straight at Robert the Bruce and spurred his warhorse on, and it charged.

As gravel and dirt sprang from under its hooves and the ground drummed, Colum's schiltron held their combined breaths, looking at the Bruce on his gray palfrey that stomped from foot to foot.

What was Bruce going to do? He watched the charging knight, unmoving, in his simple chain mail, without any iron armor, only a helmet over his chain mail coif. Was he in shock, just like the rest of them? A beast was coming for him, bringing his death. No doubt, just like Colum a few days ago, Henry knew if he finished the king, the war would be won.

Bruce knew it, too. He had a choice. Back away and run and save his life. Or confront the beast coming for him at full force, as inevitable as a storm, and come up against the impossible odds.

Bruce looked over his shoulder at his troops. His dark eyes glistened with determination. There was death in them. He opened his mouth and cried out.

It wasn't the war cry of his clan. Or any other Scottish clan. It was a roar, but it was something that brought them all together. Combined the families and clans into one nation. Bruce's roar caused a bone-deep shudder that ran across Colum's whole body, and he opened his mouth and echoed it.

"Ahhhhh!!!" came out of his throat, just like it came out of the throats of Craig and Ian by his side, and Owen behind him. And there was one more voice that he didn't think was real. And when he looked back, behind him stood Owen's wife, Amber.

They all echoed their king as one.

And then Colum knew. "Yer Grace!" he called.

Robert turned to him. "Take the ax!" said Colum and threw the Lochaber ax to Bruce. Bruce caught it and measured its weight in his hand by tossing it slightly in the air.

Then he spurred his gray horse and charged at the knight.

The earth rumbled under Colum's feet as the two headed towards and against each other. The Scotsmen around him cheered and roared.

Bruce had a smaller horse. He had minimal armor that would not protect him like Henry's iron armor would. He had no lance. It seemed sure he'd be spitted on the English knight's lance like a grilled boar.

But at the last moment, just when the horses would have met, Bruce turned his palfrey to the side, avoiding the lance, stood up in his stirrups, and crashed the ax blade into Henry's head. It sliced through the helmet, but the haft broke from the impact.

The knight fell like a stone, no doubt dead before he touched the ground. A roar of triumph burst through the air around Colum. Bruce rode close to Edward. There was a moment where he lingered and the two glared at each other—Edward in shock, Bruce triumphant. Bruce pumped his fist into the air and roared again, only louder, then turned his horse back and rode to where Colum's schiltron stood.

As he neared them, the English roared in anger and disbelief and charged after him like a storm.

"Staaand, lads!" roared Bruce, still coming towards them. "Stand!" He rode behind the four schiltrons. "Staaaaand!"

Colum tightened his fingers around the shaft of his pike. A storm was coming at them. It was a storm of war beasts and pure steel and lances. A storm of swords and rumbling hooves and the wild, searching eyes of the horses that were ridden to their deaths. Metal glistened, blinding Colum, closer and closer.

"Piiiiiikes!" roared Bruce.

They lowered their pikes, Colum and Craig and Ian in the front row, Owen and Amber and the others in the rows behind them. They were now a beast themselves. A hedgehog of steel and wood. One being. A being that stood between Scotland's freedom and its slavery.

When the first wave of beasts crashed into his schiltron, the force stole his breath away.

And yet, the only thing he could think of was *Let Danielle be safe*.

CHAPTER 30

DANIELLE KEPT STARING at the road leading between the trees, where Colum had gone with the Cambel clan and other clans following the Bruce.

A group of women came and stood by her side.

"Anything?" asked Amy.

Amy, Craig Cambel's wife, was a pretty woman in her late thirties with naturally red hair that was going silver. She wore a simple homespun dress, her hair tied back with a sort of bandanna like World War II nurses. Next to her stood Jenny, a pediatrician from New York City, and the wife of Aulay MacDonald. Catrìona Mackenzie stood next to them, as well as Kate Cambel, the wife of Ian Cambel, who fought next to Colum.

"I don't know," Danielle barely managed. "All I can hear from here are yells and...cries and..."

She stopped herself from speaking before she burst into tears. Over the past few days, she'd connected to these women, and Amber, who was fighting alongside the men, and they'd become her friends. Unlike back in the twenty-first century, she didn't need to keep people away with a job she couldn't talk about. Her fellow time travelers weren't interested in judging her personality or appearance.

The five women understood exactly what she'd gone through. Except for Catrìona, they had all been born in her century and chosen a life back in time, with minimal medical care and conveniences. All of them had chosen hardship for the Highlanders they loved.

Catrìona's husband, James Murray, the police detective from Oxford, was with clan Mackenzie, over at the eastern front of the camp together with David and next to clan MacDonald— where Colum was supposed to be had he not chosen to run off into the battle like a madman and join clan Cambel.

"'Tis all right," said Catrìona confidently as she rubbed Danielle's shoulders. "Rogene was a historian in yer time and she told us how it would all go. If she wasna heavily pregnant with her next bairn and waiting for her labor in Eilean Donan, she'd be here to tell us. 'Tis all going to be all right."

"She might have," said Danielle. "We all know the Battle of Bannockburn will be won by the Scots. But none of us know if our men will come out of there alive."

The women exchanged heavy, worried glances. She knew it was always on their minds.

"Danielle, why are you still here, sweetheart?" asked Amy gently.

Danielle glanced to the west, where the hill with her rock was. "My feet just won't move there. I'm so freaked out about Colum. I just...I can't leave until I know he's safe."

They looked at her with understanding.

"If you're sure," said Jenny.

"I'm not sure about anything," said Danielle. "I don't even know if I want to leave. You all decided life here was more important than life back there... I mean...to me, there was never anything more important than my job. But I most likely don't have that anymore. So what is left there for me? Only my family.

Though I do love them dearly. My parents and my sister are probably going mad from worry."

"Do you know that you have three passes through that stone?" asked Kate.

Danielle frowned. "No. I didn't know that."

"You went through it once, right?" said Amy, and Danielle nodded. "So you still have two passes."

The camp around them was quiet. Compared to the English camp, this one was poorer. There were fewer tents, and most of them were simple lean-tos with a single slanted roof made of canvas or sewn-together deer hides, or even just pine branches thrown in a thick layer. Unlike the English, if the weather permitted, many Highlanders slept right under the stars. Out of six thousand, only about a third possessed chain mail coifs and even fewer had real metal armor made of plates. Most had léin-tean-cròich, but a lot of them didn't even have that.

The camp was almost empty save the women—wives, sisters, and daughters—who cared for the provisions and did simple chores around the camp. Most men were now at their positions.

Four schiltrons were at the south end of the forest, facing the English. The rest—ten or so schiltrons—had already formed loosely and waited along the eastern line of New Park forest. Like those at the front, these were tight formations of men, but instead of rectangles, they formed ovals or circles, each man with a pike or a Lochaber ax. At the moment, the men stood still, with their pikes directed skywards. But Danielle had seen them train to stand in a defensive position, with their pikes and Lochaber axes directed at an imaginary enemy, and they looked like giant pincushions full of pins.

She saw Aulay MacDonald sitting on a horse in front of one of the schiltrons. The men were quiet and watched the woods.

Aulay tensed, looking east through the trees. Even from fifty feet away, Danielle could see something was wrong. He went completely still, his back as straight as a board. Then he made an urgent movement behind his back, indicating that the men behind him should be completely silent.

Danielle's heart drummed in her throat. Something was very, very wrong. Her fists clenched. She knew all the women were watching Aulay like hawks, too.

Then a loud tirade of curses exploded from his mouth, and he turned to his men.

"The English!" he cried. "A thousand head of cavalry—they're sneaking in to attack us from the back. To cut our line of retreat, nae doubt. I canna believe I almost missed it. Get ready, lads!"

There was a momentary panic among the men. It ran like a shudder of horror between them. The enemy, death, was not beyond the forest anymore where the Cambels and the Bruce himself fought.

No.

They were coming right here. They'd almost caught them. Everything could be lost, and the war could be over, no matter how well the men at the front were doing.

James "Black" Douglas rode to him and they talked quietly and nodded.

"Lads!" called Aulay. "Clifford is coming with his contingent! I noticed it almost too late, but there's still time. Let's test our pikes and see how English blood tastes!"

"Who's Clifford?" she asked out loud.

"Sir Robert Clifford," said Catrìona. "He's one of the prominent English commanders. He's known for his sly mind."

Danielle definitely couldn't leave Colum now. Nor could she sit here, useless. If she wasn't on her way to London, she'd better make herself useful and do everything she could to make sure Colum had a chance to survive. She turned to the other women.

"I'm going with them. Quickly, give me any armor and any weapon there is."

Aulay's schiltron was already moving. The ladies nodded. Amy grabbed a léine-chròich and helped Danielle into it. Kate put a chain mail coif on her, and Catrìona handed her a pike.

Danielle hugged them all in an awkward but warm group hug, and hurried towards the schiltron. She shouldered her way in among the MacDonald men, and they glanced at her in surprise. Many recognized her as Colum's odd English woman who no one liked, but she didn't care. She was going to risk her life for them today.

They moved. She felt like they were one giant wild animal. A dragon perhaps. A huge whale with countless spikes. The force moved her, and she had no choice but to follow it. Perhaps that was what it felt like for Colum, to be part of the clan. To belong to an unstoppable force that was strong as long as they had one another's backs. And they had hers. She felt it physically—back to back, shoulder to shoulder, legs shuffling against each other as they slowly crossed the field between the advancing cavalry and them.

They soon moved out of the forest and into the open field, slowly progressing forward. About a hundred yards away, the force of cavalry on huge warhorses advanced towards them. The ground drummed under their hooves. The horses were clad in armor, too, with metal plating shielding their heads, necks, chests, and hindquarters. Most of them were draped in colorful cloths of a blue-and-yellow-checkered pattern, perhaps Clifford's coat of arms. The metal of their barding glistened as they galloped across the field. The knights had their lances pointed at Danielle's schiltron.

There were dozens of them...no, hundreds!

Danielle held her breath as she kept going together with the rest of clan MacDonald.

And then there was no more time because the speed at which the horsemen charged was phenomenal.

"Pikes and axes ready!" yelled Aulay.

They lowered their pikes at an angle, and the row of men that was behind them did the same, over Danielle, and so they became a true, giant hedgehog.

The next moment, there was a crunch of flesh and the

pained, tortured neighs of the animals, and the horses and the horsemen fell one after another. Danielle planted her feet firmly into the ground, breathed, absorbing the impacts of the wave after wave of attacks. Her stomach turned and she felt sick.

She knew the several schiltrons around them did the same. The English kept trying their attacks from different sides, but attempt after attempt, they fell and sustained heavy losses. The air became thick with the scents of blood and manure and desperation. Danielle lost track of time. Attack after attack, the swords and lances of English knights flashed before her eyes, but never reached her, stopped by her pike and those of the men around her.

Then, when the light changed and it became darker, she was surprised when, with cries of desperation, the English started to throw maces, swords, and stones at the schiltron. And it was then that she first saw a man who stood right by her side fall with a mace stuck in his head.

"Hoold!" came Aulay's voice. "Hold!" He was now in the first row of the schiltron.

A sword flew right above her head, grazing the top of her chain mail coif. Horsemen kept circling them, desperate to slash, to hit, to cut their way through the wall of pikes. And after hours of holding them off, Danielle felt the tiredness in her knees. They were buckling. Her shoulders ached, and her arms shook from the exhaustion of holding the pike for so long and skewering horse after horse.

Then the horsemen seemed to get distracted and a war horn was blown. "'Tis James Douglas and his men!" cried Aulay so that everyone heard him.

The now-thin English contingent finally turned and rode away.

When she returned to camp, everything wobbled. Her knees were buckling and her legs shook. But she kept going, looking through the campfires. There were wounded men— Catrìona, Amy, Jenny, and other healers took care of them.

When she saw Colum, her stomach dropped. He sat at one of the campfires, his face in his hands, his bare torso and shoulders massive in the firelight. Jenny sat at his shoulder and was stitching it. Danielle hurried to him.

He looked up with so much sadness in his eyes. But as he recognized her, it changed to relief. Ignoring Jenny, he stood up and took her into his arms. She sank into his warmth and allowed him to surround her with the hardness of his muscles and his smell—musky and manly and so dear.

He kissed her. And the kiss was like coming home. All her tired muscles and the exhaustion of the past hours were forgotten. All she could think was how good his mouth felt on hers. How much she wanted to just keep kissing and kissing and kissing him.

When he leaned back, he looked into her eyes, and she sank in his black depths. "When I heard ye were in a schiltron I almost died. Why haven't ye left?"

She cupped his face. "I couldn't leave until I knew you were safe. What happened back there?"

"You two need a room, seriously," Jenny grumbled. "But let me finish my sutures, Colum. Then you can kiss all you want. Come back here."

He nodded and returned to his place.

"The cavalry kept launching at us," Colum said as Jenny worked on his shoulder. "They tried to come at us through the fields, to attack us from the sides, but their horses fell into the pits. So because of yer suggestion, they could only use the road and were forced to come at us through the choke point. And Bruce had trained us well to hold those schiltrons, and they were powerful against the cavalry. Nae matter how much force Edward sent at us, they all kept ending up on our Lochaber axes and pikes. Their losses were much greater than ours. Then they retreated to their camp in the east for the night. But the losses they took today are nothing compared to how large a force they still have. They're still strong. We will need to give them every-thing we have on the morrow."

When Jenny finally let him go, he scooped Danielle into his arms and lifted her up, carrying her to his tent.

CHAPTER 31

COLUM CAME out of the tent and saw Danielle sitting in front of
their private campfire, hugging her long legs. Around them, the
camp was sank into the darkness of the night. It smelled like
woodsmoke, cooking food, and pine trees. Here and there,
campfires played brightly, and around them, men sat and talked,
drank and ate, sang sad songs to mourn the fallen. But it was so
dark under the thick branches that it seemed as if black nothing-
ness separated each campfire.

Even though they were surrounded by the rest of the camp,
it felt like they were the only people in the whole world.

He went back into the tent and retrieved his woolen blanket.
When he brought it out to her, and she looked up at him, his
heart squeezed at the sadness in her eyes. He wrapped the
blanket around her shoulders and sat next to her. Cuddling into
the blanket, she laid her head on his shoulder.

"What is it, lass?" he asked.

"I don't want to leave you," she whispered.

He closed his eyes, his jaw working. He didn't want her to
leave, either. But she had a life to go back to. Family. He couldn't
trap her here where she didn't belong. This time with her had

been the happiest of his life, and he'd cherish his memories and ache for her for the rest of his days.

"Let's nae think of that now, lass." He put his fingers under her chin and gently turned her face to him. She looked into his eyes; hers were big and teary. He knew she must also be in shock and exhausted after the battle and because of her fear for him. She was made of steel, this woman. How would he ever live without her?

But he couldn't let himself dwell on that, either.

"Dinna be sad, love," he whispered. "I ken how to make ye forget any heartache."

He knew she understood the meaning of his words because the sadness on his face disappeared and was replaced by a crooked smile. "Is that so?" she asked.

"Watch me," he said and kissed her.

He tasted her soft lips, nibbled and sucked on them, his tongue gliding, probing. She tasted of otherworldly delights, and her own sweet taste that he couldn't compare to anything else.

When she was trembling and making those noises at the back of her throat that he knew meant she was burning for him as he was for her, he gently pushed her back and laid her on the ground on his blanket. The fire crackled and sent sparks into the air, setting her bonnie face aglow. He hung over her as she lay under him, marveling at her high cheekbones and her straight nose, and those big, gorgeous eyes that now looked dark and shiny. Her lips were swollen from his kisses, and her silky hair spilled over the blanket like gold.

He wrapped them both in the blanket, hiding them from the world. Then he planted a line of kisses down her throat, inhaling her sweet scent. She arched her neck to him, and he grazed his lips down her soft skin.

When he made his way down to her breasts and cupped them, she froze and he felt her look down at him.

"Colum!" she whispered. "Not here."

He chuckled and pulled the edges of the blanket tighter

around them, shutting the world away and wrapping them in a dark cocoon.

"No one will see ye, lass. My body will cover ye."

She gave a sweet whimper of surprise, and he felt his grin stretching wider. He liked her like this—delighted, excited. God's bones, he wished he could spend the rest of his life making her happy every day.

The blanket and the fire were warm, and he undid her belt and tugged her tunic over her head. Earlier, they'd gone to Bannockburn stream and bathed in a secluded grove, washing away the grime and the sweat from the battle. Now, he inhaled her clean scent and tugged the garment she called a "top" over her head, as well. He marveled at her bonnie, lean body and felt himself harden even more at the sight of her.

He drank her in, aching to remember every crease of her gorgeous body—how her pale pink nipples darkened and tightened from desire, the way her narrow waist curved into her hips. Hips that could move so sweetly and meet his own in a perfect rhythm.

He kissed one of her nipples, then took it into his mouth, playing with the hardened bud while he covered her other breast with his hand and repeated the same game with it. He sucked hard on her nipple, and she gasped loudly, squirming under him. God's blood, he loved this woman wriggling and squirming in excitement. How she could ever think she was unable to feel pleasure was out of his understanding. All she was made of was pleasure, with beautiful, sensitive flesh that sang under his hands.

He undid her odd braies and pushed them down, then relieved her of the wee, sexy "knickers." Then, still working on her breasts with his mouth and fingers, he brushed his other hand up her silky thigh and found her entrance. He cupped it, and she gasped again and jerked.

"Do ye want me there, lass?" he growled against her skin, looking up at her from under his eyebrows.

"Yes..."

"How?"

"Everything," she said.

"Nae. 'Tis nae an answer. Be concrete."

"Ahh... Your hands. Your mouth. Your cock."

"Hmmm, good."

She was opening up. As he spread her folds and found her clit with his finger, a tremor went through her, and she covered her mouth with her hand, suppressing a whimper. She was so soft and warm and sleek there, and God's bones, how he wanted her. But he had to be patient. This was likely the last time he'd ever have her. So he'd stretch out these moments. Enjoy them for the rest of his life.

He circled his fingers there while he moved to her other breast with his mouth and took her second nipple in, sucking, circling, nibbling. She wrapped her legs around him and began making grinding motions with her hips. He kept doing this for a while, slowly, and he felt her grow wetter and wetter.

"So greedy. Such an impatient lass," he murmured as he kissed his way down her torso, down her hard stomach, which rose and fell as she panted, and down to the apex of her thighs.

He spread her before him, marveling at her.

"Colum..." she pleaded.

"Aye, lass?"

"I'm—"

"Ye're the most bonnie woman I've ever kent, lass. And I want to see all of ye. All."

Because he would never see her again after tomorrow.

Then he melded his mouth with her sex and began teasing and playing with her the way he knew she liked. He listened to her body and sucked and licked the sensitive bud until she was making the noises that told him she was about to have her climax. But he had so much more planned for her. He wanted her to climax over and over and over again. So he retreated and looked at her and waited. She raised her head, and he gave her a crooked smile.

"Patience, lass."

Because this was the last time.

"Colum…"

"Shhhh," he said.

Without looking away from her, he rose over her on his knees, the blanket falling off his back, and removed his own tunic and his braies and now nothing separated them anymore. Her appreciative gaze went over his whole body, and she bit her lip. He hoped she liked what she saw. He hoped she would remember him for the rest of her life like he would remember her.

"Hands," he said as he lowered himself to her. "Mouth." He wrapped the blanket over them, hiding them away from the world again. "Cock."

Then he pushed her thighs apart, and she readily wriggled her hips to accommodate him. He wanted her so much he was shaking. He directed himself to her entrance, and when he slowly slid into her hot, sleek depths, she silently arched into him, pulling him closer with her tightly wrapped legs.

He groaned silently as he pushed deeper into her sweet, tight sex. God's blood, the pleasure of being inside her would be the end of him. He stayed frozen like that for a few moments, and when she looked into his eyes again, he said, "I love ye, lass."

She swallowed and gave him the most beautiful smile in the world. "And I love you, Colum."

Then he began moving. He wanted this to last forever. He wanted it to last for a lifetime that they would never have together. He thrust into her slowly, his gaze never leaving her face. But she was too sweet. The pleasure too much. And soon he couldn't remember what he'd promised himself because there was just her body and his body, and they were one. And like one, they thrust together, their hips meeting rhythmically, both panting, both climbing the rungs of pleasure like a single being.

Too soon, she was there—he could feel her walls tightening around him, hear the whimpers that he knew meant she was about to come apart. Her chest and neck were flushed, red and misty. His own release was right there, too, and he made a movement to pull out of her before he spilled his seed, but she didn't let him, her legs holding his hips in place.

In her eyes, he saw it, too. She'd known this whole time that this was their last night together, and she wanted to feel him come inside her just this one time.

With one more thrust, his release burst through him in a fiery, hot wave of pleasure. He bucked and froze, feeling himself spilling inside her as her walls milked him. She bit into his shoulder, muffling her cries of release, her body convulsing.

Then he collapsed on top of her. And as they both turned to the side, he spooned her, hugging her close, holding her by the waist, his mouth pressed to her back, inhaling her scent.

The fire crackled peacefully. Pines rustled softly above them. And he rocked on the waves of the pleasure of having her in his embrace. Of being close to her like this, of feeling her warm body and her stomach rising and falling as she breathed.

After a while, he quietly reached down to his belt, which lay by his feet. He rummaged in his small belt purse and found what he was looking for. He returned to lie behind her, found her hand, and slid his mother's ring onto her finger. She froze and then turned around to face him.

Her big eyes were on her hand. The ring on her finger was silver, with an aquamarine stone as blue as her eyes.

"Colum, what is this?" she asked.

"My father gave this ring to my mother before they got marrit. On her deathbed, my ma gave it to me, for the woman I would love."

"But—"

"Ye are the woman I love, lass. I want ye to have this."

She shook her head, tears filling her eyes. "No, this is too much."

"Please, lass. I want ye to look at this ring and ken that 'tis from a man that would love ye with every breath he'd take till his very last. That what ye've told yerself to be true isna. That ye can trust people. Because despite what I'd done to ye, one day, ye were brave and decided to trust me. That, most importantly, ye can trust yerself."

She clutched her hand to her heart. "I don't know what to say..."

"Say ye accept my gift."

She nodded and fell into his arms. "I'll cherish it forever."

CHAPTER 32

DANIELLE HID her face in Colum's neck and inhaled his scent. It was the morning of the next day, the twenty-fourth of June, the final day of the Battle of Bannockburn. Through the canvas walls of the tent, she heard warriors preparing for battle—quiet, tense voices, the clanking of weapons, the neighing of horses. The screams and groans of the wounded being treated made her shudder with empathy.

Colum traced the side of her face with his knuckles. Last night, after they'd made love, he'd lulled her to sleep, whispering how much he loved her. How much she brightened his world. How she gave him back a sense of wonder and love of life.

"You must go, lass," he said now. "I canna stand the thought of ye being hurt in the war."

She swallowed hard and looked down. How long had she been postponing leaving? For days now. If she did die here, her family would never know what had happened to her. They could live the rest of their lives in worry and grief. Especially her parents, who had never recovered from her kidnapping as a teen.

But the thought of going back to that life filled her with sadness. A life where she'd go home every day to her empty apartment. She may not even have a job anymore to let her hide from relationships.

Whereas this life here, in the Middle Ages, no matter how intense and dangerous, gave her love. Filled her heart with so much joy. Plus she had friends here now in the other time travelers. And no matter how much clan MacDonald had looked at her like at a traitor before, yesterday when she'd stood with the men shoulder to shoulder and risked her life together with them, their attitude towards her had changed.

"I want to make sure you make it out of there alive, Colum," she whispered. "I can't bring myself to leave until I know you're all right."

He shook his head slightly. His eyes, previously soft and dark like liquid night, gained more steel. "I will carry ye myself if I have to. Ye wilna stay."

Danielle sat up. "Colum, I thought you wanted me to stay...forever."

He sat up, as well. He was so tall, his head pressed against the slanted canvas of the tent. "Nae like this, lass. I wilna entrap ye where ye dinna want to be. I already did it when I didna ken who ye really were—and I wilna do it again."

Tears blurred her eyes. This man...noble and honorable and so sexy.

"Ye deserve the best, lass, and I want ye to be safe, healthy, and happy. And if I have to live the rest of my life without ye, then...I will do it. I want ye to have what ye want."

But why did she have a feeling that what she wanted a couple of weeks ago wasn't what she wanted now?

"So get dressed, and I'll take ye to the rock myself. I left ye yesterday and ye didna go. Instead, ye went to battle. I wilna let that happen today."

Danielle didn't have any more arguments to contradict him. He was right. That was what she'd been saying to him since the moment he'd caught her—she wanted to go home.

And now he was giving it to her.

Only why did her chest feel like it was about to burst?

They both dressed in heavy silence. She helped Colum to put on the léine-chròich and chain mail coif, and his sword belt. Colum told Aulay that he was going to take Danielle to the rock and come back and fight. He'd probably miss the opportunity to be in the schiltron. The plan of attack for today was to send most of the schiltrons off towards the English camp in echelon formation. They would go in diagonal rows with units each to the left or right of the one in the rear. There was also the light cavalry unit and the archers, which were held in waiting and used for quick and dirty attacks. He'd join the cavalry.

They made their way through the woods and towards the hill with the ruins. There were no sheep this time, gratefully. As they began climbing, her legs felt heavier and heavier with every step.

Finally, they stood on the hilltop, in the place where she, Jamie, and Liam had chatted while watching the preparations for the reenactment. It felt like centuries ago, which, of course, it was—centuries from now, anyway.

The rock was right there, hiding among the bushes and the grass, under the canopy of the trees. Her stomach wrenched. With every step she felt this was wrong. When they were at the rock, she could feel its power buzzing through the air. Colum stared at it like it were a nest of snakes.

"Is this it?" he asked, sounding as though he'd swallowed a handful of gravel.

He stood with his feet wide apart, tall and broad-shouldered. Behind him lay New Park forest and Robert the Bruce's camp. Danielle could even see the English camp that lay in the valley where the stream of Bannockburn made its huge U-turn. There, in the field between the forest and the English camp, Colum might die.

Wind picked up the dark strands of his hair and played with them. His face was proud, the strong, chiseled features so handsome he took her breath away. He was the image of masculinity and strength...and she would never see him again.

"Yeah," she said. "This is it."

He nodded solemnly and covered the space between them in three long strides and took her face between his palms. "Thank ye for coming to this time, lass, and for showing me that I can still love. That despite my sins and betrayals there's still someone that loves me for who I am. I'll remember ye and love ye till my last breath."

He leaned down and kissed her, making her head spin. She wrapped her arms around his neck and pressed herself to him as tightly as she could. The kiss was long and slow, and she never wanted it to end. There was so much tenderness in it, she could drown.

Then he stepped away from her and bowed to her as if she were a queen. "Goodbye, sweet lass, the love of my life. Be well."

She opened her mouth to say her own goodbye but couldn't. He turned away, put his chain mail coif over his head, and marched down the slope.

With her stomach turning and aching, she stood and watched his figure until he disappeared between the trees of the forest.

She couldn't bring herself to move. Couldn't make her feet walk to the stone.

Far below, the echelon of ten Scottish schiltrons marched forward in two diagonal formations, thousands of pikes high in the air. Behind them, two more schiltrons under Robert the Bruce's command followed. Archers followed close behind, and then a small contingent of Scottish cavalry—the group that Colum would join.

She needed to go. She was wasting precious time, and the longer she stood here, the longer her family would worry.

She strained her eyes to see if she could pick out Colum among the cavalry from here, but they were too far away, just ants.

She forced her legs to move towards the rock and sat by its side. The carvings glowed, and she hovered her hand over the handprint and felt that cold whoosh of air and the vibration, the feeling of being sucked in.

And yet, she couldn't bring herself to do it. Her heart pulled her towards Colum like a giant magnet.

She loved him. It was as clear as day. So why was she leaving? Why had she not decided to stay and spend the rest of her life with the man she loved?

The hope of getting her job back was still there, though slim.

But did she truly even want her job anymore? She was not the same Danielle who had come through that stone. She loved. She was loved. She trusted him, and she trusted herself. The Danielle from the twenty-first century would have never imagined she could do that.

She understood now that work had been an excuse to keep herself away from relationships, from being hurt. From trusting people only to be used and deceived, like her sweet, kind neighbor Sebastian. He'd shown her that no matter how well you thought you knew people, they could never be trusted.

And that was why she'd chosen a profession where it was her job not to trust anyone.

She'd thought she was going into it to protect people, to watch for signs of danger and stop crimes before they happened. Like she had wished she'd seen the signs in Sebastian.

But she was different now. Because she trusted Colum. He'd proved to her time and time again that he put her first. That he'd die protecting her.

He'd shown that Sìneag was right—he was the love of her life.

She didn't know how long she sat there, thinking. Hesitating. Doubting.

Hours must have passed when she heard someone calling her. "Danielle! Danielle!"

She turned and saw Kate, her golden hair flapping in the wind as she ran up the hill towards her.

Danielle stood up, her heart pounding painfully in her ears. "What is it?"

"Oh, thank God you're still here! I knew you wouldn't—doesn't matter." Kate doubled over with her hands against her knees, breathing hard. "Come on. It's Colum. He's getting himself killed."

Danielle broke into run.

CHAPTER 33

COLUM GROANED as he lifted his claymore. The cut in his side was deep and ached in a sharp, pulsating pain. His horse had been shot, and he was now on foot. Under the command of Sir Keith, Colum and his infantry had ridden out to fight the Welsh archers who had become a danger on the northern front of the battle.

Most of them had been dealt with, which allowed the main echelon of the schiltrons to progress almost into the English camp.

But after hours of battle, Colum was weak.

And what did he have to live for? His clan didn't want him. The woman he loved had just left him forever. The pain in his heart was too intense, crippling, stronger even than the pain of his torn, wounded body.

Five Welsh archers had surrounded him. And even though they were excellent bowmen, they were skilled warriors, also. They had swords and dirks for close combat.

He'd killed or wounded four of them. It was this last one, the tall one with the light one-handed English sword, who might end him.

He didn't care; why would he? This would end his miserable

life, and he would die protecting his country and his people, like he should have died with his sword brothers after Methven.

Finally, the tenth knuckle would get a name.

"Rob MacDonald," he said, raising his sword higher, ignoring the sharp pain in his side. "Ianatan MacDonald. Frangan MacDonald. Alexander Fraser. David de Inchmartin. Hugh de Haye. John Somerville. Alexander Scrymgeour. James Barclay."

He blinked away the blood that streamed from a cut somewhere on his head.

This was it. He'd go for a final blow.

"Clann Domhnaill!!" he roared and launched at the man.

The man was also wounded, but he raised his thin sword higher and ran at Colum with a similar loud war cry.

Their swords clashed in a loud metallic ring. Colum slashed and came at the man again, feeling his strength slipping away and his body weakening. They sparred, both forces equally strong, and the impact brought a shudder through him.

Somewhere far away, in a time he couldn't even imagine, Danielle was safe and well, and he hoped she would find happiness, back with her family. And mayhap she could get her job back.

"Colum!" came her voice. His imagination was playing tricks. Her voice was so sweet and beautiful, and it made him smile.

The other man's sword was raised high for one last, deadly blow.

"Colum, fight!" Her voice came closer now and from the side. "Fight!"

He raised his sword, just on instinct, and blocked the blow. Out of the corner of his eye, he saw a tall, willowy figure with golden hair running towards him.

While his sword was locked with the enemy's, he allowed himself to steal a quick glance.

His breath caught.

It was her, running towards him with a pike in her hand.

"Don't you dare get yourself killed. Fight! Fight, my love."

He didn't know if she was a vision or if it was really her. Mayhap it didn't matter. With his other hand, he went into the back of his girdle and pulled out his dirk. With a thrust, he planted it deep under the man's ribs, and the Welshman fell with a grunt.

Colum collapsed like a sack of rocks, and everything became blurry and dark. As though through water, he kept hearing her voice.

"Colum! Colum! Wake up, love!"

A warm, gentle hand lay on his head, then someone wiped his face with a dry cloth. A flask of water was pressed to his lips, and he drank.

When he opened his eyes, there was a gray sky above him, clouds rolling quickly. Sunlight broke through a dark cloud and fell on the shape above him. He strained his eyes.

"Danielle..." he murmured.

She planted a hundred butterfly-like kisses on his face.

"Come back to me," she whispered. "Come back to me. I know you wanted to get yourself killed, you fool. Come back to me. I'm not going anywhere."

He stopped breathing. "What? Nae, Danielle, 'tis nae what I want. Ye must leave. 'Tis too dangerous—"

"I don't care. I love you. Love is worth the risk. And worth the danger. My life here with you and your clan and your stupid war is a hundred times happier than my empty life back home."

He couldn't believe it. His heart was bursting with love, with gratitude. As though she'd poured a magical healing potion straight into his broken heart, he felt that it was healing and becoming whole again. He sat up and looked her over. She was unharmed. Around them was a field of death. The battle still raged about three hundred feet away, and the schiltrons pushed forward but struggled as the cavalry kept coming at them again and again.

"I choose your clan, too," she said. "I will go to battle with you. Can you still fight?"

He nodded and took her stretched-out hand. She helped him stand, and he wrapped his arms around her and kissed her properly. She tasted like something fruity and delicious, and like blood, which had probably come from his face, and like life.

"I will go and fight, but if ye think I'm going to let ye—"

She broke away from him, picked up her pike, and ran towards the battle. "Try and stop me!" she cried.

A she-warrior. That was who she was, he thought as he watched her, tall and strong, run through the field. Her hair waved like a flag on the wind, her legs pumped quickly as she moved.

His exhaustion lifted. It was as though love had healed his physical body. He knew he was still tired and in pain, but he didn't feel it as happiness burst through him. He picked up a fallen man's pike and ran after her.

When he arrived at the wall of Scotsmen, gripping their pikes and holding off the English attacks, he knew they were exhausted, too. They had spent many hours moving forward through the large field, towards the English camp.

Attack after attack, the schiltrons had managed to withstand and skewer the cavalry. Step after step moving forward. And now, having left hundreds of dead Englishmen in their wake, they were close to the English camp.

He saw the knees of the first rows of the schiltrons buckling. Their arms shook. Their faces were gray as ash. Sheer determination and Scottish stubbornness, as well as months of training and years of devastating war, gave them the power of spirit to go on.

Colum and Danielle pressed against the backs of the warriors who were in the front, giving their strength to those who fought the enemy directly.

The warriors of clan MacDonald saw them both. There was appreciation in their tired eyes. He saw Marcas, his face ashen, his eyes dark and fierce. He glanced at Colum and at Danielle and gave him a nod of approval. Hands came onto his shoulders and hers and squeezed them.

Did they forgive him? At least in part? Did they also see that Danielle was on their side?

Something deep within his soul, a tear he'd thought would never heal, came together.

They stood as one and pressed on and on until Colum could feel his own legs ache and start to give in. He didn't know how much time had passed.

Robert the Bruce himself descended from his horse and pressed against the backs and the shoulders of his army together with them.

"Hold on, lads!" he roared. "Keep moving, keep pressing! We're almost there!"

And so they did. Colum heard the neighing of the horses somewhere up front, the cries of wounded knights and warriors. The panicked, desperate yells.

And then suddenly, there was a huge relief, and Colum felt the wall of Scotsmen move forward.

"Retreat!" cried the English. "Retreat! Save the king!"

Colum exchanged a victorious glance with Danielle, and then with Robert the Bruce, whose tired eyes glimmered with a new hope. He caught his horse, then climbed into the saddle and pumped his fist holding his sword high in the air.

"Follow them! Catch the bastarts!"

As the English army ran and the Scottish cavalry chased after them, Colum turned to Danielle and pulled her into his arms. The feel of her was heaven.

"Lass, we won."

She giggled. "I know! We did."

"Are ye really going to stay?" he asked as a tingling sensation spread through his body.

"I am."

"Are ye sure?"

"I'm sure, Colum. I love you. And I choose you. I choose us. I choose love."

"I love ye, too, lass. Sìneag was right. Ye are my destiny."

EPILOGUE

COLUM WRAPPED his arm around Danielle's waist and brought her closer to him on the bench.

Two weeks after the Battle of Bannockburn, the great hall of Stirling Castle was full of people. Candles stood on the tables—and not tallow candles, real, expensive wax candles. Long tables with benches stood close to each other to host as many guests as possible. Bruce's coat of arms hung on the walls, which were partly clad with wooden paneling. Swords and shields with the heraldry of all the clans that had fought for Scottish independence during the past eight years hung on the walls, as well.

The hall was full of Highlander clans and Lowlanders who supported the Bruce. Mostly men, but also some women sat at the tables, chatted, laughed, ate, and drank. The tables were laden with feast food—grilled boars, fish, pastries, bread bowls with stew, fruit, heads of cheese. Five musicians played in a corner, one of them on the bagpipes. The king himself sat at the table of honor at the end of the hall. At his table sat all his commanders and the wives of those who were married, if they were present. Aulay MacDonald sat there with Jenny, as well as James "Black" Douglas, Edward Bruce, Sir Robert Keith, Walter Stewart, and Thomas Randolph.

In order of importance, the clans sat at separate long tables near the table of honor. Clan MacDonald had the honor to sit closer to the king—no doubt a sign of his appreciation. There were many clans Colum knew, including the Cambels, the Mackenzies, the MacDonalds, and the Ruiadhrís.

But the table that Colum and Danielle sat at belonged to a different clan. A clan that was secret and wonderful and very special.

A clan of time travelers.

Amy, Kate, and Ian Cambel. Rogene, Catrìona, and James Murray, who belonged to clan Mackenzie. Colum's cousin Anna and her husband, David. Excusing themselves from the Bruce's table for a while, Aulay and Jenny came over and sat with them, as well.

"I feel like we're in this secret society," Danielle said to the table. "This secret network of time travelers. I feel more like a spy here than I did back in my time."

Amy giggled. "I know what you mean. I only miss my husband." She looked longingly at the large doors of the great hall.

"And Amber and Owen," said Kate.

"And my husband," said Rogene. "But they'll be here soon. Honestly, there couldn't be a more important reason they're away. And it was such an honor that Robert the Bruce asked for their help."

"Why are they away?" asked Danielle. "The battle was such a huge turn for the course of the war. What else is there to do now that England is ready to recognize Scotland as an independent kingdom?"

Rogene had just opened her mouth to respond when the doors to the great hall opened with a bang, and as though called by faeries, there they stood. Craig Cambel, Amber and Owen Cambel, and Angus Mackenzie, protectively surrounding three women.

At the sight of one of them, Colum felt like he'd been

punched in the gut. It was the small, auburn-haired and pretty woman he'd bargained his honor for eight years ago.

Queen Elizabeth, Robert the Bruce's wife.

Holding her hand was a young, dark-haired woman he wouldn't have recognized. The wee lass he'd acted to protect when she was only eleven and was about to watch something she would have been burdened with her whole life.

Princess Marjorie. She wasn't a wee lass anymore. She was a young woman, her long, wavy, dark hair falling over her shoulders, which were covered with a long cloak.

The third woman must be Robert the Bruce's sister.

"Is that Queen Elizabeth and…"

"Marjorie," whispered Anna. "My sister."

"And that is Christina, Bruce's sister," whispered Colum. "She was a war hostage, too, though I didn't see her in Berwick."

Rogene leaned forward and said in a low voice, "Fun fact, Anna. Your sister, Marjorie, will be the mother of the first Stewart king of Scotland and start a whole new dynasty of Scottish kings."

Colum swallowed hard. "Your sacrifice wasn't in vain, Colum," Danielle whispered. "By protecting Marjorie and Elizabeth, you may have saved the whole line of Scottish kings and queens."

Colum felt a weak smile on his lips. His eyes watered. "Aye. 'Tis good. God almighty, I'm just glad the lass and the queen are all right. That they survived an eight-year-long imprisonment."

There was a movement between the rows of tables, and a large, dark shadow hurried down the aisle. It was the king himself who ran to his wife and fell to his knees before her, hugging her and his daughter.

The whole hall went completely silent. A king shouldn't fall on his knees and weep. But it was as though the folks in this hall were one big family. Every single one of them knew what this meant. Most of them had been with the Bruce for the past eight years.

Some of them had seen him at his lowest. The Cambels, MacDonalds, and Mackenzies had hidden him and protected him in the worst winter, when he was an outlaw and had nothing. They'd seen him when he got the news that his brothers had been murdered by his enemies. They'd seen him when he had wanted to give up to save his queen, his daughter, and his sister.

Now, seeing this powerful man who'd turned over mountains —and won back Scotland's independence stone by stone, castle by castle—being so vulnerable was heartwarming. No one judged him.

Elizabeth dropped to her knees in front of him and hugged him back. They both wept and their shoulders shook.

Colum's eyes filled with tears. "I dinna ken how I would survive if ye were taken away from me like that for eight years. I'd be a mess."

Danielle hugged his shoulders. "Me, too."

Queen Elizabeth finally stood up and so did the king. He led her and Princess Marjorie and his sister towards the table of honor. While they did that, Craig, Owen, and Amber Cambel, as well as Angus Mackenzie made their way to Colum's table. There were quick hugs and kisses between the reunited couples.

When Queen Elizabeth was given the chair of a queen, she looked the hall over. Every person there was silent, watching her with wide eyes. Then her gaze met Colum's, and her face spread in a teary, grateful smile.

Never breaking eye contact, she stood up and raised her goblet.

"Eight years," she said, her voice shaking. "Eight years my husband, King of Scots, fought to bring back peace and independence to this country. Eight years he fought alongside every one of ye for yer families. For yer wives. For yer mothers and fathers, sisters and brothers, daughters and sons. I canna tell ye how hard it was to be imprisoned by the enemy—it was much harder for ye. We all risked our lives, our sanity, our very souls for this moment. And today, standing before ye, in my first day back home, I'd like to thank one man especially. One man who was imprisoned with Marjorie and myself in Berwick Castle."

Colum's back went cold. The king's grateful gaze landed on him. Elizabeth raised her goblet in Colum's direction.

"One man who bargained his own honor to save mine. Who shielded Marjorie from the horrors of what a strong man can do to a woman."

Everyone was looking in his direction, following her gaze. Colum's hand clenched tightly around the handle of his cup. Was she really going to say this? Finally reveal the secret he had been asked to keep quiet for so long?

"Eight years ago, at Berwick Castle, Edward II ordered his man to rape me. It was a gesture, a message meant for Robert, to humiliate him, to show him to what extent Scotland had lost. Marjorie, a wee lass back then, was supposed to watch. But Colum MacDonald, the strong and honorable warrior sitting over there"—she pointed with her goblet, and now everyone was really staring at Colum, most of them wide-eyed—"negotiated that he would swear his allegiance to England only if I wouldna be raped."

Astonished, outraged gasps went through the hall. Colum felt every pair of MacDonald eyes on him.

"He betrayed his clan so that his queen could keep her honor and his princess wouldn't grow to be a shell of a woman. Colum, thanks to ye, I stand here with my honor and my dignity intact. Without Colum's choice, to protect me at the expense of his own honor, I may not have survived that imprisonment. Thanks to him, the unspeakable didn't happen and my spirit wasn't broken. So, here's to Colum MacDonald, one of the most honorable and loyal men I have a privilege to ken."

The hall erupted in cheers. But the eyes of his clansmen were the only things he saw. Finally, they looked at him with respect and gratitude. Finally, they came to him from other tables, clapping at his shoulders, squeezing them, saying words of approval and congratulations.

"We wilna have a better laird after Aulay passes, may it be many, many years from now," said Marcas.

Everyone drank, and the celebration continued. Bruce rose after a while and made a toast. He gave a speech about how they had finally achieved a great milestone in this war. He reminded them of how eight years ago he'd been defeated, as well as all his supporters. How all of them had been through a lot. Loss. Sacrifice. Tragedy.

All for their king. For Scotland. For freedom.

"Freedom is almost within our reach. England will have a hard time recovering from this defeat. King Edward II is humiliated. His nobles wilna forgive him so easily for this. 'Tis all thanks to ye, my loyal, courageous warriors and knights. The Highlanders of clans Cambel, Mackenzie, and MacDonald, who shielded me in the lowest time of my life and helped me to come back and gather my new army." His eyes met Colum's. "And my special thanks to ye, Colum MacDonald, for protecting my wife when I couldna. It cost a lot for ye to keep yer word and keep it a secret to respect Elizabeth's honor. But I promise I wilna forget this. Destiny wasna always kind to ye, but 'tis about to get better, my lad. For yer service to my queen and yer country, I will make ye a knight."

The hall gasped, and Colum's head swam from the incredible honor. "I'm so proud of you," whispered Danielle. "My knight."

Bruce turned to Anna MacDonald now. "'Tis also my honor that my older daughter, Anna, is of clan MacDonald and is marrit to David from clan Mackenzie."

He raised his cup and the clans raised theirs. "'Tis a victory. So let us drink and be merry. To Scotland. To freedom. For the human right to live in a safe country."

The hall cheered and rejoiced, and the festivities went on.

"They're finally getting it," Danielle told him. "How good of the king and the queen that they acknowledged you."

Colum had never felt so supported and loved and accepted as he did in this moment. Finally, here was everything he'd ever wanted and didn't even know he needed. His clan forgave him. His king acknowledged him. The woman he loved chose him.

He stood up and raised his cup and the hall went quiet once again.

"If I may, Yer Grace," he said. "I'd like to say a few words, as well."

Bruce nodded to him with a smile and picked up his goblet.

"What ye said, Yer Grace, about destiny... Truer words havena been spoken. Destiny hasna dealt a lot of us a good hand. Scotland, ye, my king and my queen, as well as me. But it did do one good thing." He looked at Danielle, and his breath caught in his chest. She gazed up at him, with a goblet of wine in her hand. She wore a beautiful gown, and he couldn't tear his eyes away from her—how beautiful she was. Her hair was gathered up behind her head. The dress was red, with angel sleeves and images of flowers and leaves embroidered in green thread. It made her skin look smooth and luminous and highlighted her blue eyes. No one had any doubt she was a woman—the most beautiful woman he'd ever seen.

"It did one good thing," he repeated. "It brought this woman into my life. Danielle Field of London. Aye, she's a Sassenach, before any of ye start yer quarrels, and I wilna let ye. Because nae matter where she was born, she's the most loyal, honorable, and courageous woman I've ever met. She saved my life several times, and she fought alongside ye all in the battle. I love ye, lass, and I want to marry ye."

Gasps came from around the room. "Will ye be my wife?"

And it didn't matter to him anymore if the clan loved him. If his king approved of him. If his queen cleared his name or not.

What mattered to him was that her eyes sparkled like the sea on a bright, sunny day. That her cheeks flushed in delight, and that she gave him the brightest, most beautiful smile he'd ever seen. Then she said the only word that would matter for the rest of his life.

"Yes."

~

THANK YOU FOR READING HIGHLANDER'S DESTINY. Find out what happens next, when Rogene and Angus host all our couples for Christmas in the series epilogue CHRISTMAS REUNION.

A CHRISTMAS WISH FOR LOVE AND family bridges the centuries.

READ CHRISTMAS REUNION NOW >
"What a satisfying ending to a wonderful series!"

SIGN-UP FOR MARIAH STONE'S NEWSLETTER:
http://mariahstone.com/signup

FANCY A VIKING?

And other mysterious matchmakers are sending modern-day people to the past too, also to the Viking Age. If you haven't read Holly and Einar's story yet, be sure to pick up VIKING'S DESIRE.

A captive time traveler. A Viking jarl on a mission. Will marriage be the price of her freedom?

. . .

Read VIKING'S DESIRE now >
"Fabulous! What a great way to start a new series!"

Or stay in the Highlands and keep reading for an excerpt from CHRISTMAS REUNION.

~

Eilean Donan, December 24, 1315

Rogene Mackenzie laid the last present on top of the pile of gifts under the Christmas tree in Eilean Donan Castle's great hall.

"Looks good, lass," Angus said, his voice rich and deep. Their four-year-old son, Paul, hung a small bright-red wooden horse on a lower branch. Angus tousled Paul's thick, dark hair, and the boy giggled, bringing a huge smile to Rogene's face. Sitting at the great table, among the guests of honor at the end of the hall, a nurse rocked the crib where their three-month-old daughter, Emma, slept.

Rogene straightened and rested her head on Angus's shoulder, admiring the tree. "We did well."

Tall and fluffy, the young Scots pine stood next to the large fireplace and received many puzzled gazes. Rogene knew medieval people weren't familiar with Christmas trees, but this Christmas, all eight couples with time travelers were gathering together at Eilean Donan, so she'd allowed herself this little indulgence to bring her friends a feeling of home.

The tree was gorgeous. Red and yellow wooden balls hung on its branches as well as little horses and stars, garlands of holly berries, colorful ribbons, and even real candles. The candles were, of course, a fire hazard, but Angus had carefully attached them to the branches following all precautions to keep them from burning the tree down.

A gold-colored wooden star tree topper shone in the candle and firelight. The gifts beneath the tree were packed in wooden boxes of various sizes, wrapped in red and blue fabric, and tied with golden silk ribbons, courtesy of David, who'd made sure clan MacDonald traders brought them from the kingdom of Galicia.

The hall swarmed with people sitting at the tables, eating and drinking and laughing. Children ran around, chasing each other and playing with the dogs who waited hopefully for table scraps. In one corner, a trio of musicians played cheerful music, and the space in front of them was dedicated to a dance floor— people danced, jumping around in circles, entwining their hands, laughing. Most of them were teenagers, among them Seoc, Catriona and James's adopted son, who was now fifteen years old and danced with a pretty blond girl.

Satisfied, Rogene turned around just as Amber and Owen appeared in the doorway. They were the last couple to arrive, and the rest of them had been a little worried.

She squeezed Angus's large biceps. "Owen and Amber are here!" she said excitedly.

A grin spread under his short, dark beard. "Finally."

Five years had passed since Rogene and Angus had fallen in love, and even though he now had a few white hairs in his thick, dark mane, he was still as huge and handsome as ever, and she still melted at the sound of his voice.

Rogene ushered Paul towards the group of children that played and danced in another corner of the room. Then Rogene and Angus made their way down the aisle between the long tables and benches in the great hall. As they went, they smiled and greeted their guests, including Mackenzies from all around Kintail, as well as clans Cambel and MacDonald.

When they reached Owen and Amber, they hugged. Amber's long, fur-trimmed cloak and Owen's wolfskin cloak were covered with snow. Rogene took in Amber's rounded stomach and gasped.

"Amber Ryan Cambel!" she cried. "Why didn't you send a message! Congratulations! How far along are you?"

Amber beamed and exchanged the most loving smile with her husband. "Six months."

"So were you finally ready, or was it a happy accident?" Rogene asked with a wink.

"I was finally ready," said Amber.

"*We* were," said Owen with a grin.

Since Rogene had last seen him a year ago, he'd taken on a more mature look, and Rogene wondered if it was because of the pregnancy or because he was, indeed, ready. Amber was glowing, and not just because of the pregnancy—she had always been a gorgeous woman.

"Right," said Amber. "We both were. You know, we traveled for the first few years, and then we were helping the Bruce. But after the Battle of Bannockburn, it feels like the war is won. Even though it isn't officially over."

Rogene pulled her close with one arm around her shoulders and led her towards the table of honor while Owen and Angus walked together, talking. "I'm so happy for you both. Paul and Emma can't wait to have another cousin to play with."

"And how are my niece and nephew?" Amber leaned her head close to Rogene's.

Even though the only time traveler related to Rogene was David, her brother, from the moment they'd all met, she'd felt like they were family.

"They're good," said Rogene. "You see him playing with Noah?" She pointed at the corner where Paul and Noah, the five-year-old son of Kate and Ian, built a tower of wooden blocks.

"Oh, yes," said Amber. "Good God, they grew up!"

"And there's Jenny." She pointed at a seven-year-old who ran through the tables and joined the dancing couples by the musicians. She took the blond girl's place, dance-jumped with Seoc, her red curls bouncing, her green Cambel eyes glistening with joy.

"Aw, look at her!" Amber cooed. Midway to the table, she stopped and gaped at the space next to the fireplace.

"Rogene Mackenzie," whispered Amber. "You didn't! A Christmas tree?"

Rogene beamed. "James, David, and Angus carved the decorations from wood. It must have taken them months. Then Catrìona, Seoc, and I painted them. Paul helped, of course. His are the ones with tiny fingerprints." She giggled.

"Of course." Amber grinned, her eyes on the little dark-haired head. "But where did you get so much dye?"

"David sent it over. He had the MacDonald traders bring some when they traded in Naples."

Owen stopped by Amber's side, and with a frown, eyed the large fir. "Is that the odd tree ye kept telling me about, love?" he asked Amber.

Amber nodded, her eyes tearing up. "It is. Isn't it beautiful? Gosh, I missed a proper Christmas..." She squeezed Rogene's hand.

Owen and Angus exchanged a look, raising their eyebrows. "I ken, Owen," said Angus. "I dinna understand this tradition from the future. But what my wife wants, my wife gets. I only hope it doesna send Eilean Donan up in flames."

"We still have all your traditions as well," said Rogene, pointing at the Yule log next to the fireplace, ready for burning later that evening. "And I really appreciate all the effort you and everyone made to put this Christmas tree here. You made eight people from the future incredibly happy."

Angus wrapped his hand around her waist and pulled her to him. "*Ye* did, love," he said, his voice sending a shiver through her whole body. "It was ye."

"The Christmas tree," she said as she continued leading them down the aisle between the tables, "was a German tradition that was introduced to other countries only in the middle of the eighteenth century. And I know people born in the Middle Ages are confused about it, but…I love it!"

There were branches of holly and mistletoe hung as decorations on the rough stone walls, as well. The air was thick with the scents of freshly baked pastry, grilled meat, bread, wine, and ale. Kate had been in charge of managing the kitchen and had made sure there were traditional medieval dishes, such as roast grouse stuffed with what Kate called haggis—the medieval cooks looked at her funny and said they had no idea what haggis was. She'd also made the dish she called Crazy Mary, delicious roast mutton. There was also roast pork, chicken, and honey-glazed deer, plus meat pies. There wasn't turkey or mashed potatoes, but there was ham and mashed garlic parsnips, which smelled amazing. She'd even managed to make gingerbread cookies and made sure there was a plate of them on each table.

As Rogene took her next step, a flash of red and brown passed right in front of her feet.

"Nessieee!!! Give it back!"

A dark-haired boy in a purple tunic ran after the flash of fur, his arms outstretched. It was Alexander Cambel, Amy and Craig's four-year-old, chasing Angus's favorite hunting hound. The dog loved playing with children more than chasing boars and foxes. When the hound was a puppy—the smallest and most mischievous of the litter—Angus had lovingly called her a little monster. So Rogene had named the pooch Nessie, after the Loch Ness Monster. Now that Rogene could see the dog clearly, she noticed it had a grouse's leg in its jaws, its eyes as wide and as glistening with excitement as Alexander's.

William, Catrìona and James's three-year-old son, ran after them, his gait less steady and his excited squeals even louder than the music. His head of soft, blond curls earned him adoring gazes from all guests.

When Rogene, Angus, Owen, and Amber approached the table of honor, there was a festive roar of greetings. Amy and Craig, Kate and Ian, Catrìona and James, Anna and David, Aulay and Jenny as well as Colum and Danielle were all here. Chairs scraped against the floor as people stood up to hug and greet the final couple.

When they could all sit around the table, Rogene wiped at her teary eyes. David and Anna's daughter, Alice, who was one year and nine months, slept peacefully in her father's arms. Una, the beautiful red-haired daughter of Aulay and Jenny, now almost three years old, sat in a high chair next to her mother. With a look of great concentration on her little face, she studied a picture book with wooden pages that Jenny had painted for her.

"How's everyone?" asked Amber cheerfully as she undid her cloak and handed it, with a nod of thanks, to a waiting servant. "I missed you all!"

"We missed you!" said Kate, passing a dish of glazed apples. She looked beautiful with her golden hair in a pretty updo and her gorgeous curves complemented by a deep violet dress with silver embroidered flower patterns. "We are all good. Healthy. Noah is good, too. Keeps us on our toes." She glanced lovingly at her son playing with Paul.

"He adores his mother," said Ian. "Who wouldna?" He planted a kiss on her cheek. Her smile illuminated the room. He was as huge and protective as Rogene remembered, though his previously fiery red hair had now turned to pale copper.

"Danielle, are you settled in?" asked Amber. "You must be missing things."

Danielle, a beautiful, tall blonde who had joined the time travelers' club last year, looked at Colum with a tender smile. "The only thing I miss is chocolate. And my family. I couldn't care less about the rest. I went to say goodbye to my parents and my sister. Told them I'm happy and that they don't need to worry about me. I told my sister the whole truth, and I gave her a letter for my parents. I didn't think they'd believe me if I told them the truth upfront, but I wanted them to know I hadn't died or been kidnapped. I wanted them to have closure, with time."

Colum MacDonald, a handsome, tall, muscular warrior with shoulder-length dark hair and the look of a wolf, grinned at her.

"Well done, lass," said Aulay MacDonald, towering and broad-shouldered, with long, silvery hair. He chewed happily on a crispy gingerbread cookie. "Wasna easy."

"Looking now at all of us gathered tonight for Christmas," said Craig Cambel, running his fingers through his dark mane that now showed a few silver strands. "Ye ken what I miss...or rather who? Marjorie and Colin." Nods of agreement came from Ian and Owen. "I'd like to meet Konnor, as well."

"Aye, brother," said Owen and squeezed Craig's shoulder. "I miss them, too."

"As do I," said Ian and sighed.

Catrìona sighed as she set down a half-eaten oatmeal cookie. "And I miss Raghnall."

Her blond hair was done in two buns, one on either side of her head, her cheeks flushed from the heat in the room and perhaps also the mulled wine.

"Me, too," said David. Rogene's brother looked like a proper medieval man now. He and Anna were the youngest in their little club, but people grew up quickly in medieval times, especially during a war. She was thrilled to see her brother so happy and to still have him here with her. She only wished the first few years hadn't been such a struggle for David. But she knew the challenges had helped him become the man he was today—a loving husband and father and an increasingly skilled trader.

"I miss the rascal, too," said Angus and raised his goblet of mulled wine. The rest followed him. "To those who arenae among us but who will never leave our hearts!"

They clunked their cups and goblets together and drank, and the wine, dark and spiced, spread a warm glow through Rogene's body.

Later that night, Craig stared through the open shutters at the gentle snow falling outside of the great hall. The white banks on the other side of the loch glowed dimly through the snowfall. The vast room behind him was quiet now that the clansmen from Dornie and nearby farms had returned home, the children were asleep in their chambers, and the only ones left in the great hall were the time traveler couples.

He turned back, watching Amy help gather the food trenchers and pack the leftover food—of which there was plenty—into baskets and bowls together with Kate, Danielle, and, Rogene. Those would later be delivered to the poorer families in the area so that they, too, could celebrate with full stomachs. The four women chatted as they worked. Amber talked to Catrìona and Jennifer in another corner, perhaps they were advising her about the pregnancy. He knew Jennifer was a physician of some kind, and Catrìona was a valued healer.

And while Ian, David, and James brought in more firewood, and Owen, Aulay, and Colum stood near Craig and quietly talked of the war and trade, he felt the absence of Marjorie and Colin like never before. It was a dull ache in his chest, a distant memory but also a need. He wondered if it was grief for Marjorie. She wasn't dead, not in his imagination, even though he'd never be able to talk to her again. It was more like she'd traveled to a distant country, so far away, there was no means to write to her or receive a response.

Angus came to stand by his side and peered through the open window as well. "Anything troubling ye?" Angus said without looking at him, his arms crossed over his chest.

"I just...I miss my sister, 'tis all," said Craig. Sharing his emotions still wasn't always easy, but he'd gotten better at it with the right people since Amy had come into his life. And Angus was his friend.

Angus let out a sharp exhale. "I ken. I miss my brother, too."

"Aye, Raghnall..." said Craig. "I wish he were here, too." The raven-haired warrior had been both a rebel and a terrifying man to meet in battle. They had fought together at the Battle of the Pass of Brander, and at numerous others. "'Tis strange to think he's in the future, too."

"He is, the rascal," said Angus and chuckled. "'Twas I who insisted he needed to marry. Which he did, and I ken he's happy. But I still miss him. I just wish I could see him one more time."

"All right, everyone!" Rogene's cheerful exclamation had them both turn their heads to her. "It's time for presents!"

Craig glanced at Amy, who caught his gaze, and his heart clenched at the sight of her bright, bonnie smile. It was the kind of smile that melted his heart every time he saw it, and he thanked God he was lucky enough to be able to put that smile on her face every day of his life.

The journey from their estate, Falnaird, had been difficult and dangerous given the weather, but Craig was glad they'd decided to make the trip. Thanks to the friends who lived on Cambel and Mackenzie lands along the way, they'd made several stops in warm, friendly homes and arrived well.

"Come to the Christmas tree, everyone!" chimed Rogene.

The eight couples made their way to the Christmas tree and began the future custom of exchanging presents. Craig was familiar with it by now as Amy had showered him with gifts the first year of their marriage, which he'd been very grateful for. But he hadn't realized he needed to give her presents as well, which had caused a tight smile and sad eyes from her. He never wanted her to look like that again and gave her gifts he knew she'd love, too: silver necklaces and brooches, cakes of soap from Galicia, soft fabrics from overseas, and even rare finds like Mediterranean fruits, herbs, and spices.

This was the first time all sixteen of them and the children had come together, so excitement was high.

The presents were exchanged. Craig received a beautiful dagger, a box of delicious pastries from Kate and Ian, a gorgeous belt for his tunic, carved wax candles, and sharp trimming scissors. He knew the world in the future was more abundant and the meaning of presents for Christmas was much less. In his time, presents were given much more rarely, with the highest meaning and intent, and weren't taken lightly. His chest tightened in appreciation of these thoughtful and very valuable gifts.

Then there was just one more box left under the tree. It was Craig and Amy's present that they had been preparing for a long time. His gut twisted with uneasiness at the thought of this present's recipient. He'd never seen her, although she had impacted all of them in the most profound way.

Amy exchanged an excited, sly smile with Craig.

She looked around. "Sìneag, sweetheart, this is for you!"

The rest of the couples held their breath, looking around. Craig knew all their stomachs must have tightened, like his own.

For a few long moments, nothing happened. The fire still played in the fireplace. Candles flickered in the slight draft coming from the gaps in the window shutters.

The silk ribbons on the tree ornaments glimmered. No sounds came other than the crackling of the firewood and Craig's own loud breathing in his ears.

She wouldn't come. It wasn't so simple to summon a Highland faerie, surely, as just calling her name.

And then Amy looked past him into the great hall and gave a small gasp. Then she beamed. Kate covered her mouth and grasped Ian's arm.

Like the rest of the couples, he turned around. More gasps sounded. There, next to the log prepared for lighting, stood a woman of an average height. She wore a dark-green hooded cloak. From beneath the hood, long, wavy red hair cascaded over her chest. Using both of her hands, she lowered the hood to her shoulders and a pretty, strawberry-shaped face looked at them with a shy smile. She had a small, pointy nose, rounded lips, and big, slightly slanted green eyes. Freckles were sprinkled over her nose and cheeks.

Sheepishly, she smiled at them.

Craig's throat tightened. It was her. Thanks to this creature, who had so abruptly uprooted his wife and nine other men and women from the future, all their lives had changed for the better.

Amy leaned down to the last present under the Christmas tree—a small box wrapped in bonnie green fabric.

She approached Sìneag with the gift in her outstretched hands. "This is for you, Sìneag."

The faerie looked at the box dubiously.

"What is this?" asked Sìneag.

"Maybe you know, it's Christmas now," said Amy. "Christmas is a time of miracles. A time of love. A time when everything is possible. And on Christmas, we give each other presents. We gathered here as a family, a big family that was created thanks to you. So it wouldn't be a celebration or a reunion without you. Because you're part of this family, Sìneag."

Sìneag's eyes glistened, and she touched her cheeks wonderingly, then stared at the teardrops on her fingertips.

"Open it," said Amy. "Please."

Sìneag took the box in her hands and unwrapped the fabric. When she removed the lid, she retrieved a necklace on a leather string. It was in the rough shape of a heart, a simple rock that wouldn't mean anything to anyone else. But Sìneag's eyes widened like two silver pounds.

"It's because you touched our hearts," said Amy, "and helped us fill our lives with love."

Sìneag looked at the necklace in one hand and said, "I can feel what rock 'tis made of. Ye mischievous lass"—she looked at Craig—"and lad."

"It's part of the rock that brought this woman to me," said Craig, pulling Amy closer with a hand around her waist. "A chip came off when the wall caved in a few years ago. We kent it was precious."

"Thank ye," Sìneag said. "I ken ye all went through quite some ordeals, but yer love and happiness is all I've ever wanted. And it means more to me than ye can imagine, to be called yer

family. And this gift...nae one has ever given me a gift before..."
She wiped her cheek again. "I never felt so human..."

They all chuckled.

"Would you like some cookies?" asked Kate and stretched out a plate with oatmeal pastries she'd called cookies.

"Oh, aye," Sìneag exclaimed. "I canna say nae to human food, especially from ye!" She eagerly put the necklace on and took a cookie. She bit into it and moaned enthusiastically.

Kate beamed. "I'm glad you like it."

"How are Marjorie and Colin?" asked Craig. "Do ye ken if they're well in the future?"

"And Raghnall and Bryanna?" added Catrìona.

Sìneag's eyes glinted mischievously as she chewed and swallowed. "I havena asked them yet," she said.

Then she disappeared...

Keep reading CHRISTMAS REUNION.

ALSO BY MARIAH STONE

MARIAH'S TIME TRAVEL ROMANCE SERIES

- CALLED BY A HIGHLANDER
- CALLED BY A VIKING
- CALLED BY A PIRATE
- FATED

MARIAH'S REGENCY ROMANCE SERIES

- DUKES AND SECRETS

VIEW ALL OF MARIAH'S BOOKS IN READING ORDER

Scan the QR code for the complete list of Mariah's ebooks, paperbacks, and audiobooks in reading order.

GET A FREE MARIAH STONE BOOK!

Join Mariah's mailing list to be the first to know of new releases, free books, special prices, and other author giveaways.

freehistoricalromancebooks.com

ENJOY THE BOOK? YOU CAN MAKE A DIFFERENCE!

Please, leave your honest review for the book.
As much as I'd love to, I don't have financial capacity like New York publishers to run ads in the newspaper or put posters in subway.

But I have something much, much more powerful!

Committed and loyal readers

If you enjoyed the book, I'd be so grateful if you could spend five minutes leaving a review on the book's Amazon page.

Thank you very much!

SCOTTISH SLANG

aye – yes

   bairn - baby

   bastart - bastard

   bonnie - pretty, beautiful.

   canna- can not

   couldna – couldn't

   didna- didn't ("Ah didna do that!")

   dinna- don't ("Dinna do that!")

   doesna – doesn't

   fash - fuss, worry ("Dinna fash yerself.")

   feck - fuck

   hasna – has not

   havna - have not

   hadna – had not

   innit? - Isn't it?

   isna- Is not

   ken - to know

   kent - knew

   lad - boy

   lass - girl

   marrit – married

nae – no or not
shite - faeces
the morn - tomorrow
the morn's morn - tomorrow morning
uisge-beatha (uisge for short) – Scottish Gaelic for water or life / aquavitae, the distilled drink, predecessor of whiskey
verra – very
wasna - was not
wee - small
wilna - will not
wouldna - would not
ye - you
yer – your (also yerself)

ABOUT MARIAH STONE

Mariah Stone is a bestselling author of time travel romance novels, including her popular Called by a Highlander series and her hot Viking, Pirate, and Regency novels. With nearly one million books sold, Mariah writes about strong modern-day women falling in love with their soulmates across time. Her books are available worldwide in multiple languages in e-book, print, and audio.

Subscribe to Mariah's newsletter for a free time travel book today at mariahstone.com/signup!

facebook.com/mariahstoneauthor

instagram.com/mariahstoneauthor

bookbub.com/authors/mariah-stone

pinterest.com/mariahstoneauthor

amazon.com/Mariah-Stone/e/B07JVW28PJ